THE FLIGHT TO BLUE RIVER

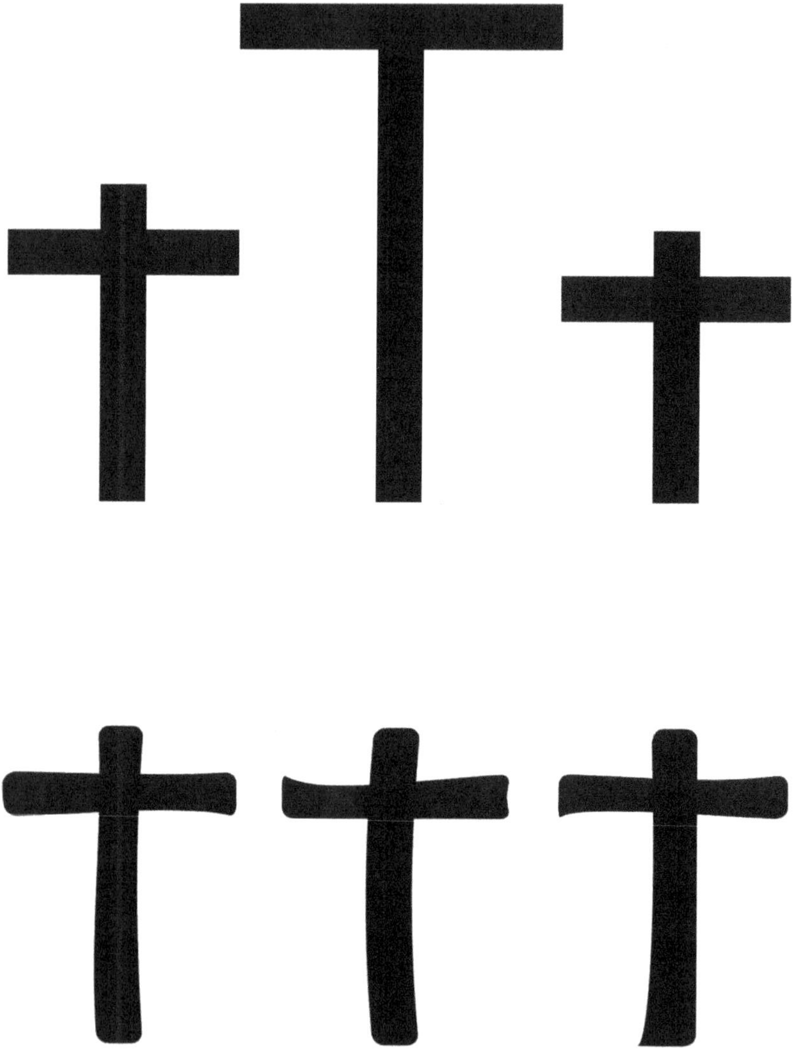

THE FLIGHT TO BLUE RIVER

THERMALS OF TIME - BOOK TWO

The Last Ditch Press
First Published in 2020

MARCUS LYNN DEAN

Published by: The Last Ditch Press - Cedaredge, Colorado
www.lastditchpress.com

ISBN: 978-1-7346746-2-0

The
Last Ditch Press

For Casey

No one, other than her mother, has so profoundly
affected my life.

ACKNOWLEDGEMENTS

This second book of the Thermals Of Time trilogy owes its very existence to those readers of *The Scream Of An Eagle* who encouraged me to continue the story. To all those readers - my sincere thanks. I hope you enjoy reading *The Flight To Blue River* as much as I enjoyed writing it.

To give credit where it is most due, I also need to thank my wife, Karen, for everything she does. Not only has she put up with me as a husband for all these years, she is a proofreader extraordinaire, without whose editorial and design assistance, this book would be sorely lacking.

Part One

In the beginning, our beginning, Mother Earth gave us life. Mother Earth is not Planet Earth. Mother Earth is the life-giver, from which all life springs.

Mother Earth gave life to all living things. To plants and animals, to birds and fish, and even the planet itself. Did you not know that this planet is a living thing?

When Mother Earth gave the first humans life, she could not know that humans were like a virus. She could not know how fast we would multiply and how far we would spread.

Mother Earth gave us life, and in turn, we brought death to so much of what once was good. Other life vanished. The corals and fish in the sea; on land, animals and plants beyond count, and wondrous birds in the air. All diminished or extinct. Even the great eagles no longer soar where once they were king.

Know you this, Mother Earth will defend the life of this planet. Man's reign will end, and the eagles will return. In time, balance will once again be restored to this world. –
Mystic Martin 2030

Chapter One

THERE HAD ONLY BEEN two weeks to go until the end of the semester, just a month to go until her twenty-first birthday. That's when the world ended. At least the world Anna had always known came to a sudden halt. Not only her junior year at the University of Oregon but basically the United States Of America, as she'd always known it, came to a sudden unexpected end.

Anna was testing a newly modified storage battery at the lab, where she'd spent a great deal of time over the past three years. Majoring in electrical engineering, she spent more time doing hands-on work in the lab than she spent studying theory in a classroom. It was getting late, but she was just about finished with this round of testing when she felt the com vibrate in her lab coat. Will was onscreen as soon as she pulled the com out of her pocket.

"You better come home," he said, without so much as a hello. The look on his face accentuated the concern in his voice.

"What's wrong?" It was all too obvious to Anna that something terrible must have happened.

"People are dying," was not the response that Anna expected.

Will worked at the McKenzie-Willamette hospital while doing his pre-med studies at the University of Oregon. He'd worked there since he and Anna arrived in Eugene three years ago. People always died at McKenzie-Willamette. So, why was Will so agitated?

"What do you mean, people are dying?" she asked.

"At the hospital," Will managed to get out, before coughing.

"I'm just about finished," she told him. "I should be home in an hour or so."

"You don't understand," Will told her before being wracked by a severe fit of coughing.

He doesn't look well, Anna thought, noticing that Will seemed too pallid, and there were beads of sweat on his forehead.

"Are you alright?" she asked, even though the answer was obvious.

"Not so good," Will managed to get out between spasms of coughing. "Hurry," he said, and her screen went blank.

Tendrils of fear were working their way through her thoughts as she hurriedly started shutting down the battery test. *What was that all about? Will is obviously sick, but he seemed just fine when we got up this morning. What did he mean, people are dying at the hospital?*

When Anna got home to the duplex they had lived in for the past three years, she found Will sitting in front of the comscreen in his favorite chair. He was wrapped up like a mummy in a blanket that he must have dug out of the back of the closet. There was a newscaster on the comscreen talking about some hurricane and an earthquake somewhere, but Anna didn't pay much attention to the com. Her attention was focused on Will. How could he stand to be wrapped up like that? It felt like it must be eighty degrees in their apartment.

She hurried across the room and didn't even need to touch his forehead to feel the heat coming off of him. *My god, he's burning up,* she thought. He seemed to be asleep.

"Will, wake up!" she shook his shoulders. *I need to get him to the hospital,* was her first thought. Then, *he just came from the hospital.* A moan and a cough were the only responses from Will.

That fever will kill him, she thought. She rushed into the bathroom and started filling the tub with cold water, as cold as it would get anyway. With high temperatures averaging around a hundred degrees lately, water from the tap was not that cold. She added a binful of ice from the ice-maker to the water. Then she ran back to Will and pulled the blanket off of him. She gently slapped his face trying to get him to wake up. Another moan was all she got for her efforts.

Will weighed about a hundred and seventy pounds to Anna's hundred and twenty, but Anna was a strong girl. You don't grow up on a ranch working cattle with a family of men without developing quite a bit of strength. Reaching under his arms and wrapping hers around him, she was able to drag him to the tub and literally drop him into the water. Even that didn't wake Will up. She had to quickly pull him back to a semi-seated position to keep his head above water. Then she faced a real quandary. She wanted to do more, though she didn't know what. Her com was back on the table in the other room, but who could she call? Will's words, "people are dying," came back to her, and she was gripped by fear. Was Will dying? Was everyone at the hospital already dead? What the hell was it?

Anna coughed, and a new fear hit. *Do I have it, too?* She didn't feel sick, but then Will had been perfectly fine less than twelve hours ago. *And now he's dying.* That thought shook her into action. She couldn't leave Will's side, she had to hold onto him so he wouldn't just slide under the water and drown.

"Raven," she yelled at her com. Anna had always called her com Raven, after the ability of the large black birds to communicate over long distances. "Raven, call the hospital." Not hearing any response from her com, she yelled, "Raven, maximum volume!"

"Which hospital?" her com asked from the other room.

"McKenzie-Willamette," she yelled back.

After what seemed like an eternity, her com informed her that no one was answering. "Call PeaceHealth," she yelled back.

After not getting through to either one of the hospitals and no answer from 9-1-1, Anna was at a loss. More than that, she felt lost. She looked at Will through tears she hadn't realized were in her eyes and could tell that his breathing was getting shallow and ragged. *This can't be happening.* The thought was a vain protest. Anna knew without a doubt that it was happening. Will Donovan, her fiancé, the man she'd followed to Oregon and lived with for three years, was dying, and there was absolutely nothing she could do.

...

Anna wasn't sure if it was the sunlight streaming through the window or the noise of the newscast coming from the comscreen that woke her up. As soon as she was awake, the events of the night before came rushing back into her consciousness. Her deep brown eyes were red and swollen from crying. She couldn't have been asleep for long, but the sun was high enough in the sky that it had to be mid-morning. Her neck was stiff from sleeping with her head on the arm of the sofa. The big comscreen on the living room wall was still on with an unfamiliar female newscaster who started sobbing on air.

A newscaster sobbing while live on the air was unexpected enough, but she really got Anna's attention as she uttered the words, *"I can't."* Anna's attention was riveted to the screen as a couple of military looking people basically picked up the well-dressed woman who had been broadcasting the news, and escorted her off-camera. A third man dressed in a much fancier military uniform took the woman's place in front of the camera. Anna didn't know much about military insignia, but she knew by the four stars that this man was some kind of general or something. She listened, almost spellbound, as the man spoke.

My fellow Americans, I am sorry you had to witness the fake news that was just forced upon you. This was a blatant attempt by certain factions in the military to sow doubt and discord among us.

Anna had slept through the news of the hurricane and the tsunami hitting the northeastern United States, so she had no idea what the general was talking about. But at least it momentarily took her mind off of Will, lying dead in the bathtub. The general continued:

Rest assured that the government of the United States is safe and secure. In order to maintain that security, the country has been placed under martial law, effective immediately. All banks and financial institutions, as well as all food production and distribution facilities, have now been placed under direct government control. A nationwide dusk to dawn curfew will take effect immediately. Please remain in your homes after dark.

The general onscreen now had Anna's total and undivided attention.

To provide security and to protect the legitimate government of the United States from the forces that assail us, all broadcast systems and all personal communications will be shut down immediately. Please leave all coms in standby mode in order to receive further updates as they are made available. Thank you for your cooperation. God bless America.

The screen went dark and silent practically before the general finished speaking. Anna sat and stared at the screen. What was that all about? She realized she was probably in shock, but that couldn't be driving her total lack of comprehension. What the hell was going on? Then she coughed and realized she didn't feel one hundred percent well. Fear gripped her again. Did she have what Will died of? She didn't really want to go back into the bathroom, but she had to pee.

She tried not to look at Will, but she couldn't help herself. It was strange, but he mostly just looked peaceful. Like he'd just decided to take a nap, fully clothed, reclining in a bathtub full of tepid water.

I need to call his mom, she thought, and then remembered what the general had said about all personal communications being shut down. Returning to the living room, she grabbed her com just as another small coughing fit took hold. Now she wanted to call 9-1-1 for herself, but the words "NO SERVICE" were prominently displayed on the screen. She felt a chill. Grabbing the blanket that she'd pulled off of Will last night, she snuggled into the same recliner where she'd found him and wrapped the blanket around herself. *Guess I'm exposed, I'm probably going to die,* she thought. In all the years of her young life, Anna had never been as scared as she was right at that moment.

. . .

The room was dark. Anna felt like she was being suffocated. It was the blanket that had her wrapped up like a mummy. *I'm alive.* The thought seemed strange until she remembered sitting in the recliner, thinking she was going to die.

She threw the blanket off, whatever fever she'd had earlier was gone. She didn't even seem to have a cough. She wondered how long she'd been asleep. Judging by the fact that it appeared to be the middle of the night, she must have slept for at least twelve hours. She was hungry. *How long has it been since I had anything to eat?* she wondered. The events of the past couple of days were fresh in her mind, but it was like she woke up in a different world than the one she went to sleep in.

Other than thinking it would be nice to have a shower, she paid Will's body in the bathtub little mind as she used the toilet and then washed her hands and face. She undressed and gave herself a sponge bath, occasionally glancing at Will in the mirror. *I have to contact the authorities,* she thought. Maybe they can get in touch with Will's mom. Since Will didn't have a father, and he was an only child, it seemed extra crucial that his mother should know of his death. *Why?* she wondered. *Do I just want someone to share my sorrow?*

Anna took one last look at Will and let the overwhelming sorrow wash over her once again before turning and walking out of the bathroom. She went to their bedroom and had a hard time deciding what to wear. She had no idea what she was dressing for. It certainly wasn't going to be just another day at school. She ended up in khaki shorts, a light chambray shirt, and her light hiking boots. She decided on the light hikers after remembering how most forms of transportation stopped working the last time the internet went offline, back at the start of the Great Mid-East War. It was a couple of miles to the police station, but Anna was used to hiking. Hiking had always been one of her and Will's favorite activities. During the past two years, the two of them had hiked trails all over the state.

Back in the kitchen, she threw a couple of frozen waffles into the toaster and waited impatiently for them to heat up. Looking at the glowing orange wires down in the toaster, she was once again amazed at the simplicity of the technology that had toasted bread for well over a hundred years. Anna had been fascinated by technology for as long as she could remember. Especially electrical technology. While most people from her generation were more into electronics and computers, Anna was fascinated by electricity itself. Fascinated by all the different methods one could use to produce electric power, and by the incredible multitude of uses for that power once it was made available. That's why she had decided to study electrical engineering. She loved figuring out the way things worked and how to make things work better.

After eating the waffles in a hurry, and checking her com one more time, Anna stuffed a couple of protein bars into her pocket and stepped out into the hot midday sun. The duplex was on a quiet street, but there was absolutely no one in sight in either direction as she looked up and down the road. It seemed not just quiet but eerily silent. On a whim, Anna decided to see if Cheryl and Jasper were home. Jasper and Cheryl lived in the other half of the duplex.

Anna knocked on the door and waited. She couldn't hear any sound from inside at all, so she banged on the door even harder. Still nothing, so she turned and started walking toward the police station. The intersection with Gilham Road was only about a quarter of a mile away, so it didn't take long to get there, but she didn't see a single vehicle pass through the intersection as she walked toward it. When she got to the intersection, it was easy to see why. Autonomous vehicles were stalled out, blocking the road in both directions. *Just like what happened during the Great Mid-East War,* she thought. To the north, nothing was moving as far as Anna could see. There were a couple of people several blocks to the south. They seemed to be walking away from her, headed in the same direction she was.

Anna started walking faster, thinking she might catch up to whoever it was on the road ahead of her. It seemed really strange that they were the only people in sight. She was just over a block away from Cal Young Road when the couple ahead of her stopped walking at that intersection. As Anna got closer, it became clear that the two people were a man and a woman, probably middle-aged or older, from the look of them. When she first saw them, the couple had been walking side by side. By the time they got to the intersection with Cal Young, the man was obviously supporting the woman and helping her walk.

As Anna got close to the elderly couple, two more people on an electric scooter came toward them from the east. The scooter was making its way west along Cal Young Road, mainly by staying on the sidewalk that wasn't blocked by dead autonomous vehicles.

Damn, wish I could have borrowed Jasper's scooter, Anna thought. Not that she minded walking, but she could have made it to the police station that much quicker.

The scooter stopped next to the man and woman, and Anna noticed that the younger looking man who was sitting on the back of the scooter was actually the one doing the driving. The other passenger was another man who was slumped over in front of the driver. The driver was holding the front passenger, who was unconscious, in place.

"I'll come back for her as soon as I get my dad to PeaceHealth," Anna heard the scooter driver tell the older man who was supporting the woman on the sidewalk. The scooter pulled away just as Anna came up behind the elderly couple.

"Let me help," Anna told the man, who she could now see was quite old. He was probably at least in his seventies, and he was now totally supporting the woman. The old lady, apparently the man's wife, seemed to have fainted or lost consciousness.

"Thank you," the old man said, as Anna grabbed the other side of the old woman and took some of the weight off his straining arm.

"Let's set her down here on the grass," Anna told him, gently pulling the couple over to the manicured grass along the side of the walk.

The old man didn't resist as Anna helped him gently ease the old woman to a lying position on the soft grass. He held the woman's hand as he and Anna knelt beside her.

"Thank you," the man said again. "She's my wife," he added, stating what was already apparent to Anna. "She's sick," he said, still not telling Anna anything that wasn't already obvious.

The old woman was burning up just like Will had been, and she seemed to be having trouble breathing. Having watched Will die, Anna knew that the old woman didn't have more than a few minutes left to live. A strange emotional coldness came over Anna. She felt detached. Detached from herself, detached from reality. Part of her felt pity for this poor old man who was about to lose his wife. Part of her was so drained of emotion that she couldn't feel sympathy for anyone, not even herself.

I'm in shock, Anna thought. *We must all be in shock. At least those of us who are still alive, that is.* That thought really shook her. She remembered how the man and woman had been walking side by side when she first saw them less than an hour ago. And now, here she was looking down at a dying woman. What the hell was it? What kind of sickness or disease could kill people so quickly?

"I'm sorry," she told the old man. "I lost my fiancé."

Anna looked the old man in the eye, and she could see that he knew his wife would die. "What is this?" he asked. "How can everyone just be dying? If this is a nightmare, why don't I wake up?"

And why are the two of us alive, and not even sick? That was the burning question in Anna's mind. "Have you been sick?" she asked the man.

"I was a little bit under the weather when I got home last night," he answered. "But Sandy was fine. Now look, she's," he paused, not wanting to say the words. "She's dying," he managed to get out.

It has to be some kind of virus or something, Anna thought. *But what virus or sickness can spread and kill this fast?* As if cued by the thought, the old woman lying on the ground drew in a ragged, rattling breath and just stopped breathing.

"No!" the old man cried. "Not Sandy. Why?" He covered his face with his hands, sobbing, and sat down on the grass, next to his dead wife.

Anna stood and looked up and down the streets in every direction. There was no one. *Are they all dead?* When she left the duplex, her only thought was to get to the police station because she couldn't dial 9-1-1. She needed an ambulance or a mortuary or someone to come and take Will's body away. That's what happened to dead people. Someone came and took them away. *What happens when the dead outnumber the living? Outnumber the living? What if it's just him and me?* She looked at the old man sitting in the grass, sobbing.

Just as despair was about to incapacitate her, Anna saw a movement out of the corner of her eye. She looked up and saw a motorcycle weaving around and between the stalled out vehicles on Cal Young Road. The motorcycle was coming toward them, and as it got closer, she could see that it was one of Eugene's motorcycle cops. *Thank god!* The feeling of relief was almost overwhelming. The police were still on duty.

The policeman stopped his motorcycle at the curb, took off his helmet and looked at Anna and the old man like he must be looking at ghosts. He looked like a ghost himself. His face was ashen.

"They're all dead," the policeman said, seemingly to no one. He, too, was obviously in a state of shock.

"Who's dead?" Anna asked, not really wanting to know the answer.

The policeman looked at her like she'd just asked a ridiculous question. "All of them," he answered.

"All of who?" Anna asked.

"The station," he said simply. "Everyone at the station is dead."

Anna looked from the policeman sitting on his motorcycle to the old man sobbing on the ground beside his dead wife. She looked up at the clear blue sky, and then back down at the totally quiet city street. She started to turn around, then stopped and turned back toward the policeman.

"Where are you going?" she asked him. But the real

question in her mind was, *where am I going?* There was obviously no reason to go on down to the police station. Was there a reason to go anywhere? If so, where? No sooner had the questions gone through her mind than she knew the answer. *I have to get back to the BR. Back to my family.* Thoughts of the Blue River Ranch, and her family, as always, were immediately followed by memories of James Mendez.

They have to be alive, was the only thought in her head as she turned away from the policeman and started walking back the way she'd come, oblivious to anything else the policeman might have said.

Anna was about half-way back home before she saw another living person. This one was a woman in her backyard with a shovel digging a hole. From the street, Anna couldn't see the hole in detail, but she knew without a doubt that the woman was digging a grave. Maybe more than one grave, for all Anna knew. *Guess I better bury Will before I go,* she thought, and she didn't bother to talk to the woman at all.

Digging a hole in the small backyard of the duplex was harder than Anna would have thought. It had taken her a couple of hours worth of hard labor in the hot afternoon sun to dig a big enough hole to be a shallow grave for Will. She leaned on her shovel and looked at the neighbor's backyard on the other side of the white vinyl fence. *What about Jasper and Cheryl,* she thought. *They must be dead, too.* Logical thinking was beginning to overcome the emotional freefall that she'd been in for the past two days. She looked at the other back yards all neatly lined up side by side, facing another row of back yards across the alley. There was no other living soul in sight. *Jesus! How many dead people are there?* She looked back at the other half of her duplex. *Can't bury them all,* she thought, as she headed inside to drag Will's body out to his final resting place.

...

Anna knew she was within ten or fifteen miles of Bend when the scooter battery finally gave out. She'd taken Jasper's electric scooter after breaking into their side of the duplex and finding both him and Cheryl dead. As she parked the scooter off the edge of the road, she remembered how Jasper and Cheryl had been when she discovered their bodies. They were in their bed. It appeared that Cheryl had died first, and Jasper had laid down beside her and wrapped his arm around her dead body. Anna had simply left them lying together in that eternal embrace.

With a backpack full of supplies strapped to her back and her pistol in the holster on her hip, Anna started walking toward Bend. There weren't nearly as many vehicles stalled out on Highway 20 as there had been near Eugene. None at all, as far as she could see, on this particular stretch of highway. The way she was dressed, with the full backpack and wide-brimmed trekking hat, she would have looked more at home in the evergreen forests that lined both sides of the road than she did walking down the paved shoulder of the highway.

The few vehicles that had stalled out on Highway 20 didn't block the road here like they did in more congested areas. Most had simply stopped in the lane they were in when the navigation systems went down, so the other lane was open. A human-driven vehicle could simply go around the stalled cars and trucks without ever leaving the pavement.

Anna had at least part of a plan brewing in the back of her mind. As many people as there were dead, she figured she could "borrow" someone else's non-autonomous vehicle and drive it however far it would go on the charge in the batteries. Then, she'd simply have to "borrow" another one and continue on. Seeing how open the road was once she got away from more populated areas, she decided she would try to stick to less-traveled roads and less populated areas. Having grown up on the Blue River Ranch near Kremmling, Colorado, sparsely populated areas with roads less traveled should feel a lot like home.

With the sun just starting to go down behind the mountains to the west, Anna decided that the next order of business was to make camp for the night. She knew she could get to Bend before dark, but the Oregon woods offered a feeling of comfort and security that another dead town could never match. She climbed the grass-covered embankment on the side of the road and disappeared into the woods.

Chapter Two

FINDING THE FIRST vehicle to borrow had been really easy. Anna hadn't even walked all the way to Bend before deciding to start taking a look at some of the farms she was passing by. Some of these places looked like they'd been prosperous for decades. Nice farms that had probably been owned and operated by multiple generations of the same family. She picked a farm about halfway between Tumalo and Bend. It had a large old red brick farmhouse that was only about a quarter of a mile back from the highway. Actually, she didn't pick this particular farm so much as Katy picked her.

The dog started barking at her before she even got to the lane that led up to the house. All black except for a white patch around its right eye and a white star in the middle of its chest, the dog looked like some kind of cross between a poodle and a border collie. It would come no closer to the highway than the fenceline that marked the farm's boundary. As Anna approached the drive, the dog kept coming out toward the road and barking. It would come to the edge of the property, look at Anna, bark a couple of times like it was trying to tell her something, and then turn and start trotting back toward the house. Then it would stop, turn to look back at Anna, and trot back out to the end of the drive to bark at her some more.

It's like he's trying to tell me something, Anna thought. She started walking toward the dog, who immediately turned and started trotting back up the lane. The dog ran a few yards up the drive, stopped, and looked back. Seeing that Anna was still following, the dog turned and went further up the lane before stopping, and once again looking back. *He's making sure I'm following.* Anna had grown up around some excellent stock dogs, and she recognized a smart dog when she saw one.

"Good dog," she said, by way of encouragement. The dog said nothing, just turned and padded on up the lane.

With Anna following, the dog went straight up to the back door of the farmhouse, raised a paw and scratched at the door. It whined or whimpered a little as Anna caught up. There was an expression of sadness in the dog's brown eyes. Anna reached down and patted the wooly fur on top of the dog's head. "It's okay," she said as she scratched behind the dog's ears and looked at the black leather collar around its neck. There was a metal tag on the collar with the dog's name, Katy, engraved on it. "So, you aren't a he at all, are you?" Anna said as she continued petting the dog.

Katy looked from Anna back to the door and scratched at it again. "Okay, okay," Anna said as she first knocked loudly on the door, and then when there was no sound at all from inside the house, she reached down to turn the doorknob. To her surprise, the door wasn't locked. Anna had no more than pushed the door open a crack when

Katy knocked the door out of her hand and bounded into the house.

Anna followed Katy and found herself in an old-fashioned mudroom that led into a homey kitchen. She could hear Katy whining further on into the house. Following the sound, she walked into a spacious living room. Katy was sitting on her haunches in front of a large sofa, whining at the obviously dead woman stretched out under a blanket. The woman couldn't have been dead more than a day. Anna was surprised to see that she was quite young, probably just a few years older than herself. For some reason, she'd envisioned nothing but old people living in this old farmhouse.

Anna found another body in the master bedroom. A man who was probably the dead woman's husband. The man had obviously died before the woman downstairs, and the smell of death permeated the air in the bedroom. Anna closed the bedroom door and went back downstairs in a hurry.

...

That had been the day before yesterday. "Well, it looks like time to start walking again," Anna told Katy, as the old F-150E came to a stop on the edge of Highway 26 just east of Vale, only a few miles from the Idaho border. The old electric pickup truck that she'd commandeered at Katy's farm had done well. Over three hundred miles before the battery died. At that rate, it would only take a couple more vehicles and a few more days to get home.

Katy had come with Anna, of course. If it was Katy's farm, since Anna didn't know the dead people's names, then the truck, which she found in the old metal shop, must have also belonged to Katy. The dog certainly seemed at home in the passenger seat with her head hanging out of the open window.

Katy pulled her head back inside and looked at Anna. Why are we stopping? She seemed to be asking. "Out of juice," Anna answered the unspoken question as she reached over and scratched behind Katy's ears. "Hungry?" she asked. Katy didn't answer. She just pricked up her ears and tilted her head slightly. Anna wasn't sure if it was a questioning look, or if the dog was simply turning her head into Anna's scratching fingers. One thing Anna was sure of was that Katy really liked being scratched behind the ears.

Anna stepped out of the truck with Katy right behind her. She opened the back door and grabbed one of the cans of Allpro that she'd stashed behind the driver's seat. The Allpro had also come from Katy's farm. Anna had found what looked like a lifetime supply in the massive pantry of the old house. Using the spork from her backpack, Anna scooped about half of the Allpro into Katy's bowl, which she'd also brought from the farm. Then she poured some water into the other half of Katy's two-sided bowl.

Katy lapped up some of the water and just looked at the Allpro before looking up at Anna. With a sporkfull of the Allpro already in her mouth, Anna had to laugh. She swallowed the Allpro and said, "Not very good, is it?" to Katy, who kept looking down at the bowl of Allpro then back up at Anna with a questioning look on her face. "Guess I'm not sure that it's real food either," Anna told the dog, as she threw the half-full can of Allpro into the back of the truck.

Katy looked extremely grateful as she scarfed down the

half of a protein bar that Anna gave her, before dumping the Allpro out of the dog's bowl. There wasn't enough room in Anna's pack for Katy's bowl, so Anna rigged a way to tie it on. She was glad to have Katy's company, but she didn't want to share dishes with her.

This part of the world was truly farm country. They were in a broad flat valley of fields full of the spring greenery of young crops. As they started walking toward Idaho, Anna couldn't help but wonder at the vagaries of climate change. What made this part of the western U.S. so much wetter than most of the parched land? Maybe it was just close enough to the Pacific Northwest that it got spillover moisture. Whatever it was, Anna knew that it wasn't much farther south or east in either direction, before she'd get to the real drought-stricken parts of the country. The last time she talked to her folks, they'd told her there had been practically no snow at the Blue River Ranch during the previous winter. As Anna walked along, with Katy right beside her, she wondered if her parents and brothers were okay. Her dad had seemed so happy when he heard that she was coming home soon. That was back a few days ago when she and Will had been planning on going home for a visit at the end of the trimester. Not in her wildest nightmare would she have dreamed she'd be going home this way, crossing a dead and dying land. Going home alone, with Will dead and buried back in Eugene.

There was an emptiness in Anna's heart where Will used to be. A hollowness inside where something had been carved out. Maybe it wasn't just Will. Maybe it was the overwhelming loss of everything. Life, as she'd always known it, was gone. What about her mom and dad? Her brothers? What about Chuck Pierson, who was more like a grandfather to her than just her dad's employer? And what about James? *God damn you, James!* The thought was unbidden and shocked her. *Why? Why did he do it? How could he just cut it off like that? And why can't I stop thinking about him?*

Anna shook her head and reached up to brush the tears from her eyes. She hadn't even realized she was crying until she stumbled and almost tripped on a rock at the edge of the road. Wiping her eyes with the back of her hand cleared her vision, but she knew she had to get her emotions under control. Yes, the man she had agreed to marry was gone. And yes, she had loved Will. But as she thought about it, she came to a sobering realization. Losing Will wasn't as bad as losing James had been. She'd lost James a long time ago, whether he was alive or not. And now, here she was trudging along toward Idaho, hoping against hope that she would find him again. Hoping to find him and hating him all at the same time. Hating him for leaving. Hating him for the fact that she wouldn't even be here if he hadn't broken her heart in the first place.

Katy, who was a few paces ahead, stopped suddenly and forced Anna to look up from her wandering thoughts. The dog's ears were pricked up, and she had her full attention focused toward an intersection that Anna could see about a quarter of a mile ahead. A sign on the shoulder of the road told her they were approaching the Oregon Highway 201 junction. At first, all she noticed was a couple of stalled vehicles right at the intersection. Then she saw what had caught Katy's attention.

There was one car, from here it looked like an older

Tesla, that was pulled off on the right-hand shoulder of the road. Anna noticed that the driver's door was open just as a woman stepped out of the car and stood up. Anna had been looking down, not paying any attention, but Katy must have heard the car door open. Anna wasn't close enough to tell for sure, but it looked like a young woman. She definitely had long blonde hair that she was pushing away from her face as she turned and saw Anna. The woman waved, and Katy's tail started wagging. Anna raised her hand and waved back.

Anna picked up their pace, almost running. It had only been a couple of days, but it would be so nice to talk to another living human.

"Hi," the girl yelled as she reached down to pet Katy, who had run on ahead.

"Hi," Anna said as she got close. "God, it's good to see somebody else alive." The woman was definitely young. Probably even younger than Anna.

"Oh my god! It really is." The blonde girl was almost giggling as she reached up and grabbed Anna by both arms. "I'm Heather," she said. Her blue eyes were glistening with tears, and Anna couldn't tell if it was joy or sorrow.

"I'm Anna," she said and realized there were tears in her own eyes, as well. Heather had a huge smile on her face that matched the one she knew was on her own. She put her arms around the total stranger, and they stood hugging each other in a silent embrace.

Katy barked, and Anna pulled herself away from Heather. She looked down at Katy, who seemed to be wanting a hug too. "And this is Katy," she said as she stooped down and did give Katy a hug.

Chapter Three

AS THE THREE of them, Anna, Heather, and Katy, walked south on 26 toward Nyssa, the two young women were eagerly sharing their life stories. Sharing simple human companionship was such a treat that they practically forgot to even look for their next vehicle. Anna learned that Heather was a year younger, just twenty years old. She had been going to school at the University of Washington in Seattle when the sickness hit. Now, much like Anna, she was trying to get home to learn the fate of her own family. Home for Heather was Pocatello, Idaho. Deciding to travel together didn't actually even require a decision. Anna figured they might have to split up before they made it all the way to Pocatello. Or maybe not. Depending on what route she decided to take, Pocatello wasn't much out of her way at all.

Walking and talking, they'd covered about five miles when Anna spotted an old Tesla Cybertruck parked in a driveway just off the road. Nyssa was just down the road, but there was no guarantee that there would be anything available there. "Let's try that one," she told Heather, pointing toward the truck.

"What if there's somebody there?" Heather asked. Having driven her own Tesla all the way from Seattle, "borrowing" someone else's car still seemed a lot like stealing to her.

"Guess we'll find out," Anna answered as she started walking up toward the front door of the house.

After ringing the doorbell and waiting, knocking as loudly as possible and waiting some more, then ringing the doorbell again, there was still no answer. Anna tried the door, but it was locked.

"What now?" Heather asked. She'd stood back off the edge of the porch watching nervously while Anna pounded on the door.

"Well…" Anna walked past Heather letting the word hang in the air. She walked up to the Cybertruck and found it locked as well, which did not surprise her at all. The truck was still plugged into a wall charger, so it probably had a full battery. She continued on around to the back of the house with Heather right on her heels.

Banging on the back door was as futile as knocking on the front door had been. All of the racket on the outside was answered by dead silence inside, and Anna was pretty sure that dead was the operative word. She looked around for an easy way to break into the house. All they needed was the fob that would grant them access to the Tesla.

Heather watched with trepidation as Anna grabbed a rock from the border of a flower bed and used it to shatter the glass window that made up most of the top half of the back door. A siren immediately started going off in the house. The burglar alarm was deafening, but Anna was undeterred. She calmly used the rock to break out the shards of glass that were still sticking out of the frame where she wanted to reach inside. Anna reached carefully in through the broken window and unlatched the door. Heather was looking around wildly like she expected the police to show up at any minute.

The wailing siren was really deafening inside the house. Fortunately, Anna didn't have to go far. She spotted the cute brass basket on the wall as soon as she stepped inside. It was hanging just inside the door with a couple of car fobs and some other keys filling the small basket. The control for the alarm was directly below it, a flashing red light keeping time with the siren. Anna grabbed both of the fobs and got back out of the house as fast as she could. The blaring siren was a lot easier on the ears once she was back around the corner of the house.

She tossed one of the fobs to Heather, who had preceded her back around the house. Heather had to pull her hands down away from her ears to catch the fob that Anna threw her way. It turned out that Anna would only have needed one of the fobs. They were identical; apparently, one for him and one for her. She pushed the unlock button, and the truck's lights flashed. As she disconnected the charge cord and closed the charge access door, she thought of something that she'd noticed inside the house. There'd been a light on in the kitchen. The old farmhouse didn't have any solar panels or a wind turbine, and there hadn't been any sound of a generator before the burglar alarm drowned out everything else.

The power grid must still be live here, she thought. For Anna, who was well on her way to becoming a full-fledged electrical engineer, the fact that the grid was still functioning raised some interesting questions. Were there people somewhere still alive at some of the power grid control centers, or were the computerized systems still working autonomously? Probably the latter, she decided, as she put her backpack and Katy in the back seat of the Cybertruck. As bad as her ears were ringing, she could only imagine what Katy must be feeling. She waited for Heather to deposit her suitcase in the back and get in before pulling out of the driveway and heading south. The rolling bag that Heather had pulled all the way from her car, along with Anna's backpack, didn't leave much room in the back seat for Katy, but the dog didn't seem to mind.

Through the ringing in her ears, Anna heard Heather ask, "what if somebody comes back for this truck?"

Anna looked over at her and then back at the road before answering. "Guess they'll just have to find another one," she said.

...

The bridge was blocked. Anna looked it over. Two autonomous freight haulers had apparently both shutdown as they met each other right in the middle of the Highway 26 bridge across the Snake River. They'd both tried to pull over to the shoulder as they coasted to a shutdown. The result was that the two semis were sitting diagonally on the bridge, blocking not only the travel lanes but the shoulders as well. Having a bridge blocked only a couple of miles from where they'd "borrowed" the Tesla was not a good sign.

"Guess we could go back up to I-84 in Ontario," Heather suggested.

Anna thought about it, but it didn't seem like a very good idea. If Highway 26 was blocked, a highway as busy as I-84 was probably impassable. She didn't know the area very well, but she made up her mind to keep working their way south, figuring there had to be another bridge across the Snake River somewhere upstream. At the end of Nyssa's main street, she turned left on State Highway 201. At first, with the highway headed back due west, she thought maybe she'd made a mistake.

"Do you know where this road goes?" she asked Heather.

"Not really," Heather said, "but it seems to be going the wrong way to me."

Anna was just about to turn around when she saw a highway sign stating, **_Adrian 12._** "Do you know Adrian?" she asked.

Heather thought for just a second before answering. "I'm not sure, but I think Adrian is another little town on the Snake River. I don't see how, though," she added, "since we're headed away from the river."

Looking up the road, Anna thought she could see that it was going to turn to the south, so she continued on. With a few jogs, the road did indeed continue mostly south, and there were very few stalled vehicles to go around. Katy was whining, so Anna stopped the truck and put her backpack and Heather's suitcase in the back. Katy obviously needed more room to stretch out. As Anna was reaching in to get her pack out of the backseat, she noticed some kind of atlas sticking up out of the pouch on the back of her seat. It was an ancient topographic atlas of Idaho. Anna instantly realized what a treasure such an atlas was. Now that coms and GPS enabled watches and all of the other technological marvels of the 21st century were gone, old fashioned printed maps were worth their weight in gold.

Finding that atlas was really lucky. How hard it might be to get through Boise had been worrying Anna for a while. After studying the maps, she and Heather agreed to just keep following the Snake River south and east all the way upstream to the crossing near Hammett. That would put them almost halfway between Boise and Twin Falls before hitting Interstate 84.

The Highway 78 bridge just east of Hammett was wide open, and they crossed old U.S. 30 in downtown Hammett right at dusk. Just north of town, there was a wide sweeping curve to the east just before 78 got to the I-84 on-ramp. As they rounded the bend and the interstate came into view, something wasn't right. There was a semi parked across the road blocking the entrance to the interstate. Not only that, but there was a small group of people standing in the middle of the road in front of the semi.

Shit! Anna thought. They were now close enough to see that there were four men, all wearing orange jumpsuits, and all four were armed with rifles.

"Fuck!" Heather screamed as Anna cranked the wheel hard to the right, and they bounced down the highway embankment, crashing through low scrubs of brush and busting through an old wire fence. At the bottom of the embankment, a two-track road followed along the edge of an old irrigation canal. All four wheels of the Cybertruck gained purchase as Anna swerved onto the half-ass road and avoided driving straight into the ditch. The canal ran almost parallel to the interstate heading east, and Anna didn't waste any time once she was on the canal road. Katy, who wasn't buckled in like Anna and Heather, was doing her best to keep from bouncing all over the cab, as Anna floored it, and the Tesla nearly flew down the rutted old canal road.

Anna only stayed on the canal road for about a quarter of a mile before slowing just a little and turning back across a sagebrush-covered flat toward the interstate. Bouncing Katy clear up against the roof one last time, she pulled back up onto the interstate and stomped on the throttle, heading east.

The interstate wasn't as totally devoid of vehicles as the backroads had been, but Anna only had to zig and zag around a few cars and trucks.

"The charge might last longer if you slow down a little," Heather said as they slid a little bit sideways coming out of a tight spot between two autonomous freighters.

A glance at the speedometer showed they were traveling at over a hundred miles an hour. Another quick glance in the rearview mirror didn't show any sign of pursuit, and a quick look at Heather staring straight ahead with both hands latched firmly to the oh shit handles convinced Anna to ease up on the throttle. Heather's face, light-skinned to begin with, was definitely a whiter shade of pale.

Anna, with their speed slowed to a more manageable level, studied the road behind for any sign of anyone who might be following them. "Sorry," she told Heather. "I just kind of freaked out."

Heather was starting to relax her grip on the grab bars and feeling a little better about riding with a madwoman behind the wheel. "Guess I totally forgot about the prisons," she said. "What the fuck do you suppose those inmates were up to?"

"Don't know," Anna replied, "but it sure didn't look like they were up to anything good. What do you mean, prisons? How many prisons are there?"

Heather finally let go of the grab bar and gave Katy's head a pat where it was sticking up between her and Anna's seats. "I don't really know," she answered. "I just remember that most of Idaho's prisons are in the Boise area. Even Idaho's own super-max is somewhere south of Boise. We must have slipped right past it."

That little bit of news didn't make Anna feel good at all. She wondered how many evil people had survived. *Probably about the same percentage as decent people,* she thought. *If ten percent of the population was basically evil, then ten percent of survivors probably are as well.* It was definitely not a very comforting thought.

Working her way slowly around another semi and a tanker stalled just underneath an overpass, Anna's thoughts were interrupted by what she saw ahead. They'd just come by the second Glenn's Ferry exit, and it was probably a good thing they weren't running along at a hundred miles per hour. Interstate 84 used to cross the Snake River a quarter of a mile or so ahead of them. Now, the interstate ended at a ragged hole where the bridge used to be. There were blasted remains of what looked like some kind of military vehicles on both sides of the missing highway.

From this point, where Anna had stopped to try to make sense of the scene before them, one couldn't see down into the river, but she guessed there were probably more remains of military vehicles. It reminded her of scenes from old war movies. Some kind of military convoy had apparently been blown up. For some reason, the memory of the general taking over the newscast a few days ago came to mind. The general who had replaced the newscaster to inform the world that all communications were being shutdown. In Anna's mind, the picture of that general saying, "God bless America," followed by the image of a blank comscreen momentarily replaced the scene of destruction before them.

The westbound bridge had also been hit by the bombs or missiles, or whatever had destroyed the eastbound side. The other bridge wasn't totally destroyed, but it was definitely impassable.

"What the hell?" Heather said, just as Anna decided she didn't need to see any more. She pulled down into the grassy median and up onto the westbound lanes on the other side. Nervously scanning the horizon for any sign of the convicts, she headed back toward the west. Not for long though. Just as Heather was wondering what Anna had in mind, she took the exit to Glenns Ferry. Instead of turning left into town, Anna turned right onto old U.S. 30 and punched it.

For a little over a mile, the girls rode in silence. Each lost in their own thoughts. Anna continually watched the rearview mirror, but she didn't see any other vehicles moving anywhere. The old highway made a curve around a hill that blocked any view of where they'd been.

"Do you know where this road goes?" Anna asked, even though Heather didn't seem to know this part of Idaho any better than she did.

"Other than King Hill, I guess not," Heather answered. They'd both seen the road sign stating that it was four miles to King Hill.

"Check the map," Anna told Heather. She really wanted to check it herself but didn't want to stop. Not with some kind of prison gang somewhere behind them.

While she was driving, Anna glanced at Heather thumbing through the pages of the topo atlas. It was pretty obvious just from a few passing glances that Heather had no idea how to use the old paper maps. Not too many people did, of course. With the built-in nav screens in vehicles, not to mention the self-driving capability of most cars, people's understanding of printed maps had atrophied over the years.

Thank God Dad taught me how to read maps, Anna thought. There wasn't much to the community of King Hill, but she decided to use what there was to get off of the highway long enough to figure out what route they should take to get to Pocatello. She turned left onto Idaho Avenue after checking the rearview one last time to make sure no one was following them. It was getting pretty dark under the old trees that lined both sides of Idaho Avenue, and Anna couldn't help but notice that there was no artificial light anywhere. The streetlights weren't coming on at all. She wondered if the entire grid was finally down, or if it was just here.

After just a couple of blocks going north, Idaho Avenue made a sweeping curve to the east, and Anna pulled off onto a tree-lined driveway where she knew there was no way they could be spotted from old U.S. 30. "Let's take a look at the map," she told Heather, as she clicked on the other overhead light.

Heather handed the atlas to Anna, but instead of just studying it herself, Anna spread the book open on the console between them. While Katy seemed to watch with rapt attention from the backseat, Anna gave Heather a quick lesson in using the old topographic atlas. They decided they would avoid the interstate for as long as they could. Some of the back roads that Anna planned on using would be gravel or even dirt, and it might take quite a bit longer to get to Pocatello than it would otherwise, but they would be on U.S. 26 and Idaho State Highway 24 most of the way. Remembering the state of disrepair that Highway 9 was in back home, Anna figured that 26 and 24 probably hadn't had the best of maintenance over the past few decades either. And the lesser roads she planned to take from Minidoka to American Falls might be in terrible shape. Anna was glad the vehicle they'd found was a Cybertruck. *If we can make it in anything,* she thought as she backed out of the driveway, *this should work.*

As she pulled back out onto Highway 30, her thoughts turned to another abandoned road and another time. The bittersweet memories of meeting James on a dirt backroad a few years ago were as fresh in her mind as if it had happened yesterday. The wondrous joy she'd felt making love in the woods was followed, as always, by the terrible pain of the next day's text message. Anna could still recall word for word the last she'd heard from James Mendez - *My Dearest Anna, I can't see you anymore. I can't explain. You have to forget about me; about us. I can give you nothing but misery, and more than anything else in this life, I want you to be happy.*

Chapter Four

THE MORNING SUN was just bringing light to the eastern sky as Anna was jolted awake. Heather was driving, trying to carefully work her way across another washed out section of some old gravel road somewhere north and east of Lake Walcott. Katy was whining in the back seat. *Probably needs to pee,* Anna thought. *So do I.*

"Let's take a break," she told Heather. "Katy and I need to get out." It had taken them all night to drive just a couple of hundred miles. The roads had been worse than Anna feared. Especially after they turned off of U.S. 26. The whole world's infrastructure really had been going to hell over the past several decades. *Good thing we had passenger trains,* Anna thought, remembering how she got from Kremmling to Eugene in the first place.

After squatting beside the road to relieve herself, something that Anna was obviously a lot more comfortable with than Heather, Anna rummaged around in her backpack for something to eat. She still had Allpro and some of the protein bars that she'd brought from Eugene, and they'd liberated a couple of gallons of bottled water from an old country store in Shoshone. Finding some more food in the abandoned store would have been good, but the place had mainly been stocked with Allpro. Since she already had more in her pack than she'd ever want to eat, Anna passed on acquiring any more of that particular delicacy.

The Allpro did taste better this morning. Even Katy wasn't turning up her nose at it. *Must be pretty hungry,* Anna thought, meaning all three of them, based on the way Heather seemed to be shoveling down her share.

After breakfast, such as it was, Anna started driving again. She figured they had to be getting close to American Falls as the scenery started changing from mostly barren low rolling hills to old leveled agricultural fields that were now just as barren as the hills and flatlands surrounding them. Unlike the area around Bend, this area was far enough east that it was definitely in the grip of the drought that was plaguing most of the western and southwestern United States.

"This country is starting to look familiar," Heather said. She was really looking the country over, seeing familiar terrain from an unfamiliar back road that she'd never been on.

The terrain didn't look much different to Anna, except for the dried up circular fields and what looked like mostly abandoned run-down old farmhouses and outbuildings. The farm fields were like giant crop circles in a desert. The remains of pivot irrigation systems still strung out across many of the old parched fields. Decaying pipes and machinery waited for an era that would never come again.

Anna noticed that the road seemed to be improving

dramatically, just as she caught the glimmer of water ahead. Looking off to the southeast, she could see giant wind turbines in the distance. *Back to civilization,* she thought. *Or what used to be civilization.* The thought was accompanied by mixed emotions. What would they find when they got to Heather's home? Looking over at her blonde traveling companion, Anna could see that Heather was probably even more anxious and nervous than she was.

The automatic braking system kicked in hard before Anna even saw him. The boy darted out from behind a mostly dead hedgerow lining a driveway. He jumped in front of the truck, frantically waving his arms up and down for them to stop. Anna slammed on the brakes. A totally unnecessary habit, as the Cybertruck was already coming to an abrupt halt. The boy, who appeared to be no more than twelve or thirteen years old, ran around to the driver's side of the Tesla as soon as he saw that it was stopping.

"Please help me," the boy was pleading as he came to Anna's open window. He was a sandy-haired boy with freckles, and Anna could see the tears in his eyes and the desperation on his face. "Please," he begged again, "my mother's sick. She's so sick."

It wasn't just desperation on the boy's face. Anna could see that he was also in shock. She had the realization that the sickness, as she'd come to think of it, must have hit this area later than it did Eugene. She tried, but couldn't even remember how many days it had been since she'd buried Will. The recent past, from Will's call asking her to come home from the lab, to right now was just kind of a blur. *I was in shock, too,* she thought.

"Get in," she told the boy, as her thoughts turned

to her own family and her youngest brother, Cody, who wasn't much older than this boy. Maybe the sickness hadn't even hit Colorado. Maybe she would get home to find the Blue River Ranch just as she'd left it. Even as she had the thought, she knew instinctively that would not be the case. She looked at Heather as the boy was crawling into the back seat with Katy. Anna didn't know Heather that well, but she knew her well enough already to see that she was torn between sympathy for this boy and a desire to just get home to her own brothers. Any kind of delay this close to home had to be really tough for Heather.

The reason the boy was in shock was evident as soon as they stepped into the living room of the old farmhouse. There was a dead man, obviously the boy's father, on one half of the L shaped sofa, and a dead girl, who was probably the boy's younger sister stretched out on the other half.

"In here," the boy said, leading them right past his sister and father like they weren't even there.

The moaning sounds from the bedroom that the boy led them to told Anna how sick his mother was before she even saw the woman. It was like Will all over again. The woman was all wrapped up in blankets on the bed. Before even getting close, Anna knew from the ashen dry look of the woman's skin that she was burning up from fever. She also knew that the comatose woman on the bed was beyond any help that anyone could offer.

Anna heard Heather sobbing behind her and knew that was not what the one person here who could still use their help needed. Not that she blamed Heather for losing control of her emotions. To get this close to home, after hoping against hope to find home untouched, and then to see this, the same sickness that she and Anna had fled, was just too much.

Anna took the boy's hand and asked him to show her where to get a cloth and some cold water. Knowing that the woman would be dead soon was no reason to do nothing. She could at least go through the motions of trying to help. Bathing the fevered forehead with cold water was not for the sake of the dying woman, but for the sake of the boy.

...

Jeremy, that was the boy's name, said he didn't want to pray anymore. He said he'd prayed enough already; that he'd prayed and prayed, but they all still died. Anna was exhausted, and she had blisters on her hands from digging the three graves in Jeremy's back yard. She found that she was disappointed in herself for growing so soft over the past couple of years in Oregon.

Heather was even more exhausted than Anna. She hadn't grown up doing a lot of hard physical work like Anna had.

Burying Jeremy's parents and his sister hadn't been the first option after his mother succumbed to the sickness. At first, Jeremy had insisted they drive into American Falls to the Mormon church that the family attended. He'd hoped to find the Bishop and make arrangements for funerals. What they'd found in American Falls was about the same as what Anna had found in Eugene that first day. A few survivors wandering around in shock, but not much else. There was no one at the church, so Jeremy directed them to the Bishop's house. They'd knocked on the door, rang the doorbell and pounded on the door some more. Jeremy wanted to go inside when no one answered, but Anna led him back to the truck. She was pretty sure of what they would find inside.

It was getting dark by the time they finished burying Jeremy's family, and as much as Heather wanted to get home, they decided to spend the night in the old farmhouse. After a few nights on the road, it would be good to sleep inside a house for a change.

Anna, who was most definitely in charge by now, rustled up a pretty good meal of fried eggs and Allpro before they discussed any sleeping arrangements. After a meal that was mostly eaten in silence, Anna decided to boil the other dozen eggs that she found in the refrigerator so they could take them along when they hit the road tomorrow. The power was already out, so the eggs would just end up spoiling anyway. Fortunately, the cookstove was such an antique propane burner that it didn't require electronic ignition.

"Will you stay with me?" Jeremy asked Anna.

The question just came out of the blue, and she didn't have a ready answer. She'd been thinking about what to do about the twelve-year-old boy, but she hadn't figured it out yet. She couldn't just leave him here alone to fend for himself.

"Well," she answered, "I was hoping maybe you could come with us. Don't you think that would be best, Heather?" she asked, trying to get Heather involved in this too.

"I think that's a great idea," Heather answered, and Anna could feel the empathy toward Jeremy that was shared by the two young women. "We can all go home to my house," she added. "My brother, Scott, is just your age. You guys will get along great."

Even as she said it, Anna could see the worry on Heather's face and feel the concern growing deep inside her own being. What if their brothers didn't make it? What if they found their own families dead or gone along with most everyone else? It was a thought that Anna refused to let stay in her mind. She was relieved when Jeremy brought her back to the here and now.

"But this is home," he said. "I've never been anyplace else."

Anna bent down to his level to look him in the eye. "We can't just leave you here, Jeremy," she told him. "We need to stick together now. We'll stay here tonight, and then tomorrow we'll head out together. Please say you'll come with us." She had no intention of leaving such a young boy all alone, but it would be much better if it was his decision to go with them.

He searched Anna's eyes before answering. "Okay," he said finally, "guess I don't have any reason to stay here anymore, do I?"

Chapter Five

HEATHER DROVE the rest of the way to Pocatello. She was up before sunrise, refreshed even though she didn't really sleep that much at all. She was so anxious to get home that she wouldn't let Anna fix them any breakfast other than the eggs she'd boiled the night before. Heather didn't even want to give Jeremy time to pack anything, but Anna wasn't about to force him to leave home with nothing but the clothes on his back. As it turned out, Jeremy didn't have a lot more than the clothes on his back anyway. Still, his family was doing better than many before the sickness hit. They had a home and, based on what she saw in the kitchen, plenty to eat, which was more than most people had.

As Heather wound her way around and through the stalled traffic on I-86, Anna was surprised to see a couple of vehicles making their way in the opposite direction over in the westbound lanes. Anna had never been to Pocatello before, so she kept looking for any signs of prosperity, wondering if the people here had fared better than anywhere else. It was disappointing to see that was not the case. The few businesses Anna could see from the interstate seemed dilapidated and just flat worn out. They all had the obligatory bars on the windows if they had windows at all, and, though no one was in sight right now, Anna could imagine the armed security guards that must have stood watch when the businesses were open. Most would have also had at least one armed guard posted in the store or shop at night.

Heather worked her way around and through Pocatello, avoiding the interstates, which were jammed with a lot of disabled cars and trucks. They were almost out of the city at what Anna thought had to be the very southeast end of Pocatello when Heather pulled to a stop in front of what must have been the most affluent neighborhood in this part of Idaho. "That doesn't look good," she said as she saw the gates to the gated community standing wide open.

Anna didn't even have time to respond before Heather drove through the gate and wound her way down a totally deserted looking winding street with mega-mansions from another age on either side. Heather turned into a long winding driveway that led up a slight grade to one of the most imposing old homes.

My god, Heather's rich, Anna thought, then corrected herself, *was rich.* Being wealthy didn't mean much now, but the imposing antebellum-style house that they were parking in front of reminded her of James. Not that this house was really that big. It was designed to look bigger than it really was. It was like a miniature version of some grand old southern mansion. Anna used to dream of seeing the Mendez estate in Castle Pines, but that was not to be.

There was no sign of life, and Anna feared the worst as she opened the back door to let Katy out. Katy was off and running just as soon as her feet hit the ground, so many unfamiliar smells assailing her from every direction, that she seemed to have a hard time deciding what to explore first.

Jeremy got out and looked all around, obviously in awe of this place that was so much different from the home he'd always known just a few miles down the road. This didn't just seem like a different home to him; it seemed like a different world. As if he'd just stepped out of the Tesla onto the surface of a different planet entirely.

As the other three took in their surroundings, Heather literally bounded up the wide front steps and attempted to just open the front door. It was locked. Almost frantically, she punched her code into the keypad and heard the comforting click of the door unlocking. Pushing the door open and stepping through in one motion, she was lucky she didn't get shot. Inside the house, she came face to face with the business end of a shotgun. At the other end of the gun was the oldest of her younger brothers.

"Jesus Tom, you just about scared me to death," Heather exclaimed, as Tom lowered the gun.

He not only lowered the gun, he just let it drop to the floor before throwing his arms around his older sister. That's how Anna and Jeremy found them when they got to the top of the stairs. Anna couldn't see Heather's face. Her back was to the door. She could see the face of the boy that was hugging her, though. The resemblance to Heather was amazing, right down to the natural blonde hair. What Anna really noticed, though, was the swollen red eyes. She knew the tears coursing down the boy's cheeks weren't tears of joy, and her heart went out to both Heather and her brother.

An intense longing to see her younger brothers, Cody and Ralph, came over Anna. She remembered the last time she'd seen them, standing at the depot waving goodbye. That was a couple of years ago. *That's how I'll always remember them,* she thought. The train car's window framing them like a picture. She felt the tears on her cheeks and realized she wasn't just missing her brothers, she was mourning. *No! They're still there. They're still alive. I'll see them again soon.*

...

Anna woke up early as usual. Not wanting to wake the others, she lay quietly in bed thinking. She'd been here at the Smith home for a week now. Strange how she hadn't known Heather's last name until they'd arrived at her home. Anna could imagine that last names wouldn't matter as much as they used to, now that so much of the human population was gone. She wondered, once again, how many people had survived the sickness. Did any of her family survive? Maybe the sickness hadn't even hit Kremmling or the BR at all. Pocatello seemed to be about a week behind Eugene, as far as the sickness was concerned. Heather's mother and little brother, Scott, had both died the day before they got here. Why did the sickness kill so many, yet spare a few? What determined who lived and died? It didn't seem to be genetics, or was it? If it was in one's genes, why did Scott and Mrs. Smith die, but not Tom or Heather? And what about Mr. Smith? Tom didn't know what had happened to their father. Mr. Smith had been away on some kind of business trip back east when the world stopped. Tom, and now Heather, had both resigned themselves to the fact that their father had probably been either a victim of the tsunami that hit the east coast or the sickness that was wiping out everyone else.

Anna crawled out of the comfortable bed and slipped quietly over to the window of what had been Heather's parent's bedroom. The master suite was on the top floor, with a large picture window providing a view to the east. An orange glow was just beginning to light up the sky above the mountains. Anna wanted nothing more than to head off into that rising sun. To hit the road for home, to find whatever awaited her at the Blue River Ranch. Looking down on the large backyard that ended at the edge of the Portneuf River, she knew that she couldn't leave. Not yet, anyway. She couldn't just leave the others here alone to fend for themselves, and they didn't want to go with her. Anna had become the leader of their little tribe because she was the most capable, but none of them, not even Jeremy, wanted to follow her to Colorado.

After burying Heather's mother and brother, it had been a hectic week getting the Smith home set-up to be as self-contained as possible. The house already had a large enough array of solar panels, but the PV system was designed to just feed power into the grid. There was no battery backup, and the PV system was designed to just shut down if the grid went down. The grid had gone dead the day after they got to Pocatello. Anna had spent most of the last week scrounging tools, batteries, controllers, and other components to convert the PV from a grid-tied system to a totally off-grid system.

Heather and Tom hadn't been as much help as Jeremy, but they tried, and Anna tried to teach them all everything she possibly could. Neither Heather nor Tom seemed to have much mechanical ability, but Jeremy, even though he was only twelve years old, showed real promise. Anna found herself wondering if it had something to do with growing up on a farm instead of in the city.

Just one more major project, Anna thought, as she looked down at the small creek that they called the Portneuf River. The small stream was a mere shadow of what the river had once been before the mega-drought. *It may not be much, but at least it's water.* Anna turned away from the window, got dressed, and headed downstairs to start the day. Today she would go back into Pocatello to find a pump, a pressure tank, pipe, and the rest of what they would need to turn the running creek into running water for the Smith house. The city water had stopped flowing before Anna and Heather got to Pocatello, and packing water from the creek one bucketful at a time was a real pain. The water would still have to be boiled before drinking, but there was nothing she could do about that. First, she'd get them running water; then, she could head out for Colorado.

. . .

Anna pulled the Cybertruck up to the large detached garage, and Jeremy got out and ran around to plug it in. The wall charger was now powered solely by the PV system, and it drew a lot of juice, but keeping the Tesla charged up was one of Anna's priorities. She damn sure wanted a full battery whenever she could finally head for home.

The bed of the truck was filled with everything that she and Jeremy had picked up for the water system. Most of it, they'd gathered up at the old Home Depot store, which someone else had broken into long before Anna and

Jeremy arrived. It had been somewhat eery finding their way around the darkened store and carrying what they wanted back out to the truck. Birds were flying around inside the store, and Anna had found herself jumping every time she heard one of them make a strange noise. Who else might be foraging at Home Depot? As it turned out, they didn't see anyone else at the store and only a handful of people anywhere along the way back and forth.

Anna could hear voices coming from the backyard as she carried the pump toward the gate in the privacy fence that separated the yard from the driveway. She stopped abruptly at the gate, hearing a voice she didn't recognize. It was a man's voice, definitely not Heather or Tom. Setting the pump down quietly, Anna was about to turn back to the truck to get her gun, when the gate opened.

"Looks like you can use some help," a man that Anna had never seen before said. He was probably ten or fifteen years older than Anna, not as old as her dad, but not young enough to be part of her generation either. Seeing the startled look on Anna's face, he held out his hand. "I'm Richard," he said, as Anna shook his hand, "and you must be Anna."

"Richard lives just down the road," Heather explained. She and Tom followed Richard out of the gate and grabbed as much as they could carry from the Tesla while Richard picked up the pump and carried it into the yard.

· · ·

The installation of the water system took a lot less time and was much easier with Richard's help. Richard had been an excavation contractor before the sickness. When it came to plumbing and waterworks, he had more experience and expertise than the rest of the group combined. With his help, it only took another five days to get the water system installed and functioning properly. Richard had even gone so far as to get one of his battery-powered electric backhoes from his old business to help. They used the backhoe to dig a sump in the creek to pump out of, and to bury the waterline underground so it wouldn't freeze next winter.

Richard had more or less invited himself to not only work with the little group to get the waterline installed but to move into the big house with them. His wife died from the sickness, and, being childless, he didn't have much reason to stay home.

The group had canvassed the neighborhood to see if there were more survivors, but they didn't find any. After getting the water system up and running, Richard had suggested that, since they had the backhoe, maybe they should bury the neighbors who'd died. Or, at least the ones closest to their house. It was a pretty gruesome task by the time they got started. Some of the neighbors had been dead for well over a week by the time they got to them. But they persevered, broke into houses, and buried all of their closest dead neighbors. Using the backhoe to dig the graves, the project only took a couple of days. Not only did they bury their neighbors, but they also liberated a pretty overwhelming supply of food stocks from their neighbor's pantries and storerooms.

Anna had been in Pocatello for fifteen days, and each day the desire to get home to Colorado grew stronger than the day before. Her desire to get away from Idaho was also fueled by awareness of another problem that was starting to develop. With two young women at the sexual prime of their lives now living under the same roof with one sexually mature man, and no other potential sexual partners around, personal relationships were bound to become strained.

I have to leave today, Anna thought, as she lay in bed fighting against a strong desire to just go crawl in bed with Richard. *Why am I so damn horny? What is it about death that brings out such strong sexual desire in people?* Anna knew it wasn't just her. She couldn't help but notice the way Heather looked at Richard. It was only a matter of time before Richard would be ready to move beyond grieving for his wife. Only a matter of time until Richard felt the same sexual attraction that both she and Heather did. And then there was Heather's brother, Tom.

Yesterday, Anna caught Tom masturbating in the garage. At fifteen years old, he was probably still a virgin, but his young body was as physically ready for sex as it was ever going to get. Having younger brothers herself, Anna was not at all surprised that Tom would be masturbating. What did shock her was her own reaction. She had to force herself to look away, to give the young man the privacy he deserved.

Even now, lying in bed as the sun was rising in the east, Anna was picturing young Tom standing in the garage. She fantasized about what it would have been like if she had just walked in and introduced him to real sex.

An orgasm sent tingling sensations from her head to her toes. She hardly even realized she was masturbating, as she dreamed of taking the virginity of a fifteen-year-old boy. *I do have to get out of here,* she thought, as she crawled out of bed and stepped over Katy, who was sleeping peacefully on the floor, oblivious to the activity in Anna's bed.

Chapter Six

A NNA TOOK HIGHWAY 30 from McCammon, Idaho, to Interstate 80 near Little America in Wyoming. She was starting to get worried about finding another vehicle to "borrow". Having wasted a couple of hours and several miles of the Cybertruck's range looking for a replacement vehicle in Kemmerer, the day and driving range were both getting shorter as she approached Little America. Anna and Katy had left Pocatello early that morning after very emotional goodbyes with the four friends they'd left behind.

"What do you think, Katy," she asked the dog, who was curled up in the passenger seat, apparently tired of looking out the window at the barren desert that southwest Wyoming had become. "Should we check Little America, or just go on to Rock Springs?"

Katy raised her head off of her paws and looked at Anna as if to say, "you're asking me?" Anna checked the range again, she still had about 75 miles of range left. Plenty to get to Rock Springs, but that was about it. Anna didn't even have to look at a map to know they would run out of battery somewhere between Rock Springs and

Wamsutter. Being just a few hundred miles from home, Anna knew this part of the world much better than she knew Idaho. This part of the world had been empty and barren forever. Southwestern Wyoming was one of the few places in America to remain nearly unchanged for at least a hundred years.

Better check, Anna thought as she took the Exit 68 offramp. She hadn't found a useable vehicle in Kemmerer, would Rock Springs be any batter? From I-80, she couldn't tell if the old Little America parking lots had any cars in them or not. The trees that had been carefully nurtured to turn Little America into an oasis were mostly dead now, but they still blocked the view from the highway. Based on how empty I-80 was, she didn't have very high hopes as she pulled under the overpass and headed into the iconic travel stop.

There were a lot more vehicles than Anna would have guessed at Little America. Even stranger than there being quite a few semis of various sorts and several cars, trucks, and SUVs, there were a couple of military vehicles of some kind parked over in one corner of the truck lot. She drove slowly through the auto parking lots looking for suitable transportation to replace the Cybertruck that had served so well. Her nerves were on edge, with the military vehicles reminding her of the blown-up bridges back in Idaho. Staying as far as possible away from the military trucks, Anna cruised the auto parking area, her senses on high alert. Even Katy sat up straight in her seat with her head out the window, testing the air with her nose.

Anna didn't need a nose like Katy's to take in the overriding smell of death in the air. It seemed extra strange that there didn't seem to be a single living person in the whole area, just that insidious smell of decaying human flesh. The vehicles all seemed to be of the autonomous variety, and Anna was just about to give up when she spotted a car off by itself, parked behind the old restaurant. At first, she couldn't tell what it was, it looked old, older even than the Cybertruck. As she got closer, she realized it was a Chevrolet Bolt. *God, I haven't seen one of those for a while,* she thought. She parked the Tesla and got out to take a closer look. A Bolt would never have been her first choice, but, seeing the cord running from behind the building to the charge port on the car, it might be her only choice. Anna had no doubt that there wouldn't be any power flowing through that cord now, but maybe the car had been fully charged before the power died.

Katy, freed from the confines of the truck, took off on her own while Anna walked up to the Bolt and tried the door. It was locked of course. *Now what?* The fob for this one car could be on a dead body anywhere. It was odd, though. There weren't any dead people just lying around. She'd seen some bodies in some of the cars in the parking lot, and she was sure she'd smelled more than she'd seen, but there weren't any just lying around. Maybe someone's still alive. Anna suddenly had a strong sense that there were more than just dead people left at the Little America travel plaza. For some reason, that wasn't a comforting thought.

Wishing Katy wouldn't have gone off exploring, Anna grabbed her old .40 caliber Smith and Wesson handgun out of the console of the Tesla. Her dad gave her the gun for her sixteenth birthday. He also made sure she knew how to use it. The weight of the gun belt wrapped around her waist gave her a little better feeling as she walked around the corner of the restaurant. The Bolt was probably one of the employee's cars. If that was the case, the owner was most likely inside the building, either dead or alive.

As she came around the front of the building, she caught a glimpse of Katy running between a couple of semis out in the truck parking lot. She hollered, but the dog kept going, seemingly intent on something other than Anna. The entrance door to the restaurant was standing wide open, blocked that way by a rock someone had placed in front of it. A little chill went up Anna's spine. Were there still living people here? If so, what kind of people?

Walking through the open door, Anna just about gagged. Based on the smell, the only people in the restaurant were dead people. The horrific sight inside left Anna no further hope of finding anyone alive. There were at least eight decomposing bodies in the restaurant's booths. It looked like they had just laid down in the booths and died. Another woman's body was sprawled out on the floor with flies and maggots crawling in and out of her gaping mouth and nostrils. The sight and the smell were too much. Anna bent over and wretched up the last of the protein bar she'd eaten an hour or so ago.

She turned and rushed back out into the open air. She couldn't do it. She'd just have to find another car. There was no way she was going to search those dead bodies for a key fob. She'd just have to find something at Rock Springs.

The unmistakable loud crack of a gunshot stopped her instantly. It sounded like it came from over behind the semis where she'd last seen Katy. Anna froze. She couldn't see anyone or anything besides the trucks that had been parked out there all along. She pulled the slide back and let it go, jacking a shell into the chamber of the gun that was in her right hand. The pistol had almost magically jumped from her holster into her hand. Grabbing the gun and cocking it had been a nearly instantaneous reaction, made without any conscious thought at all.

Who shot the gun? Why? She was pretty sure that it wasn't aimed at her. A quick look around let her know there was no place very close to hide even if she wanted to. Why should she hide? Just because someone shot a gun didn't mean anything. The sound of gunshots was a fairly common occurrence anywhere in the rural mountain west.

"Hey," she yelled as loud as she could. "Who's shooting?" Her yell was answered by silence. The fact that no one answered scared Anna more than the gunshot had. "Katy, here Katy," she yelled as she took off running back toward the Tesla. Coming around the back corner of the building, Anna froze. Someone was looking in the window of the Cybertruck. It was a man dressed in some kind of desert camo military uniform.

The man saw Anna at just about the same time she saw him. He also saw the gun in her hand that was now aimed directly at him.

"Whoa," he said, raising his hands above his head. He was a large man, but he didn't seem to be armed. "Easy ma'am," he said with a definite southern accent. "Just looking's all, no need for weapons."

Anna lowered the gun as the absurdity of the situation struck her. Here they were, two of the few people left alive in the whole area. Why would anyone want to harm anyone else now? *Then what about the gunshot?* With that thought, Anna started to raise the gun again, but it was too late. She felt the blow to her head that knocked her to the ground and had the fleeting thought that it must have been someone else shooting the gun. Her world faded to black as she lost consciousness.

Chapter Seven

IT WAS A NIGHTMARE like nothing she'd ever had before. She was tied down somehow, laying on her back. Her arms were stretched out to her sides. She struggled to free a hand to push the man that was on top of her away. Her legs were spread wide apart, held that way as securely as her hands. She could feel the man thrusting as she struggled and squirmed, unable to escape. She felt the man shudder as he thrust hard one last time.

"My turn," she heard a voice say, and Anna regained full consciousness, realizing it wasn't a nightmare at all. At least it wasn't a sleeping nightmare. This was really happening. She was being raped. Worse, she was being gang-raped.

"Sure," the man said as he crawled off of her. It was the same man that had been looking at the Tesla. She could see him much better now. As he buttoned up his pants, Anna looked up at his face. He was older than her, probably in his thirties. She couldn't help but notice, as she had before, that he was a big man. When she had seen him from a distance, she could tell how large he was, but now, close up, she could see how muscled he was as well. He had close-cropped blonde, almost white, hair. She felt totally consumed by hate as she looked into his pale blue eyes. Eyes that screamed crazy. Here was a truly insane man.

He smiled down at her. "Go ahead, Curt," he said. "Get some while you can. She's a real keeper." He looked up apparently at someone named Curt, who wasn't visible to Anna. "After this, though, she's all mine, understand?"

"Sure Sarge," Curt said. He must have understood, alright. She watched in horror as he stood over her and pulled down his pants before kneeling between her legs. Through blurred vision, she saw that Curt was smaller in every way than the other man. "Don't cry," he said, "you should enjoy this as much as me." Anna didn't even have to see Curt's eyes to know that he was as crazy as the first man, the one called Sarge.

Anna had pulled into the Little America parking lot in the early afternoon. It was late in the day by the time the man named Curt crawled off of her. Anna could feel the earth beneath her back. She could feel that she was totally naked, stripped, and staked out on the bare dirt. She could feel the ropes biting into her wrists and ankles, and the scrapes and scratches where her back, and especially her butt, had been ground into the hard dirt. She had been concentrating on feeling all of those abrasions to avoid feeling what was happening to the rest of her body. Now that the men were finished with her, she just hurt all over. She could feel the sun burning her naked body even this late in the day.

"Now what?" she heard the man called Curt ask. Then she saw Sarge come around from behind her to stand between her outstretched legs. She was afraid that he was going to rape her again, but this time he just raped her naked body with those crazy pale blue eyes.

"You're mine now. You understand?" he said.

Anna, almost involuntarily, shook her head yes. She understood that she had no other choice.

"Cut her loose. Put her with the others," Sarge told Curt. Then he looked back down at Anna. "You run, I'll kill ya. Understand?"

Anna nodded her understanding again, as she felt Curt cutting the rope loose from her left wrist. She did understand. She understood that she hated these two men like she had never hated anyone before, especially Sarge. She understood how much she'd like to cut Sarge's throat to watch him bleed out and die. But she also realized that she would have to bide her time and wait for the right opportunity.

Curt let her get dressed, except for her shoes. She'd been wearing her light hikers when they stripped her, but he told her to carry them. Apparently, he was afraid she'd make a run for it if she had shoes on. *Not much chance of that,* Anna thought. *Not with him holding a rifle on me. And not with my head throbbing like this.*

Curt forced her to walk ahead of him while he trained the rifle on her back. He directed her toward the back corner of the lot where the military vehicles were parked. Thankfully, he'd let her put her socks back on. The scorching asphalt still burned the bottom of her feet, even through the socks. He forced her to walk between two semis that seemed out of the way. Coming out from between the two trucks, she saw why the man forced her to come this way.

Katy was lying dead in a pool of blood in front of one of the semis. The dog that had been her closest companion for weeks, a gentle thing that would never hurt anyone, had been killed for no reason by the man walking behind her. As tears filled her eyes, she heard the man laugh. *I'll kill him, too,* she made a silent vow to her dead friend.

Anna kept on walking. She wouldn't give the crazy sonofabitch the satisfaction of seeing her grief. He herded her to one of the military vehicles that she hadn't really noticed before. It was like nothing she'd ever seen. It was an armored truck with obviously extreme off-road capabilities. The cab had no windows at all, just slots that were probably more to shoot through than to see out. The truck had to either be autonomous, or else it had to have cameras projecting the road ahead on a screen for the driver. The cab wasn't what really caught her attention, though. The truck had an enclosed bed that was about thirty feet long, and probably ten feet tall. There was a row of window-like openings about a foot high all down the side, just below the roof. The windows were covered, not with any kind of glass, just vertical bars. It was like a mobile armored prison or jail cell, with no insignia to identify which branch of the military it belonged to. The only symbol of any kind that might help identify the truck was three black crosses painted on the side of the cage. The three black crosses looked like they had been painted on the side of the truck by hand. Other than the three black crosses on the sidewall, what really grabbed Anna's attention was on the roof. The entire top of the truck was covered with solar panels that were angled to capture the maximum amount of solar radiation. Without being able to get a better look, it appeared to Anna that they were somehow mounted with some kind of tracking system to keep them always turned toward the sun.

Curt didn't allow Anna any time to study the PV system but forced her to the back of the truck. Stepping around the back corner, trying to stay on the shaded part of the hot asphalt, she was confronted with the fact that this wasn't so much a mobile jail cell as it was a cage. The entire back of the van box was open to the elements. Open that is, except for the solid steel bars running from the floor to the ceiling with a barred door right in the center. Anna watched as Curt touched a button on the side of the van, and a set of steps silently slid out from under the door and lowered to the pavement.

"Stay back or your dead," he yelled at the back of the truck as he pushed another button. Anna heard the click of the locks unlatching, and the cage door automatically swung inwardly open. "Get in," he said, waving the barrel of the gun at her.

Walking up those steps and into that cage was as hard as anything Anna had ever done. Part of her wanted to just make a break for it and accept the bullet or bullets that would bring an end to the nightmare. In the end, it was hatred, plain and simple, that kept up her will to live. She had to live. At least long enough to kill these two monsters.

The interior of the cage on wheels was dim but not dark. There was plenty of light from the row of barred windows along the top of each side and the barred open end of the cage. There were three other people, all women, sitting on built-in benches at the front end of the steel cage. Besides the benches, the only furnishings in the van were another small bench near the door of the cage and a bare mattress lying on the floor against one side. The little bench at the rear of the mobile cell was only big enough to accommodate one person, and it had a round hole in the seat. It was obviously a toilet. Anna heard the cage door lock behind her as she walked toward the front of the van. Even with the ventilation provided by the barred openings, the late afternoon heat was stifling. The outside of the truck was painted in light-colored desert camo, but the heat coming off the steel wall that had been facing the sun all day was still intense.

The first two things Anna noticed about the three other inhabitants of her cage was they were all women, and they were all darker-skinned than she was. As she got close enough to see their eyes looking at her, she noticed that they all had a vacant hollow stare. It reminded her of pictures she'd seen in history books of prisoners of war, or the images of Nazi death camps. Anna was shocked to see that one of the women wasn't a woman at all. She was just a girl, no more than thirteen or fourteen years old. She appeared to be Native American, and, if possible, her stare was even more vacant than the other two.

"You been raped yet?" was the first thing any of the three said. It was the one that appeared to be the oldest. She was a Black woman, who Anna guessed to be about thirty. The question seemed like a strange thing to ask, but it let Anna know that all three of them had also been raped, even the young girl.

Anna sat down on the floor against the sidewall of the van a few feet from the others before answering. She knew she didn't really need to respond, the answer had to be written all over her face. "Yes," she answered simply, "two of them."

The woman sitting between the Black woman and the girl was probably about Anna's age. She seemed to be Latina, but darker-skinned than most. She looked at Anna with that vacant stare that wasn't quite as empty as it appeared. "Just once?" she asked.

Anna wasn't sure she understood the question. She'd just told them there were two of them. "There were two men," Anna answered. "Both of them raped me." She held out her wrists toward the other three, thinking maybe the rope burns and cuts could make them understand.

"Just once?" the Chicana girl asked again, incredulously. Anna just stared at her, wondering if she had lost her mind or something.

"There's only two of them," the Black woman said. "What Sonia wants to know is if they both only raped you once. Those are the horniest two crazy sonsabitches I have ever seen. Shit, they took turns a couple of times on poor Jasmine there. Made us watch while they did it. Poor girl hasn't spoken since."

Anna looked over at the young Native American. The look in Jasmine's eyes was especially haunting. She looked like the caged animal that all of them had become. Anna felt so sorry for the young girl that it helped push her own trauma to the back of her mind. "I'm Anna," she said softly to the girl.

"What is your tribe?" Jasmine asked Anna to the utter surprise of the other two women. With Native American ancestry from both her mother and father, Anna did look more native than a lot of the people on tribal rolls, but she had never been listed on any tribal roll that she was aware of. She didn't even know from which, or from how many tribes she was descended.

"I don't know," Anna said, and she wished she did know. It had been a long time since she'd felt that longing to know her ancestry. Probably not since junior high school when others called her Pocahontas. The nickname, meant to bully or shame her, had just the opposite effect. Anna wore the nickname proudly. No one had called her Pocahontas for a long time. Probably not since she had insisted the would-be bullies call her that all the time. Since then, she'd had the derogatory, injun, thrown at her a few times, but not many.

"I am Shoshone," Jasmine told her with pride. And Anna could see how genuinely proud the girl was of her own ancestry.

"I'm Flo," the Black woman said, jumping into the conversation. "And in case you haven't noticed, I'm a Black woman. Since I've been in this cage the longest, guess I should fill you in. The first thing you need to know is these ain't no ordinary crazies. No, Sarge and Curt are both some special kind of crazy. They're white supremacists, for one thing. They seem to think if you don't have lily-white skin, you ain't good for anything but killing or fucking. The only reason we're alive is for fucking. Those assholes actually think they're breeding us. They think they're going to raise their own crop of slaves. Can you believe that shit? What kind of person plans to use their own children for slaves?"

Anna and the other two listened while Flo told her story. Apparently, Flo hadn't told this entire story to either of the other two before now. She said that she'd kind of lost track of time, but that she'd been taken about two weeks ago. She and her husband, Ben, had both survived the sickness when it wiped out most of the rest of Sacramento. They'd been on foot, crossing Interstate 80 on the outskirts of the city when they saw the truck heading east on the shoulder of the freeway. Flo and Ben had thought it must be some kind of U.S. military or National Guard coming to help survivors, so they waved their arms and waited for the oncoming vehicle. Flo paused for a bit, with a mixture of emotions ranging from anger to grief playing across her face.

"They shot Ben before they even got to us. Don't know if it was Sarge or Curt. I heard the impact of the bullet hitting Ben in the chest, and the thud as his body was driven to the ground. I didn't understand. Ben was just dead on the ground with a pool of blood starting to form around him. I didn't understand…" Tears were forming in Flo's eyes, and for a moment it seemed that she couldn't go on. "One more dead nigger. That's the first thing Sarge said when he got out of the truck." Flo was finally able to continue. "At first, I wondered why they didn't just kill me too if they were trying to wipe out Black survivors. It didn't take long to figure that one out, though."

She said they didn't rape her right then, but threw her in the cage and headed east. It was when they stopped somewhere by Truckee that they dragged her out of the cage, and Sarge ordered her to strip while Curt held a gun on her. When she didn't comply immediately, Sarge hit her in the face so hard that it knocked her flat. "Now, take off your clothes, or you're a dead woman." He'd told her.

Flo had another short breakdown before continuing.

"Should have just let them kill me," she said softly.

There seemed to be some kind of catharsis in talking that Anna somehow triggered in the other three. Why they hadn't told each other before, Anna couldn't guess, but they seemed to be telling their stories for the first time.

Sonia was next. When Flo fell silent, she told them how she had been taken near Elko, Nevada. Like Anna, Sonia was a ranch girl. She'd grown up on a ranch on the Humboldt River west of Elko. Unlike Flo, the sickness left Sonia totally alone. The rest of her family had all died within two days of each other. Where Sonia lived had been pretty well removed from the rest of the world. Her dad had been some kind of prepper isolationist. From what Sonia said, it sounded like her father had been prepared for almost anything. Anything except the sickness that wiped out everyone that is. She'd been homeschooled her whole life. Occasional trips into Elko were her only contact with outsiders. When everyone else in her family died, she hadn't known what to do. There was never a com of any kind on the ranch, so she had no idea that it wasn't just her family. Not until she got out on Interstate 80, that is.

She was headed into Elko to get help when she encountered Sarge and Curt. Sonia had been driving her dad's old Chevy pickup but got stuck when she tried to go around some semis that were stalled in the middle of I-80. Her dad's old truck was just two-wheel drive, and she high-centered in a washout on the shoulder of the interstate. That's when she first saw other dead people. Other than her family, that is. Walking toward Elko, she'd come across a dead man and woman lying in the median in the middle of nowhere. She was pondering the dead couple and all of the stalled autonomous vehicles on I-80 when she saw the camouflaged military truck working its way slowly up the shoulder of the interstate toward her. "I thought they would help," she said and fell silent.

No one spoke for a while. All four women seemingly lost in their own thoughts. Then Jasmine said, "I was a virgin. It wasn't supposed to be like that. It hurt so bad," she sobbed.

Anna got up and sat down beside the poor girl. She put her arm around Jasmine and held her while Jasmine cried on her shoulder.

"What do they want?" Anna asked, as much to herself as any of the other three. "I mean other than fucking and, apparently, trying to raise slaves. Are they collecting sex slaves, or what?"

Anna didn't really expect an answer, so she was surprised when Flo answered, "You got it exactly right. They want slaves period, not just sex slaves. That first time, when Sarge was raping me, he told me I should feel honored. Honored because I was going to bear him lots of slaves. It seems, from what I've overheard, that some crazy white supremacists had a plan to overthrow the government and take over the old south. They call themselves The New Army Of God. They plan on turning back time to their good old days when white men ruled, and people of color were nothing but slaves."

The question that immediately popped into Anna's head was why they hadn't just enslaved Flo's husband instead of killing him. She posed the question to Flo, whose answer was as crazy as the two lunatics that had captured them. "They don't think they can trust any modern men of color to yield to becoming slaves. So, they figure they'll just breed their own slave stock. What I can't figure out is what they plan on having slaves do. Pick cotton? I do know Sarge and Curt, at least, plan on breeding us all just as fast as they can. Like I said, I never knew men that could fuck as much as those two can." Flo leaned close to the others then and whispered, "Wouldn't they be disappointed if they knew my birth control implant will last at least eleven months or so."

Anna felt the truck start to move as she had the thought, mine will last even longer. It wasn't much, but there was a little comfort in the knowledge that at least she couldn't get pregnant. That probably wasn't the case for poor Jasmine, who was still sobbing on her shoulder. Anna guessed that it was also probably not the case for Sonia. Sonia hadn't said so, but Anna had the feeling that Jasmine wasn't the only one who had been a virgin. It was impossible to imagine a worse way to lose one's virginity than to be raped by two crazy men. Guess I should be thankful. At least it wasn't my first time. The thought didn't provide any comfort at all. If there was one thing Anna didn't feel, it was thankful.

Chapter Eight

"WHAT IF NOBODY'S THERE?" Anna could hear the two men talking outside the cage. It was Curt's voice asking the question.

"Somebody's gonna be there," she heard Sarge answer. "You think we're the only two motherfuckers that survived this shit?"

It had been about a week since Anna was taken captive. From the snippets of conversation she'd overheard, she knew that Sarge and Curt were members of some kind of white supremacist group. Flo had called them The New Army Of God, but Anna never heard Sarge or Curt use that name at all. Whatever they called themselves, they were imbedded in the U.S. Army and Marines. Apparently, they hadn't been as successful in the Air Force, Navy, or Space Force; but Curt and Sarge seemed to look down on those branches of the military as much as they looked down on people of color. From conversations Anna had overheard, this group of white supremacists had all agreed to meet up in Kentucky after staging a revolution to take out the United States Government. The plan was to begin with Kentucky and start a whole new nation. A new white-ruled slave state, based on the model of the old Confederate South. Curt and Sarge talked about killing niggers and Mexicans with relish. They, not just Sarge and Curt, but the movement they belonged to, planned to exterminate any people of color that couldn't be assimilated as slaves. The movement's planners obviously didn't count on the sickness doing so much extermination for them, but that was something no one could have predicted or planned. In actuality, the sickness had probably killed as many members of The New Army Of God as it did anyone else. *I hope it killed them all,* Anna thought, even though two of them were still very much alive.

After traveling every night for the past six days, Anna had no idea where they were, other than a long way east of where they started. It was getting light enough to really see the surroundings through the bars at the back of the truck. They were definitely in a much greener place than any she'd seen since western Oregon. They were parked on the outskirts of what seemed to be a small town somewhere, maybe Nebraska or Kansas. Anna had never been east of Colorado before, so the terrain was totally unfamiliar. Through the bars, she could see that they were parked next to a bridge. There was an old sign on the bridge that filled her with longing and memories. The sign on the bridge read, ***The Big Blue River.*** How she longed to be back at the Blue River in Colorado. The longing to be back home was at least as intense as the dread of what she knew was coming next.

Sarge and Curt followed the same routine every day. Every night, as soon as the sun went down, they traveled for about four hours. Anna figured that must be how long the batteries lasted on a full charge. Then, they'd stop somewhere, usually in, or close to a town of some kind. Wherever they stopped, they'd wait out the rest of that night and the following day. Anna was sure they remained stationary all day, every day, in order for the PV panels to recharge the batteries. Apparently, the solar tracking mechanism couldn't function while they were in motion.

For the four captives, the growing light didn't bring the promise of a new day. It brought the promise that one or two of them would soon be fucked again by Sarge and Curt. It wasn't so much rape anymore, as it was simply being fucked. None of the women resisted at all, resistance was futile and only made it worse. All they could do was endure. What Flo had told Anna that first day about Sarge and Curt being the horniest two men she'd ever known was definitely right. Anna couldn't understand how or why the two men started off each day by fucking one of the women, but they hadn't missed a morning yet. She used to think her fiance, Will, was horny, making love to her at least three or four times a week. Not that she'd had anything against that. Anna enjoyed making love with Will as much as he did, maybe more. There was nothing enjoyable about being fucked by one of the monsters she could hear talking outside the cage, though. Not that Curt ever got another chance to fuck her. No, Sarge may have been crazy, but he was definitely in charge, and he was true to his word. Anna was strictly his own private property. Curt always got his choice of any of the other three.

"I'm going to let you go first this morning," Anna heard Sarge tell Curt as the two men came around to the back of the cage. "Pick whichever one you want. As long as it isn't Anna," he added quickly.

Flo looked questioningly at Anna. "Now that's a first," Flo whispered, having obviously overheard the two men's conversation as well as Anna had. Anna wasn't sure if Flo meant that this was the first time Sarge had allowed Curt to go ahead of him, or if she meant it was a first that one of the women was off-limits to Curt. It may not have been as noticeable to Flo as it was to Anna that she was Sarge's favorite.

"Damn, I don't know, Sarge," Curt said, looking through the opened door to the cage. "What I'd really like is some white pussy for a change."

"Save that for the sisterhood," Sarge told him. "There'll be plenty of white women once we get to Kentucky. True Aryan women worthy of being wives. Those are the women we need to bring back our glory. We can rebuild the Aryan race later. Right now, we have to make colored babies." It wasn't clear how many white women of some sisterhood Sarge expected to find in Kentucky, but it was clear that whatever cult they belonged to expected white power to retake control of the world.

"S'pose so," Curt answered as he walked into the cage. "You, Jasmine, get your tight little Indian cunt over here."

Jasmine didn't even hesitate. Her spirit had been completely broken. The young woman was pulling off her clothes as she walked to the mattress that was never used for sleeping.

The women were always fucked right there in the cage in front of the others. That bothered Anna as much as the act itself. She always made herself look away, usually at whichever man wasn't doing the fucking. Whoever that was, he'd invariably be holding his rifle pointed at the other three women while mostly watching the sex being performed by the other. Like dirty old men at a peep show, Curt and Sarge watched each other fuck with rapt attention.

I *wonder if the other women watch when Sarge fucks me?* Anna wondered absently, staring straight at Sarge through the bars. Sarge, of course, wasn't staring back at Anna. He obviously had other things on his mind. The rifle was pointed at the three women in the front of the cage, but his eyes were fixed on the activity on the mattress. *He's probably trying to decide between me or seconds on Jasmine,* Anna thought. She hoped Sarge would choose the young girl and leave her alone this morning, and then she was ashamed of herself for wishing that on anyone.

The sounds coming from the mattress and the intent look in Sarge's crazy eyes told Anna that Curt was about to finish. Then Sarge's head exploded, followed by the reverberating sound of the blast of a high-powered rifle. That was followed immediately by another blast from the gun that was falling from Sarge's dead hands.

Everything seemed to happen at once. The blast that blew up Sarge's head knocked him instantly to the ground. Curt jumped off of Jasmine and headed to the open door, but he wasn't fast enough. Anna tackled him from behind as he was running down the stairs toward the rifle he'd left at the back of the cage. Anna didn't even hear the sound of the gunshot that had been meant for Curt. She was totally unaware that she'd saved Curt from the same sniper that killed Sarge. The focus of her whole being was to get to the rifle before Curt did. He was still scrambling to get back to his feet by the time Anna grabbed the gun. She pulled the trigger the first time, hitting him in the chest as he turned toward her. That first shot no doubt killed him, but Anna pulled the trigger again and again, the dead man's body bouncing each time another round tore into it. It still wasn't enough. Anna turned the rifle on the lifeless form of Sarge lying on the ground and emptied the rest of the magazine into his dead body.

She heard Flo telling her, "it's okay Anna, they're dead," as she came back to the now from the murderous rage that had taken her outside the confines of time. Anna let the gun slip slowly to the ground as the red blur of rage slipped from her vision, and she turned back to face the other women. Flo was standing at the top of the stair, looking down at her. Jasmine was naked, sitting up on the filthy mattress with the faraway stare of someone in total shock. And then there was Sonia. She hadn't moved from the bench at the front of the van. She was right where she'd been when the violence erupted, only now she was slumped down with her head bowed forward, her chin resting against her chest just above where blood was spreading from the little hole right between her breasts. The reflex action of Sarge's trigger finger had claimed one life, even in death.

Chapter Nine

"ANOTHER COUPLE of these assholes came through here about two weeks ago." The Black man was answering Anna's question about how he'd known from a distance that Sarge was not just some kind of active duty military. "They shot my brother in law and were about to rape my sister, but I got them first. It wasn't just no count assholes like these that served in the Marines, you know. I was a sniper back in my younger days."

From what Anna had just witnessed, he must have been a good one. Having just killed a man herself, she couldn't help but wonder how different it must have been to kill someone in a war. To kill people that you had absolutely nothing personal against. Anna was still shaking, almost sick from the adrenaline that had overwhelmed her just a few minutes ago. She literally felt sick to her stomach. Sickened as much by the strength of rage and hatred that had festered inside her for the past week, as by the knowledge that she'd just taken a human life.

"Well praise the lord, that's all I gotta say. Hallelujah and thank you, Mr.?" Flo didn't even give the man time to tell her his name before throwing her arms around him in a bear hug embrace.

"Daniel Day," the man said, extracting himself from Flo's embrace. "Just call me Danny," he added, looking up into the cage and then quickly averting his eyes from Jasmine's naked young body.

Jasmine was still standing at the top of the stairs in the open cage door, staring at the scene below. Her blank detached stare was unlike anything Anna had ever personally seen before. Anna was reminded, once again, of pictures she'd seen in history books of the prisoners who were freed from the Nazi death camps at the end of World War Two. It was a look of total shock and disbelief, wondering if what they were seeing was even real.

Seeing Jasmine in such straits focused Anna's mind back away from the rage and the killing of just a few minutes before. She shook her head, as if to clear out cobwebs, and climbed the stairs to help Jasmine. With neither of them saying a word, Jasmine allowed Anna to lead her back to where she'd dropped her clothes. She just stood there, staring down at the little pile of clothes until Anna reached down and gave her panties to her. Jasmine dressed herself, but only as Anna handed her clothes to her, one piece at a time.

"It's been a long time since I've seen one of these," Danny was telling Flo as Anna led Jasmine down the stairs out of the cage. He was looking at the mobile prison.

"Where'd it come from?" Flo asked.

Jasmine had a firm grip on Anna's hand like she was never going to let go. Anna looked at the Black man that had killed Sarge with one shot. He was even bigger than

Sarge but older. Anna guessed the man must be about the same age as Clyde, her dad. He had the rifle that had killed Sarge slung over his shoulder. It was a high-powered hunting rifle with a scope, not a military rifle at all.

Danny, still looking over the mobile jail cell that had brought them here, said, "They used them for prisoner transport in the desert back in the day. I thought they'd all been destroyed." He looked at the three recent inmates of the mobile cage. "Where do you think they got it?" he asked the women.

"Must have been somewhere in California," Flo answered. "They killed my husband and took me in Sacramento. I figure they must have come up from LA or somewhere else in southern Cal. Where they got this thing, though, I couldn't say."

Danny absently pushed one of the buttons on the side of the van, and the cage door slowly swung shut and locked. "I'll be damned," he said. "Ya'all been in that cage all the way from California?"

"Just Flo," Anna answered. "Jasmine here is from Idaho, and they took me in Wyoming. I'm Anna," she added, realizing she hadn't even told him her name. "Where are we, anyway?" she asked.

"Blue Rapids, Kansas," Danny replied, looking at the women with a new sense of wonder. "All the way from California," he seemed to mutter to himself while looking at Flo. "All the way from California in a cage." A renewed look of hatred came over him as he looked past the women at the two dead men behind them.

Anna, holding the hand of the youngest victim, thought of the other prisoner who'd shared their cage. None of them deserved what Sarge and Curt had done, but Sonia, especially, didn't deserve to die. They were all survivors, up until just a few minutes ago. Even the two men that she'd gladly kill again if she could. There was something flawed about the human race. It seemed like the sickness had wiped out most of humanity. How could anyone who had survived the sickness rape and kill other people? How did anyone get to be like Sarge and Curt?

"Do you have a shovel I can borrow, Mr. Day?" Anna asked.

Danny, mistaking Anna's intention, said, "No way we're burying these sonsabitches," he said. "They don't deserve to be buried. No, we're gonna put these two out with the ones that killed Ned. Let the buzzards have at 'em."

"Not them," Anna said. "I need to bury Sonia. She didn't deserve to die. She deserves a decent burial, Mr. Day."

"Don't you worry about her," Danny said. "And please, just call me Danny. Me and the boys, we'll bury the other young lady, just like we have so many of the townsfolk."

...

Danny Day and his two sons had buried most of the people that had once been their neighbors in Blue Rapids. And they'd done it the hard way, hand-digging so many graves that adding one for Sonia was no problem at all. True to his word, Danny drug the bodies of Sarge and Curt out into a field south of town and left them there to rot. Maybe buzzards could get some good out of them, after all.

There were more survivors in the little old town of Blue Rapids than Anna would have guessed. Members of four different families had all survived the sickness. But none of the families had survived intact, and of the survivors, only three, Danny and his sister, Doris, and a man named Lucas were very much older than Anna.

. . .

"We need to find a bigger inverter," Anna told Charlie. Charlie was Danny's oldest son. He and his younger brother Noah were the only two of Danny's five children that survived the sickness. He was just a year younger than Anna, and though he wasn't nearly as well educated, he had an innate mechanical aptitude that was amazing.

Sometime between the death of most of the town, and that day nearly a week ago when Danny's marksmanship facilitated an end to Anna's nightmare, the eight remaining survivors of Blue Rapids, Kansas, had all banded together. There had been nine survivors, before Doris's husband had been killed. Like a long line of Black men before him, Doris's husband was murdered simply for being Black. For Anna, it was disheartening to know how much racism had survived the pandemic. The Blue Rapids survivors had formed into a sort of tribe, or extended non-biological family, and taken up residence in a large, ancient farmhouse on the edge of town. The old house was made out of cut limestone that must have come from a quarry somewhere nearby.

The farmhouse and surrounding farm had always been the home of the youngest of the survivors. Amelia was a toddler with blonde hair and bright blue eyes who wasn't old enough to have any idea what had happened to her family. When Anna asked her how old she was, the girl just said, "Four," and held up four little fingers for emphasis.

The other members of the Blue Rapids clan were an older man named Lucas, and two women, Valentina and Olivia. Valentina reminded Anna of Sonia. She was a Chicana woman in her mid-twenties. Besides little Amelia, Olivia was the only other anglo in the group. Olivia, like Anna, had just recently turned twenty-one years old.

It was mid-afternoon, and the entire group, all eleven of them, were in the basement waiting out the hottest part of another July day. The basement was one of the main reasons the clan had taken up residence in this old farmhouse. Not only did they find a lot of food stored in that basement, but it was cool down there, even though it was well over a hundred degrees outside.

"I need to go potty," Amelia interrupted Anna and Charlie's discussion of the PV system they were trying to get up and running.

"I'll take her," Olivia said, getting up out of the old plastic lawn chair and taking Amelia by the hand. Going potty meant climbing the old wooden stairs to one of the two bathrooms on the main floor. Thanks to Charlie, the old house actually had some running water. Though it hadn't been used in decades, he had been able to tap into the old well out behind the house. The remains of the windmill that had once been used to pump water from the well were of no use, so Charlie had rigged up a solar-powered pump to get water from the well to the house. The only problem being the pump was too small to supply much water, and it had no battery storage, which meant the running water was only available when the sun was shining. Anna made it her mission to get the Blue Rapids clan set up with all the power they'd need. Not just to have full time running water, but to power the air conditioner. Sitting out the worst heat of summer in a basement that was really just a cellar was not how anyone wanted to spend their time.

"I've looked, Anna," Charlie told her. "There just never was much solar power here in Blue Rapids."

Anna had looked through the town enough to know that Charlie was right. They weren't going to find what they needed here. As bad as she hated the thought of leaving the security of this place, she knew they were going to have to look elsewhere. But she had no idea where to start looking. She really didn't even know where in Kansas Blue Rapids was located.

"Are there any bigger places anywhere near here?" she asked.

Charlie didn't answer immediately. He seemed to not want to answer the question. Finally, he said, "Manhattan. Guess we're going to have to go to Manhattan." It was easy to see that Charlie didn't want to go to Manhattan at all.

Anna knew that Manhattan, Kansas must be a reasonably large city since it was home to one of Kansas' major universities. Still, she had no idea where it was in relationship to Blue Rapids.

"How far?" she asked.

"I don't want you going down to Manhattan," Danny said, before Charlie even had a chance to answer. "We can live without electricity if we have to."

Danny was the leader of this little clan, and Anna didn't really want to go to any city of any size anyway. Growing up in rural Colorado, and seeing how much worse everything seemed in the cities she'd been to, even before the sickness hit, she was afraid of how dangerous cities might be now. It didn't dawn on Anna that Manhattan was probably no bigger than Pocatello. There was nothing rational about her fear of a strange city. After the ordeal she'd been through, Anna was mostly just scared, period. How many other white supremacists or others like them were there? Being surrounded by this Blue Rapids clan of basically decent people, couldn't erase the fear of others. The only thing she wanted anywhere near as much as the security she felt in this clan was to be back home in Colorado with her family. And she had a new fear now. She feared more and more that she wouldn't find her family alive. Seeing how few people had survived, and how no families had survived intact, she had accepted the fact that she would probably never see all of her family again. Would she see any of them? Would she be better off just staying here and becoming one of this new clan? A tribe of survivors.

Anna's thoughts were interrupted by Charlie. "Maybe we can find something up at Marysville."

Anna had no more heard of Marysville than she had Blue Rapids. "Is Marysville very big?" she asked.

"It has a Walmart," Danny answered, which was really not much of an answer at all.

"Four or five times as big as Blue Rapids," Charlie clarified. "And probably twenty times as well off," he added. "At least they were a lot better off before the sickness hit."

"How far is it?" Anna asked, thinking they might have to put the rolling cage back together again to drive to Marysville. Anna and Charlie had already started dismantling the hated vehicle to make use of its PV collectors, tracking system, and batteries.

"It's only about twelve miles up the road," Charlie said.

Anna figured a twelve-mile hike to get to Marysville wouldn't be a problem, but carrying an inverter back, if they found one, would be. They'd already told her they were pretty sure there were no usable vehicles in Blue Rapids, but Anna really didn't want to put the old military prisoner transport back together. The solution, she decided was to walk to Marysville and find not only an inverter but a vehicle to use to haul it back. Danny and Charlie agreed with her plan, but it was too hot to head out right away. After debating whether they should do the trek after the sun went down, or wait until tomorrow, they decided to head out well before dawn in the morning.

It was easy walking on old Highway 77. The nearly full moon in a totally clear sky illuminated the potholes in the old asphalt. *Better shape than Highway 9,* Anna thought, remembering how broken up the old highway in front of the Blue River Ranch had become. Charlie and Anna were walking side by side, headed north in the middle of the old southbound lane, facing into the non-existent oncoming traffic. Not only was there no traffic on the old highway, it didn't look like this road had ever had much traffic. They walked about two miles before they saw any vehicle of any kind.

There was some kind of old abandoned factory or something on the west side of the road. The hulking remains of the large metal buildings had been visible for at least a half-mile before they got to it. For the longest time, it seemed like the old highway was going to run right into the ghostly factory. There was an old autonomous electric delivery truck of some kind parked half in and half out of the main drive into the old plant. The way it was parked, it looked like its navigation had cut out at the exact instant it was turning in to the place.

"What's that?" Anna asked Charlie, pointing at the old factory.

"You mean the truck or the old gypsum plant?" Charlie asked.

"A gypsum plant," Anna mused out loud. "I thought Gypsum was the only one."

Not knowing anything about the town of Gypsum, Colorado, Charlie didn't know what Anna was talking about, so he tried to clarify. "They used to make wallboard, you know, sheetrock, back in the day. Course it's been at least ten years since it shut down."

"Last I knew, the one back in Gypsum, Colorado was still operating," Anna told him. "I guess not anymore, though."

On a hunch, Anna turned off of the highway and walked around the stalled delivery truck into the main driveway entrance to the old factory. She was wondering why a delivery truck would have been headed into a place that was obviously abandoned.

"Where are you going?" Charlie asked, following Anna. "I thought we were going to Marysville."

"Just want to check it out," Anna said over her shoulder.

"Well, I don't think there's anything to see here," Charlie told her, hurrying to catch up. "It used to be something to see, though. I don't remember much about it, but Pop says the day they shut this plant down was the day the town of Blue Rapids died."

Charlie was telling her all about how most everyone

that lived in Blue Rapids, including his dad, had been employed at the gypsum plant back then. Anna was half-listening, but mostly wondering why a factory that had been closed for at least ten years still had a perfectly maintained ten-foot chainlink fence around it. With razor wire on top, no less.

There was a wide gate across the main, or maybe the only entrance to the plant. It was as tall as the fence, and it too was topped with razor wire. The gate was one of those that rolled sideways to open, actuated by an electric motor. On the side the gate opened from, there was a small guard shack. It seemed typical for any kind of factory or business. It had one-way glass windows that would allow someone inside to see out, but no one to see in. The glass was also no doubt bulletproof. There was a steel door on the side of the guard shack. Anna was surprised when she pushed down on the latch, and the door opened.

Her surprise turned to shock when she looked over the interior of the guardhouse. There were two comfortable looking chairs in front of a control panel that had way too many switches and buttons for merely opening and closing the gate. The bright green and red electric diodes and a brightly illuminated display screen were what really caught Anna's eye.

This place has electricity! She thought. *How?* The display screen above the control console was split into six windows, each with a different view from security cameras that were in and around the facility. The cameras would have allowed someone in the guardhouse to monitor the entire perimeter of the old factory.

"Jesus. What is this place?" she heard Charlie ask

behind her.

Anna didn't answer, but then Charlie probably didn't really expect an answer anyway. As she looked from the monitor and console to an open trapdoor in the floor on the other side of the small room, she too wondered, *what kind of place is this?*

Chapter Ten

ANNA WAS WEARING her old .40 S&W on her hip, and Charlie was carrying the M4 that he'd taken from Sarge's dead hands, but it was still spooky going down into the tunnel below the guardhouse. Charlie insisted on going through the trap door first. Anna followed, once Charlie reached the floor, which was about ten feet below the guard shack.

There was a tunnel opening in the wall on the side away from the steel rungs of the ladder. The tunnel was about three feet wide and seven feet tall. It had smooth concrete walls, floor, and ceiling, and was amazingly well lit. There was a row of LED lights down one side of the ceiling. Orienting herself with what she'd seen from the outside, Anna thought the tunnel headed straight toward the big steel building that she'd seen from the road.

The tunnel ran too far into the distance to see what was at the other end. "What the hell do you suppose this is?" Charlie asked.

Anna was beginning to have an idea of what it was, but she wasn't sure. "Only one way to find out," she answered, and started into the tunnel. Charlie didn't even object to letting her lead the way.

It was a good two or three hundred yards to the other end of the tunnel, and it seemed like they were going slightly downhill the whole way. Near the end, but not quite to it, there was a thick vaultlike steel door standing wide open, just like the trap door had been at the guardhouse. If that blast door had been closed and locked, it would have taken some powerful explosives to blow it open. It would also, no doubt, bring the whole tunnel down. *Good thing it's open,* Anna thought. *But why? Why is this place not all sealed up?* She took her pistol out of the holster and jacked a round into the chamber before going on.

On the other side of the open blast door, Anna and Charlie found themselves in a small room or chamber. The only light in this room, which was about ten feet square, came from the LEDs of another control console of some kind on one side of the room. There was another door in the wall opposite the red and green glow of the console.

Charlie, who had let Anna lead the way through the tunnel, insisted on taking the lead once again. He walked over to the closed door and turned the knob. With Anna right behind him, he walked through the door and stopped. "What's in there," she asked, trying to see into the darkness beyond Charlie.

"It's pitch black in here," Charlie answered, "I can't see a thing."

Anna reached around to the wall inside the door, feeling for the switch she was sure would be there. Sure enough, her fingers found a switch and flipped it.

"Holy shit!" Charlie exclaimed. He stepped further

into the room, and Anna followed into what looked like some kind of brightly lit underground warehouse. It was huge. The wall adjacent to the door had a rack of some sort of assault rifles that looked a lot like the one Charlie was carrying. There were metal ammunition boxes on the floor beneath the guns. Probably enough ammo for a small army. Starting about twenty feet away and going straight back into the room as far as they could see, there were rows of industrial shelving. The shelves were filled with all kinds of supplies. From the door, Anna could see case after case marked Allpro. Another rack was full of toilet paper, of all things.

In the corner off to her left, there was the cage of a freight elevator that was big enough to accommodate the small forklift parked next to it. The elevator had to be how all of those supplies had been lowered into the room. Next to the freight elevator, there was another door. Anna headed straight for that door while Charlie wandered off toward the stacks of food and supplies. Before she even opened the door, Anna was now absolutely sure of what she was going to find on the other side.

She'd heard of rich people building bomb shelter bunkers in some pretty weird places, like abandoned missile silos, but she never would have expected to find one beneath an abandoned factory. This particular shelter must have either been built to support multiple families or one huge family. On the other side of the door to the warehouse storeroom, Anna walked into an industrial kitchen, complete with two separate electric cooktops and two full-sized electric ovens and a massive side by side commercial refrigerator freezer.

Just as Charlie came into the kitchen from the warehouse, Anna walked through the next doorway into a massive great room or hall. It was about thirty feet wide and fifty feet long. At the end near the kitchen, there was a long dining table with seating for up to sixteen people. Beyond the dining table was a room with enough easy chairs and sofas for the sixteen diners to relax after dinner. There was a giant entertainment screen of some kind high on one wall of the great room with rows and rows of old-fashioned paper books beneath it.

At the far end of the great room, a hallway led between two doors. One marked Men and the other Women. Anna walked right past those facilities and into another room that was just about as large as the great room. This was the last room, the sleeping quarters. There were eight beds inside half wall cubicles along each of the sidewalls. In the center of the room, there were an additional eight smaller cots. The whole thing looked like some kind of luxurious barracks, but a barracks, nonetheless. It gave Anna the heebie-jeebies. She couldn't imagine being locked in this place for any length of time, no matter who was here with her.

"You check the men's, I'll check the women's," she told Charlie, who was just walking into the sleeping quarters. There was no one but the two of them in the whole place, neither living nor dead.

The bunker may have been empty, but Anna still couldn't wait to get out. She led Charlie, who was pretty much speechless, to the freight elevator back in the warehouse-sized storeroom. Inside the cage of the elevator, there were no buttons, just a single lever about waist high near the door. The lever was in the middle of its slot. Anna closed the cage door and lifted the handle to the top of the slot. The large elevator was amazingly quiet as it lifted them skyward.

Anna guessed that there must have been at least twenty feet of earth between the ceiling or roof of the storeroom and the surface. It was getting light as they came to a stop above ground. At the surface, the elevator came to a stop inside the remains of the old gypsum plant. The sun had yet to come up, but the glow from the eastern sky was enough to illuminate the interior of the giant old building. It was more like an enormous courtyard now. The roof was gone as well as parts of the surrounding walls. Much of the floor space was covered with an array of solar PV panels. The panels were mounted on short pedestals with tracking mechanisms to follow the sun. They were all facing due east, waiting for the morning's first rays of sunlight.

"Guess we don't need to go to Marysville after all," Charlie said. "Bound to be everything we need right here."

And then some, Anna thought, as she made her way past the solar panels to the other end of the factory. She couldn't help but notice that the south wall of the old factory had mostly been demolished, but not the other three walls. Even the lower half of the south wall had been left intact. Enough of the wall remained to shield the existence of the solar panels from outside view.

At the far end of the factory, there was a smaller building that was still intact. It had pre-cast concrete walls and a steel man door. "This has to be the battery and control room," she told Charlie, as she tried the steel door. It was locked. The first locked door they'd come to in the whole place. Anna looked at the numeric keypad on the wall beside the door and wondered how hard it would be to guess the right code. Nearly impossible, no doubt. There had to be another way in, though. This was just a man door. If the kind of equipment she was looking for was on the other side of that wall, it would have been taken in through a much larger doorway. "Come on, let's look outside," she said, leading the way back to the overhead shop door near the elevator.

Just outside the shop door, on one side, there was a trailer that looked like a temporary construction trailer. On the other side of the door, an old F-250 pickup truck was parked facing the factory wall. Anna and Charlie walked around the old Ford truck and down the length of the building to another overhead door that Anna knew had to lead into the battery room. There was another keypad next to that wall, but no other way to open the door. This part of the old factory seemed to be completely intact. There were no windows in the concrete walls. *Probably vented through the roof,* Anna thought.

"If we had some tools, we could probably break in," Charlie said, but Anna was starting to think along a different line. She was still trying to wrap her mind around the bigger picture, and she kept coming up with more questions than answers. Who had left the doors unlocked, allowing her and Charlie access in the first place? Why? Why had they left the guard shack open? Would they be back?

Suddenly she had an idea. She walked back to the construction trailer without saying anything to Charlie. She walked right up the metal steps and opened the door. Somehow, she'd known it wouldn't be locked. The stench that came out of the trailer was unmistakable to everyone who had survived the sickness. It was the smell of rotting human flesh. Anna forced herself to go inside, Charlie didn't follow. Inside, she found exactly what she'd known she would. This was not a construction trailer at all. It was living quarters. With a bedroom at each end, it had been living quarters for at least two people. One of whom, though no longer living, was still there. This trailer was where the guards had lived. It was permanent housing for full-time security guards, for a never used shelter.

The other guard, or guards, must have left the guardhouse open, Anna thought, *wonder if they planned on coming back. Not likely. They would have locked the door if they expected to be back.*

Turning to go back outside, Anna saw a keyring hanging from a hook beside the door. She grabbed the keys and went straight to the Ford pickup. Judging by the thick layer of dust that covered the old truck, it hadn't been driven in a long, long time. It was a pleasant surprise when the old internal combustion engine fired up almost as soon as she turned the key. Anna knew that the propane tank in the bed of the truck was probably the main reason it was still able to run. If it had been gasoline or diesel powered, the fuel most likely would have gone bad long ago. The people who built this place had really planned for the long term.

Anna hit the switches to open all of the side windows of the old truck. The air in the cab was so stale she could hardly stand it. There was no telling how long it had been since anyone else had been inside. Looking out the open driver's side window, Anna saw a huge propane tank that she hadn't really noticed before. *Must be at least ten thousand gallons,* she thought. *A lifetime supply for this one old truck. Then again, maybe whoever owned this place planned on bringing some more propane-powered vehicles.*

"Wait," Anna told Charlie, who was just crawling into the passenger seat. She turned off the ignition. "Let's lock this place up first."

Anna explained what she had in mind to Charlie as they took the elevator back down into the storeroom. Anna went straight to the control room at this end of the tunnel. She figured that one of the guards had got sick and died. With no coms and no way to know what was going on, the other guard, or guards had abandoned their post.

"Why didn't they take the truck?" Charlie asked.

"And why didn't they lock up?" Anna answered his question with another question. Both were questions with no logical answer.

She found the switch and turned on the control room lights. The long desk had a computer console and a large monitor at one end, and several loose-leaf style books standing up on a shelf at the other. Anna randomly pushed a key on the computer keyboard, and the monitor flickered to life. It had the same camera views that they'd seen on the screen in the guardhouse. She looked over at the books at the other end of the desk. Each of the loose-leaf binders had a label on the spine. They were maintenance and operations manuals for the entire shelter. There were two large manuals marked *PV System*, another marked *Appliances*, but one small loose-leaf was the only one that really mattered to Anna at the moment. It was marked *Security.*

Reading through the manual as quickly as possible,

Anna discovered that the various keypads throughout the complex were programmable from this main control room computer. Both the trap door in the guardhouse and the blast door at this end of the tunnel could also be remotely opened and closed using this computer. Anna and Charlie studied the manual together. They closed and locked the tunnel doors. Then they cleared any existing access codes in the outside keypads and put in two new ones. Each of them chose a code they could easily remember.

They left the elevator open and walked around to the entrance gate to make sure the codes they'd programmed into the keypads worked. The door on this side of the guardhouse was locked, but Anna's code did indeed open the door. She relocked it, and Charlie tried his. Both codes worked perfectly. With Anna staying inside the guardhouse just in case, Charlie went out the other door and locked it behind him. His code worked just fine on that door also.

It was mid-morning by the time Anna drove the old Ford truck through the gate and waited for Charlie to close the gate and lock the guardhouse door behind him. The odds of one of the owners making their way to this shelter from wherever were pretty slim, but wouldn't they be surprised if they did get back here only to find they couldn't even get in.

Chapter Eleven

Anna rechecked all of the connections for the umpteenth time, closed up the breaker box, and started flipping the switches on the control panel. The dials and gauges came to life, indicating that the system was working.

"You did it!" Charlie exclaimed. He grabbed Anna and gave her a celebratory hug.

"We did it," Anna said, pulling back away and looking into his eyes.

The two of them had been working together all day, every day for the past few weeks. They'd put together a solar electric system that would provide all the power that the farm, as everyone was now calling their little commune, could ever need. And they did it without using anything from the bomb shelter at the old gypsum factory except the old Ford pickup that they borrowed to haul the components from Marysville.

After discovering the gypsum factory shelter, Charlie and Anna had locked the place up and took the pickup back to the farm. They'd both wondered if maybe the Blue Rapids Clan should just move to the shelter and forget about living at the farm. It may have been the easiest way for the group of survivors to go on surviving, at least in the near term. But none of them, Charlie and Anna included, much liked the idea of living cramped up in a bunker underground. Of course, Anna had no intention of living in Kansas at all, so she refrained from the decision making process.

The whole group decided that they didn't want to move to the gypsum factory, but they also agreed not to steal anything from there if they didn't have to. Danny didn't want to take anything just in case the rightful owner or owners eventually showed up. Anna didn't think that was very likely, but she agreed with the rest of them that it might be wise to just keep the place intact as a backup plan, should they ever need it. Danny, who was, after all, the group's real leader, finally agreed that they could at least "borrow" the old Ford pickup truck. Charlie and Anna had used the old pickup a lot. They had made multiple trips to Marysville to obtain all of the components and supplies they needed. Fortunately, they hadn't needed to go anywhere besides Marysville.

Looking into Charlie's eyes that were as deep a shade of brown as her own, feelings that Anna had been suppressing oozed to the surface. Working side by side, she'd come to admire Charlie's capabilities and his intellect. She'd also found herself admiring his athletic body more and more as he worked shirtless through many a hot afternoon. After the ordeal with Sarge and Curt, Anna had been pretty sure she would never be interested in sex again. Now, as her lips met Charlie's, her body was more than just interested in sex. It was a yearning that couldn't be suppressed.

Not just a craving for sex, but for that deepest sharing of human companionship. It was not a desire to share with just anyone. She wanted to give herself to Charlie, and she wanted Charlie to be hers. Was she falling in love with this man?

Anna pushed herself back away and looked into those dark brown eyes again. "What about Olivia?" she asked. It wasn't much of a secret that Charlie and Olivia sometimes slept together, just like everyone knew that Danny had been sharing his bed with Flo. The way the world was anymore, it just seemed natural that people would seek out love and companionship wherever, if not whenever, they could.

Charlie lowered his gaze. "I don't know," he said. He shook his head slightly, "I guess I just don't know." He looked back into Anna's eyes. "I know it's not right, but I want both of you. I can't help it." He started turning away, before almost whispering to himself, "I love both of you."

Anna watched Charlie walk out of the garage that they'd converted into the battery and control room. She found herself thinking about polygamy. *Is that what we're coming to?* She wondered. Discounting Lucas, who was probably too old, and Amelia, who was definitely too young, the Blue Rapids clan consisted of six women and three men. Anna couldn't help but wonder if that ratio held true for survivors everywhere, or just here. If men had succumbed more readily than women, the odds of finding her family intact back on the Blue River Ranch were slim. *Slim to none,* she admitted to herself. *And what about James?* A wave of sorrow washed over her. Not for James. James was still alive. She wouldn't let herself think otherwise. No, the grief she felt was for her family. No matter how much she tried to suppress it, she couldn't rid herself of the feeling that some of her family, if not all, were gone.

Watching Charlie walk away, she had the thought that maybe she should just give up on the idea of ever going home. She looked at Charlie and thought about what it might be like to just live here for the rest of her life with this new "family" that she'd found in Blue Rapids. Could she genuinely love another man, other than James or Will, or was love what she really felt for Charlie? That she felt lust was undeniable, but love was not so easy to pin down. *And what about Olivia?* She thought, asking herself the same question that she'd just asked Charlie. *Can I love Charlie and share him with Olivia? I like Olivia, but could I be happy as a sister wife?* It was a question Anna had never ever considered. Growing up on the Blue River Ranch, she had always just dreamed of marrying her childhood sweetheart, James, and raising a family on the ranch. Just like her parents before her. And now, here she was considering a life as a sister wife in Blue Rapids, Kansas. *Another* BR, she thought absently, just as Charlie yelled back at her, "Come on, let's check out the air conditioner."

Anna wasn't really surprised when Charlie crawled into her bed that night, and she didn't tell him no. She just moved over to make room and asked, "does Olivia know?"

"She does," Charlie answered as he wrapped his arm around her.

I'll talk to Olivia tomorrow, was Anna's last thought of the other woman before succumbing to thoughts of only one thing. The feeling of Charlie's naked skin pressing against her own washed away any notion of resisting the desire that was coursing through her body. At that moment, that desire was all there was. At that moment, her entire being existed for just one thing. She pulled Charlie over on top of her as much as he got there by his own motivation. Anna and Charlie lost themselves in each other, in the eternity of that one brief moment in time.

…

It was still early in the morning. The sun had only been up for an hour or so, but it was already getting too hot. Anna and Olivia were pulling more of the never-ending supply of weeds that always tried to take over the garden. They were working side by side, with only the row of corn stalks between them.

"Do you ever feel jealous?" Olivia asked.

Anna stood up, stretched her aching back, and looked around. She and Olivia were the only ones working here in the northwest corner of the enormous garden. The garden had been planted too late in the year, but it was better than no garden at all. Anna searched her feelings. *Do I ever feel jealous?* She asked herself, echoing Olivia. She could see the sun glistening off Charlie's naked back, where he was hoeing a row of okra a few rows over, oblivious to the conversation between the two women he slept with.

"I guess I really don't," Anna answered. And it was true. "How about you?"

Olivia stood up and stretched as well before answering. She, too, looked over at Charlie then turned to look at Anna.

"Not anymore, I guess," Olivia said. "I have to admit, though, I was at first." She laughed. "I actually cried that first night when he told me he was going to sleep with you. Funny, if you'd have told me a year ago that I was going to be sleeping with Charlie Day, I'd have thought you were crazy. Let alone, sharing him with another woman."

Anna hadn't thought about it much, but now she wondered if Olivia had feelings for Charlie before the sickness. The two had grown up together right here in rural Kansas. Or had they? Come to think of it, Olivia had never told Anna where she lived before everybody died. Charlie had shown her the little place a few blocks over where the Day family had lived, but Olivia never talked about where she lived before. As a matter of fact, thinking about it now, Anna couldn't remember Olivia ever talking about before at all.

"Did you and Charlie, I mean before?" Anna asked.

"Oh, God no," Olivia laughed. "If my parents knew I was sleeping with Charlie Day, they'd roll over in their grave. You have noticed that he's Black and I'm white?" she asked sarcastically. She brushed a lock of her long blonde hair back up under the sunbonnet that she always wore and laughed again. "Of course, that doesn't mean I didn't have my fantasies."

"So, you did know Charlie. Before I mean?" Anna asked.

"Knew of him, more like it," Olivia answered. "My parents mostly kept me away from the Black folk and the poor white trash here in town."

Anna and Olivia both went back to weeding while Olivia told Anna all about the life she'd lived before. Anna was astounded. She never would have guessed that Olivia was from a wealthy family that didn't actually live in Blue Rapids but on an estate south of town. Olivia had never attended the public schools that Charlie went to. Hers had been a life of boarding schools and high society.

As Olivia talked about the boarding schools she'd attended, Anna thought of James Mendez, and how she used to wish she was at Colorado One with him, instead of the dilapidated old public high school in Kremmling. She thought of James and, once again, felt the tug of a love that she knew would never die. *I may not be jealous of sharing Charlie with Olivia,* she thought. *But how would I feel if it was James?* That was followed by other thoughts. *Why do I keep trying to compare Charlie and James? James is just a glorified memory. I don't even know what kind of man James grew up to be. I love Charlie Day. He's kind, intelligent, and great in bed. At least when he's in my bed and not hers.*

"Hello there," someone yelled from out on the road. It was a strange man's voice, and the yell brought Anna and Olivia, as well as the rest of those working the garden instantly to their feet. Anna had her hand on the gun she wore on her hip before she even knew she'd reached for it. Before she realized that anyone who meant her harm wouldn't have just yelled hello.

It wasn't just a single man out on the road in front of the garden. It was a whole group of people. There were two men, three women and a couple of children. Everyone working in the garden put down their tools and headed out to the road. Having strangers in their midst was the most exciting thing to happen in Blue Rapids since Danny Day shot Sarge.

The group of strangers consisted of one Black man and a Black woman, one white man, and two white women. The children, one boy and a girl, both belonged to one of the white women. Other than the mother and her two kids, the group was entirely unrelated to one another, but they had quite a tale of how they came to be traveling together in a group.

Some of them had come all the way from Hopkinsville, Kentucky, near Fort Campbell. As Anna listened, she realized that had to be where Sarge and Curt had been headed. Apparently, some kind of revolt in the military had hit Fort Campbell about the same time that the sickness did. Ben and George, the two men, had been friends since childhood. George, the Black man, told how Ben, his white friend, had saved him. It seems Ben caught wind of how white supremacists were taking over Fort Campbell and planning to enslave or kill all the Black people. By then, both men's families had died of the sickness.

"I didn't really have a choice," Ben said. "I could have joined them, been one of the ruling whites in the community, but I'd rather be dead and buried with my wife."

Melissa and her two children, Damon and Sarah, had been Ben's neighbors. Ben had helped Melissa bury her husband, and when he decided to escape what was coming to Hopkinsville, she chose to go with him. The four of them had fled in Ben's original Mach E Mustang in the middle of the night, stopping only long enough to pick up George, who lived on the other side of town.

Ben told them the Mustang had about fifty percent charge when they left Hopkinsville, and they'd only made it a couple of hundred miles before running out of juice somewhere just outside St. Louis. They'd walked the rest of the way, picking up the other two women, Poppy and Kathleen, along the way.

"Where are you headed?" Danny asked the group of strangers.

"Reckon we don't rightly know," George answered, and Ben, who'd done most of the talking up to now, shook his head in agreement.

"We've just been heading north and west to get as far away from that Fort Campbell bunch as we can," Ben said. "Don't know how much farther we can go," he added. "All this walkin's kind of hard on the little one." He reached down and gave the little girl a gentle pat on the head.

"You go much farther west, you're likely to run out of water," Anna told them. "I haven't seen it for myself, but from what I've heard, what used to be the great plains, is mostly just a great desert now."

"Maybe we should just go north." It was Poppy, the Black woman, who hadn't spoken at all up until then.

"Well, for now, why don't you come in and have lunch with us," Danny invited them in. "Get out of this heat and take a load off."

Everyone but Anna headed to the house. Spending the hottest part of the day in air-conditioned comfort had become the normal routine in Blue Rapids. As the others walked toward the house, still talking, Anna gazed to the west. Against her will, she had an uncontrollable longing to cross that great unknown. She needed to know the fate of her family. And yes, she still had an undeniable longing to find James Mendez.

Chapter Twelve

THE OLD SMITH PLACE, as Danny and Charlie called it, was the nearest neighbor to the Farm. The two houses were less than a quarter-mile apart. It hadn't taken much convincing to get the refugees from Fort Campbell to stop walking and take up residence at the old Smith place here in Blue Rapids.

People are herd animals, just like horses. Anna, for some reason, had been thinking about Pintada and the other horses back home at the Blue River Ranch in Colorado. She was sitting in the living room of the Smith house, enjoying the first cooling breeze from the old window AC unit that she and Chalie had installed. Getting the Smith house set up with its own PV and water system had been difficult. The former Smith house didn't have a well, so they had to run a water line all the way from the farm. It had taken Anna, Charlie, and George at least three weeks. It would have taken even longer if it had been just Anna and Charlie. George had once been head of maintenance at a processing plant back in Kentucky. He was old enough that Charlie and Anna did most of the physical work, but his expertise, especially with the water system, was invaluable.

Nobody really kept track anymore, but Anna figured

it had to be mid-September or so. Satisfied that the
Smith house was now ready for occupancy, she went back
outside to the battery shed where George and Charlie were
monitoring the system controls.

"AC's working great," she told the two men. "All good
in here?"

"Finer'n frog hair," George answered. "Let's tell the
others we can move in." He was obviously excited at the
prospect of being able to get out of the Farm. The big old
limestone house, totally adequate for nine, had seemed tiny
and cramped with sixteen people all living under one roof.

It was barely lunchtime when Anna, George, and
Charlie finished testing the systems. The entire clan spent
the rest of that day getting the newcomers situated in their
new abode. It was quite a relief for everyone involved. Now,
near midnight, Anna lay awake in her bed, unable to sleep.
Having a bedroom to herself seemed strange after sharing it
with Melissa and her two children for the past three weeks
or so. Anna found that she was missing their company.
She especially missed Damon and Sarah, the two children.
Anna had enjoyed their company more than she could have
imagined. Children had a way of giving one hope for the
future. *I want children of my own,* she thought, and the
realization startled her. The desire to have children was
accompanied by another longing. Charlie hadn't shared her
bed since the others moved in. Now, Anna found herself
resenting the fact that he'd apparently chosen to spend this
night with Olivia instead of her.

She got up, walked over to the window, and pulled the
curtains open. Her bedroom was on the second floor, and
her window faced west. Anna stood at the window, looking

out across the moonlit night to a place she couldn't see. She looked out toward home and thought about her past and her future. Anna found it odd that she hardly thought about Will at all. It made her sad somehow that she didn't miss Will like she missed James. It just didn't seem right. She'd spent years with Will. They'd shared everything, and yet the one man she really missed was James Mendez. Maybe that was it. Maybe it was the mystery of James. By the time Will died, there was hardly any mystery left at all.

As Anna got back in bed, she knew it was more than that. You don't get to choose who you love, or why, or for how long. What Anna knew, as she tried to go to sleep, was that the physical yearning she felt could have been partially satisfied by making love with Charlie, but she had a deeper longing. It was an insatiable desire that could only be satisfied by finding James; by exploring the mysteries of love interrupted. He has to be alive. He has to be alive, was the mantra that finally put her to sleep.

"Where's Sarah?" Amelia asked. Amelia and Sarah had been nearly inseparable at the Farm. The two girls, one four and the other five, had become more like sisters than friends. Now, with Sarah living at the Smith house, Amelia was somewhat lost.

"She's at home. We can go see her after breakfast," Doris told the little girl. Danny's sister Doris, more than most others in the group, had taken on the role of mother for the young orphan girl.

Breakfast without the group from Kentucky seemed strange to Anna, too. It seemed odd that a house with nine people still in it could feel as empty as the Farm did this morning. *It's the kids,* Anna thought. It was the lack of the two other children that made the Farm seem so quiet.

"Sarah lives here," Amelia said. "Here's home. I want her to live here with me."

Is this home for me too? Anna thought. *Amelia should live with Sarah. Where should I live?*

After breakfast, it was Anna and Olivia's turn to clean up. Everyone else was already out taking care of morning chores. Even old Lucas was out sitting in the yard watching Sarah and Amelia happily playing together. The two little girls were indeed inseparable.

"I'm pregnant." Olivia didn't even look up from the sink as she said the words. Her voice betrayed very little emotion. Maybe just a touch of fear, more than anything else.

Anna didn't know how to respond. "Are you sure?" she asked.

Olivia said she was pretty sure she was pregnant. She told Anna that she hadn't been on any kind of birth control and that she had now missed two periods.

"Are you happy?" Anna asked.

Olivia looked at Anna and just sort of had a meltdown. She smiled and started crying all at the same time. "I should be happy," she stammered. "I am happy. It's just, it's just… it wasn't supposed to be this way. I was supposed to be married. I was supposed to live in a normal family, in a normal world," she sobbed.

Anna took Olivia in her arms, letting her sob on her shoulder. The two women really had become sister wives in all but name. "I'm happy for you," Anna told her. "And I'm happy for Charlie, too." She found that her own eyes were wet with tears. "I'm happy for all of us," she said. "It's good to bring new life into this world – this world that has seen so much death."

That was the moment when Anna made up her mind to leave. In reality, the decision to leave had been made before she ever decided to stay. But at that moment, the decision to leave crystallized in her mind. She'd spent the past three months with this group of people who had become like a second family to her. She loved them all, but she knew she had to leave. It was time to search for what had been left behind in another life. Anna had to know the truth about a love she'd carried for as long as she could remember. Her love of James was like a slow-burning ember in her heart. It might flicker at times, but it could never be extinguished.

...

It took several days to get ready to leave. Charlie took her to Marysville in the Farm's old propane-powered Ford to find some mode of transportation. Finding a suitable vehicle wasn't an easy task. It seemed like most people in this part of the world hadn't been driving electric vehicles at all, let alone non-autonomous EVs. In the residential areas of Marysville, they found nothing but antiques as old as the Ford truck they were riding in. The biggest problem was, all of the old antiques they found were either gasoline or diesel powered, and most looked like they hadn't been driven for a long, long time. Most people in Marysville had probably just been relying on the various forms of mass transit for many years before the sickness hit.

They did find one good thing, though. Clear out on the southeast edge of Marysville. Anna and Charlie were just about to turn around to search another area when they saw a man standing in front of an old farmhouse holding a rifle in front of him. The man didn't raise the rifle or seem threatening at all, so Anna didn't even reach for her own gun. Instead, Charlie and Anna stopped and got out of the truck and walked up to the man with their hands in the air. "You can put your hands down," the man told them. "It's good to see others still alive." The man introduced himself as two women, and a young boy came out of the house behind him.

Besides those four people, it turned out that a whole clan had taken up residence in that farmhouse and the one next to it. There were eight of them altogether, and they seemed to be living together, much like the group back in Blue Rapids only without the modern comforts of electricity and running water. Charlie was so excited to find a group of neighbors living just twelve miles away that Anna didn't think she was ever going to get him to stop talking so they could resume their search for transportation. As it turned out, the time spent visiting was time well spent. Probably for everyone. Charlie promised the Marysville group that he would come back to help them set up their own PV and water systems, and for their part, the Marysville group told Anna where she was most likely to find a vehicle. There was a manufacturing facility in Marysville that had still been actively producing farm equipment when the sickness hit. Not that farm equipment was going to do Anna any good, but the owner of the business had also been somewhat of a collector of cars and trucks.

...

Sure enough, they'd found an old Tesla Model Y at the manufacturing plant. The old SUV had less than a quarter charge when they found it, but they also found a wall charger in the same metal building that housed the small collection of mostly antique vehicles. Back at the Farm, it only took a couple of hours to get the wall charger wired up and charging.

Now, with the car fully charged and ready to go, it was hard to say goodbye. It was early morning, but the entire Blue Rapids clan had gathered to see Anna one last time before she left. Everyone, except maybe the children, knew this was probably more than a temporary goodbye. Anna knew she would most likely never see any of them again.

She hugged each and everyone and wished them all the best. When she came to Charlie last, he held her tight and whispered in her ear, "I love you Anna. I hope you know that."

The road was blurred with tears as she drove away. *I love you, too, Charlie,* she thought. *Like I loved Will before. Why is it never enough? Damn you, James Mendez!* She cursed to herself as she headed west on Highway 77. The Blue River Ranch was no longer Anna's destination. No, Anna had decided that if home is where the heart is, the BR might no longer be her home. She wiped the tears from her eyes and tried to focus on the road. The road that now led to a place Anna had never been. In time, she would return to the Blue River Ranch, but first, she was going to Castle Pines.

Chapter Thirteen

ANNA DIDN'T KNOW much about Kansas, but she figured the shortest route to Castle Pines, Colorado would be to travel due west as much as possible. Although in what seemed like a previous life, she'd never been any farther east than Limon, she knew Colorado geography well enough to easily find her way to Castle Pines once she crossed the state line.

Expecting the plains to be dry and actually seeing it with her own eyes were two very different things. It was hard to believe how fast the terrain changed from farms and fields that were drying up in the early autumn heat to a near-desert that had dried up years ago. Anna knew enough American history to know that this part of the country was once the breadbasket of America, if not the world. Now it reminded her of far western Utah or Nevada. It really was a desert. And it wasn't just the countryside that had dried up. The towns along the way had all been abandoned long before the sickness.

It was already the middle of the afternoon, and Anna had driven less than a hundred miles. The roads out here, mostly just secondary routes back in the best of times, were crumbling and decayed to the point of being nearly impassable in places. She could tell by the trees that she was coming into another town. *Probably another ghost town,* she thought. Most of the trees were no longer green but looked like ghosts themselves. Dried up and dying, just like the country surrounding them. Some of the trees still had a few green branches, but most were merely death still standing.

The faded sign at the edge of town said Jewell City Limits, but that meant nothing to Anna. It might as well have said Timbuktu. Anna wished, once again, that she had an old fashioned paper map to figure out where she was. She knew she had been traveling mostly due west on an old Kansas highway numbered 148, and that she wasn't too far south of the Nebraska state line. Other than that, she could have been anywhere.

Jewell was definitely a ghost town. It looked like no one had lived there for at least ten years. After driving past the abandoned homes and businesses, Highway 148 came to an abrupt end at a T intersection. Anna looked at the old dead traffic light swinging in the wind. She turned on the air conditioning, which she'd been using as little as possible to conserve motive power for the car. *God, it must be a hundred twenty degrees out here,* she thought. A quick glance at the touchscreen told her it was actually just one hundred seventeen outside. She scanned the road north and south, trying to decide which way to go. There was a sign directly across from where she sat that said I-70 was sixty-one miles south, or U.S. Highway 36 was eight miles north. Anna decided, as much as she hated losing the sixty miles, she might be better off going south to I-70.

She had no way of knowing if Highway 36 would be in any better shape than Highway 148 had been. Interstate 70, on the other hand, had always been the main east-west route across both Kansas and Colorado. As soon as she was headed south, she switched the air conditioning off again and opened all of the windows. She was afraid the Tesla wouldn't have enough battery to get to Colorado, and she knew that getting stranded out in the middle of this desert would probably be fatal. She took another drink of hot water from the jug she had in the passenger seat and decided if she could stand to sweat out the rest of the day, she'd drive the rest of the way after dark.

It must have been about midnight when the Tesla finally ran out of battery and came to a stop. Interstate 70 had been surprisingly easy to travel. Other than working her way around a few stalled semis and even fewer passenger cars, the worst part was the drifts of sand and dirt that had blown across the highway. It was a good thing the old Model Y had all-wheel drive, or she probably wouldn't have been able to make it. As luck would have it, the moon was nearly full, so Anna hadn't even needed to use the headlights. Not that the lights would have shortened her range much anyway, not like the air conditioner, but Anna had conserved all she could. Still, she was just west of Burlington when the car came to a stop.

At least I made it to Colorado, she thought, *even if it does look just like Kansas. What now?* She was somewhere about halfway between Burlington and Stratton, so she strapped on the backpack that she'd prepared before leaving Blue Rapids and started trekking west. She was pretty tired, having been awake for a good eighteen hours by then, but she figured if she had to walk, she better walk at night. She didn't want to end up like the remains of others she'd seen scattered along the interstate. People that had probably died of exposure when their autonomous vehicles shut down in that great desert.

She'd only walked a mile or so before she came across another one. The corpse was so far gone that Anna couldn't even tell if it had been a man or a woman. She wondered as she passed by if the poor soul had died of exposure or the sickness. No one would ever know. She thought about how many had died. *Must be hundreds of millions just here in America,* she thought and wondered if anywhere on earth had fared any better.

The moonlight was bright enough to make out a sign beside the highway that said it was sixty miles to Limon. Anna knew she was in good enough shape that she should be able to walk at least twenty miles a day, or night more likely. With the night more than half gone already, she decided that she would hike to Stratton and then find someplace to shade up and wait out the heat of the day. Maybe, in Stratton, there would even be another vehicle she could use. As she walked past another desiccated corpse on the shoulder of the road, she doubted that would be the case.

· · ·

Anna's feet and legs ached. It was getting harder and harder to keep putting one foot in front of the other. Unable to find a vehicle in Stratton, she had hiked at a bruising pace all night, every night, for three nights in a row. The sun had already been up for a couple of hours, but she had to keep going. She could see Limon off in the distance, maybe three miles away. It was already getting hot, and it had been at least four hours ago that Anna drank the last of her water. She knew she had to get to Limon and find some water, or she would die. She would just be another one of the dead people scattered along the old interstate highway.

There was no sign of life at the travel stop and charging station on the north side of the interstate, but Anna approached the place with extreme caution. There hadn't been any indication of anyone at Little America, either. There were a few autonomous semis plugged into the row of truck and bus chargers, but only one car at the car charging stations. It was one of the newer autonomous Volkswagens, so she was out of luck as far as finding transportation.

Though she was dying of thirst, Anna carefully explored the entire perimeter of the building with her gun in hand. She even looked inside all of the vehicles in the parking lot. Satisfied that she was the only one there, at least on the outside of the building, she studied the interior of the store through the glass front with bars on the windows before going inside. She pushed the unlocked entrance door open and checked between the aisles and behind the counter before relaxing at all.

The interior of the travel store smelled terrible, but it wasn't the smell of dead people. It was the smell of rotten foodstuffs. The shelves seemed fully stocked, and an overstuffed mouse scampered out of Anna's way, as she went straight to what had been the refrigerated section at the back of the store. Through the glass doors, it appeared that no one had taken anything out of that section, either. Anna put her gun back in the holster on her hip and grabbed one of the glass bottles of water. She drank slowly at first, knowing that too much, too fast would make her sick. The warm water tasted like heaven. It was so soothing to her parched lips and throat. She pulled the bottle away from her lips, realizing that she'd guzzled over half the bottle. *Go slow,* she told herself. *It'll make you sick.*

After filling the plastic bladder in her backpack with water, and stuffing it full of non-perishable food, mostly Allpro, Anna found a real treasure back in one corner of the store. It was an old folded up paper map of Colorado. Not only did it have the state's roads and highways on one side, on the other, it had street maps of the state's major cities. Anna had been wondering since starting this journey how she was going to find the Mendez place in Castle Pines. She still remembered the address from the cards she'd sent to James years ago, but knowing an address and finding it without a map were entirely different things.

She sat outside the store, her back against the wall in the shade on the north side of the building, and studied her newfound treasure. After debating the pros and cons, she decided that she would only follow I-70 to Highway 86 and then take 86 to Castle Rock. From there, she could follow I-25 north to Castle Pines. She decided that she'd search Limon first in hopes of finding a vehicle to borrow. The thought of walking another eighty miles was not very pleasant. She knew she could do it, probably take four full nights of hiking, but finding something to drive would be so much better. *Even an old bicycle would be great,* she thought, as she painfully stood up and stretched.

It didn't take much searching through Limon to tell it had been mostly abandoned before the sickness ever hit. Limon, like most places in eastern Colorado and western

Kansas, had shriveled and died along with the Ogallala Aquifer. As the water dried up, so did the town. A train of the familiar blue water tankers sitting on the tracks at the edge of town told Anna where Limon's water had come from in recent years. What she couldn't figure out is why there seemed to be no people in Limon at all, neither living nor dead. There were just a few houses in Limon that appeared to have been recently inhabited. Those were the ones Anna searched. Invariably, the houses looked like someone had just left for the day and failed to return. From rotten food in refrigerators to dirty dishes in sinks, the homes appeared to have been abandoned all at once. Some had beds neatly made, and in others, the bed, or beds, were unmade, like people had been in too big of a hurry to make up the bed before leaving.

Where did they go? She wondered. Anna was about to the west end of town, and the heat was getting unbearable. It was the middle of the day, and she'd been on her feet for a good eighteen hours. She decided to shade up and get some sleep before continuing her trek west after nightfall. She'd all but given up on finding any kind of transportation.

The house she was walking past looked a lot like the others that she'd already explored. The front of the house faced south, so Anna, after knocking on the door and getting only silence for an answer, walked around through the side yard to find a place in the shade. She was delighted at what she found on the north side of the house. There was a covered patio with lawn furniture, including a chaise lounge with the cushions still intact. That lounge chair looked more inviting than anything Anna had seen in days, but before she stretched out, she decided to check out a shed in the back corner of the yard. Inside the shed, she found not only a bicycle but an electric bike. Even more surprising, the battery had nearly a full charge.

It was the middle of the night when Anna woke up. It took a moment to remember where she was. She'd awakened from a nightmare. In the dream, she was riding a strange horse up the lane to the Blue River Ranch, but the ranch was gone. It wasn't just gone, it was as if it had never existed. It was the strangest thing. The lane from old Highway 9 was still there just as she remembered, but it led to nowhere. Where her home and the other ranch buildings should have been, the lane just disappeared into the trees that lined Spider Creek. The thought, *you can never go home again,* came unbidden to mind and filled her with dread.

Chapter Fourteen

ANNA WAS ONLY about five miles out from Limon, riding west on the eastbound side of I-70 when she saw the lights. At first, she couldn't tell what or where the lights were. The lights came into view some distance ahead as she topped a gentle rise. Anna stopped immediately, putting her feet down, standing stationary astraddle the bike, she could tell that the lights weren't moving. It was definitely artificial lights on the ground, not stars or something stellar just above the horizon. As Anna studied the lights, she thought she could make out some kind of building off to one side. It looked like it had to be a large building or group of buildings fairly close to I-70. Anna could feel the tiny hairs on the back of her neck stand up. Something about artificial light in the middle of nowhere was frightening.

Wishing she didn't have to, Anna rode slowly toward the lights. As she got closer, she could see they were spotlights shining on an object or objects that weren't yet clearly visible. She knew what the lights were shining on before she could clearly make out the crosses. The three black crosses, even though illuminated by the spotlights, didn't stand out much against the midnight sky. But there they were, three large black crosses. The biggest cross in the middle must have been at least forty feet tall, with the two on either side no more than half that.

Anna wanted nothing more than to turn and flee. The Modern Times Church compounds with the three black crosses in front had never bothered her before. Before she'd been kidnapped and raped by men who'd painted the same three black crosses on the side of a military prisoner transport truck, that is.

She got off of the bike and pushed it along the edge of the highway, staying as far away from The Modern Times Church compound as she possibly could. She kept the bike between her and the church as she walked, like the bike was some kind of talisman that could ward off evil. It truly was a compound, not just a single building, and like the rest of the Modern Times Church compounds that Anna had seen, it was surrounded by a tall wrought iron fence. Now that she was close enough, she could see the dim glow of other lights inside the compound. The place obviously had its own electrical power.

Are people in there? she wondered. *Maybe that's where the people from Limon went.* Not that she had any intention of finding out one way or another. The compound was built on a hill on the opposite side of I-70 from Highway 86. Seeing she was at the onramp from Highway 86 to eastbound I-70, Anna jumped back on the bike and accelerated as fast as she could up the ramp. The little e-bike only had a top speed of about thirty, but Anna was going almost too fast to make the turn onto 86 at the top of the ramp. She was watching her rearview mirror as much as she was watching the moonlit road ahead, willing the bike

to go faster as she sped past the sign that said it was forty
miles to Kiowa.

Anna couldn't shake the feeling of fear. It was with her
for the rest of that ride. The ride ended when the e-bike's
battery went dead just before she made it to the small
abandoned town of Kiowa. Having to dodge potholes big
enough to swallow both her and the bike, and traversing
stretches where the road was just gone, it took the rest of
the night to make it that far. In the early light of dawn, she
could see the remains of the small town no more than two
miles away. Pedalling the e-bike without any battery assist
seemed harder than walking, so she dropped the bike off
the shoulder of the old road and started walking toward
the buildings in the distance.

Since leaving Blue Rapids, Anna had passed through
and passed by many towns, both large and small. Now she
found herself afraid of the little old ghost town ahead of her.
There was no sign of anything to fear. Certainly, no black
crosses or compounds that she could see. Looking back over
her shoulder every few steps, Anna knew she wasn't really
afraid of what was in front of her. It was what lay behind
that was so terrifying. Was the Modern Times Church evil,
or had some evil people just commandeered their religion?
Evil in the name of God? She wondered. *How much evil has
been done in the name of God?*

...

The smell was overpowering at first. The closer Anna got to
the city, the worse it was. Especially when the wind blew out
of the west. It took a few hours for Anna's nose to become
desensitized to the terrible smell of death that grew stronger
as she made her way through the ever denser suburbs and

slums approaching the city. It was mid-morning, getting hot already, and Anna was exhausted. She'd walked all night after spending a restless day in the shade of an old barn on the edge of Kiowa.

Anna knew it was only another two or three miles to Castle Rock, and she had a decision to make. Should she keep going, or find someplace to sit out the heat of the day? She was coming up on what looked like a major intersection. There was some kind of old warehouse on the south side of the road that was tall enough to make a large area of welcoming shade. She sat down with her back against the warehouse wall, had a sip of precious water, and studied her map. Using her finger for a scale, Anna figured it was about ten more miles to the Mendez address in Castle Pines. It seemed odd that she hadn't seen another living human for so many days in a row. It was especially strange as she got closer to the Denver metro area.

She didn't have to see the bodies to know the area around the warehouse was still densely populated, now with dead people. The smell told her all she needed to know about that. Anna wasn't exactly hidden, but she felt like hiding, just in case there were people around who were still alive. *Don't be so paranoid,* she told herself. *It wasn't just evil people that survived the sickness.* She found herself thinking about the good people she'd left behind in Blue Rapids. One man in particular. *I should have just stayed there,* she thought. *There's nothing here but death.* Sitting in the shade of the warehouse trying to decide what to do, it wasn't the fear of being seen, but exhaustion that finally won out. Anna bowed her head and closed her eyes. It was dark when she opened them again.

It was too dark. The sky was full of stars, but the moon was not yet up. Somewhere in the distance, Anna heard the unmistakable yipping of a pack of coyotes. Their cries only adding to the eeriness of being in a totally dead, totally dark cityscape. Deciding she could see well enough to walk by starlight, and knowing she just needed to get to I-25 and then follow it north to Castle Pines Parkway, she stretched her aching legs and set off.

The quarter moon came over the horizon behind her as she walked. By the time she got to I-25, it cast a ghostly light on the surreal scene before her. It looked like some kind of field base for the army had been plopped down under the highway overpass. She could see the remnants of some sort of banner hanging from the overpass above the camp, but she couldn't tell what the banner said. The only part she could still make out was a red cross. *At least it isn't three black crosses,* she thought. Whatever the camp was, it was as dead and quiet as the rest of Castle Rock. Silent except for the coyotes anyway. The coyotes were much closer now. It sounded like they were just on the other side of the interstate, somewhere over on the west side of the abandoned army camp. There was a slight breeze out of the west that carried not only the yapping of the coyotes but the overpowering smell of a lot of rotting flesh.

From the top of the overpass, Anna could see the source of both the stench and the howling coyotes. Less than a quarter-mile to the west, a large pit had been excavated. The heavy equipment that had been used to do the excavating was all still sitting around the perimeter of the pit. There was even a large dump truck with its bed up in the air. It sat there next to the edge, frozen for for all time in the act of dumping bodies of the eternal dead. Anna didn't want to get one step closer to that pit. In her imagination, she could see the tangled mass of bodies in the bottom of that hole. She had no desire to see them with her eyes.

Interstate 25 was totally clear of vehicles, which seemed surprising considering the amount of traffic that had once flowed north and south. There were a few vehicles pushed off to the side of the road and abandoned. There were none of the autonomous freight trucks that Anna would have expected. And the only people she saw were the remains of a few bodies scattered along the shoulder and in the median.

As she started walking west on Castle Pines Parkway, Anna had a small problem. She couldn't remember the map well enough to know the twists and turns to get to Castle Lane. She couldn't even remember which street she needed to take from Castle Pines Parkway, and there wasn't enough light to read the map by moonlight. She seemed to remember thinking that she would be on Castle Pines Parkway for at least two or three miles before heading south on…? Not being able to remember the name of the street was frustrating, but she was sure she'd remember it when she saw it.

Anna could feel the excitement building up inside. She was less than five miles from the Mendez residence. As she walked, she imagined the reunion that was now only an hour or two away. *They'll all be asleep,* she thought. *The guards probably won't even let me in the gate.* James had told her enough about the Mendez estate to know it was walled in and protected by a private army. She hadn't given that fact much thought up to now. *Damn it! I need to wait until daylight,* she decided, but her pace picked up instead of slowing.

North Briar Road. The name of the street where she needed to go south popped into her head long before she got there. North Briar Road climbed at a steady grade, as it wound its way up the hillsides. The road was empty until coming around a curve, Anna saw a vehicle in the road ahead. She froze as soon as she what it was. It was some kind of military vehicle that looked both armored and armed. It was just sitting there stopped in the middle of the road. Fear gripped her. Anna didn't know what it was, and she wasn't sure she wanted to find out.

Hoping she hadn't been spotted by anyone, she retreated back around the bend in the road and climbed up into a thicket of dead brush to hide. She found a bare spot in the brush to sit down and rest and to ponder her next move. She considered working her way through the brush up past the military vehicle. She listened intently, but only the night sounds of animals disturbed the stillness. It would be daylight in a few hours. She stretched out on the soft earth to rest.

The ground that she woke up on didn't feel anywhere near as soft as it had when she laid down. She had no more planned on falling asleep than she'd planned on running into the Army, or whatever that vehicle was. The sun wasn't up yet, but it was definitely light. She stood up, stretched, and brushed the dirt off as well as she could before putting her pack back on. She sucked the last few drops of water out of the hydration bladder. It was barely enough to moisten her throat, let alone quench her thirst. *James will have water,* she thought, remembering how close she was to the Mendez Estate.

The armored vehicle was still there, exactly where she'd seen it last night. Anna peered at it through the brush. *Abandoned?* She wondered. At least it didn't have any black crosses painted on it. She approached the vehicle cautiously and walked right past, breathing a sigh of relief that it truly did seem to be abandoned. From the way it was covered with dust, it had probably been sitting right there for months. *What was the army doing up here in the first place?* She wondered as she made her way up the hill to Castle Lane.

It was just a few hundred yards up the hill to where Castle Lane ended at the gated entrance to the Mendez Estate. Seeing the rock wall that James had described, and knowing she had made it to his home was the most wonderful feeling Anna had experienced in a long time. The feeling was extremely short-lived, though. The massive wrought iron security gate was standing wide open.

No one challenged her as she walked up to the guardhouse. She stopped just long enough to open the unlocked door and look inside. It was empty. She walked on up the driveway around the curve to where the house came into view. The mansion was pretty much as she had always imagined it would be. Robert Mendez, James' father, was, after all, one of the richest men in the world. The only thing that seemed totally out of place was the water truck sitting on top of a landscape berm in the center of the circular driveway. Seeing the hose running from the truck to the house, buoyed Anna's emotions once again. Someone had arranged a backup source of water for the place, which meant they'd survived the sickness.

She was so excited that she practically ran the rest

of the way up the steps to the big double front door. She pushed the doorbell button and pounded on the door as loudly as she could. After waiting as long as she could stand to wait, she reached down and tried the latch. To her surprise, the door was not even locked. "Hello," she yelled into the open doorway. There was no answer. She walked into the large foyer and hollered some more. Still no answer.

Instead of going further into the house, Anna went back outside. As she was running up the steps to the house, she'd noticed an open door on the large stable looking building that she knew, from James' description, had to be the car barn. James had told her that his mother called it that, much to the chagrin of his father. Thinking James might be out there in the car barn, she hurried to the open door, hollering as she went, but getting only silence in return.

The automobile collection inside the car barn was absolutely astounding, but that's all there was. There were only cars and trucks, with no sign of anyone or anything else inside the vast warehouse. Anna made her way back to the house and found her way to the kitchen. She could hear a faint humming noise that was coming from the refrigerator. She flipped on a light switch, and sure enough, the place still had power. Remembering how thirsty she was, she tried the tap at the kitchen sink. The water that came out was a little bit rust-colored and definitely warm. It must have been from the steel tank on the water truck, but it tasted wonderful to Anna.

Someone must still be living here, please let it be James, it was almost a silent prayer. A prayer to whom, Anna couldn't say. She was about as non-religious as a person can be.

Maybe he went somewhere in a vehicle from the car barn, she thought. *That would explain the barn door being left open. Maybe he's just out scavenging supplies or food.* She looked in the refrigerator. There wasn't much there, so she opened the door to the pantry. The pantry seemed pretty well stocked. Not only was there plenty of Allpro, there were a lot of other canned goods and non-perishables. She'd looked in the refrigerator, now she checked out the freezer. The freezer was stocked even better than she would have guessed. It was full of frozen meats and frozen vegetables. There was even a tub of chocolate ice cream. Anna couldn't remember the last time she had eaten chocolate ice cream or any ice cream for that matter.

So, I'll just wait for him to come home, she thought, slipping out of her backpack and hanging it on one of the barstools. She found a bowl and a spoon, having decided to treat herself to some of the ice cream. *James won't mind.*

The ice cream was good but not as good as the ice cream of her memory. Of course, that was homemade, and this was not. A thought nagged at her as she finished the bowl of ice cream. *What if it isn't James that comes home.* Anna felt, as much as heard, the air conditioning unit kick on. *Must be getting hot already,* she thought, and decided to check out more of the estate before it got unbearably hot. That's when she found the graves.

It had obviously been a beautiful flower garden back when it had water. Now it was obviously just a cemetery. *Eight graves?* She wondered. The graves were all unmarked, and they were all relatively recent burials. Anna could tell that one of the graves was a little bit newer than the other seven. *Who's buried here?* That was the troubling question. *And who did the burying? It had to be James,* she thought. *James must have buried...buried who? His mom and dad? That's only two. Who else? Security guards? A maid, housekeepers?* There were too many possibilities to even think of them all. Anna went back inside to wait for James. No use wondering about it, James would be able to tell her everything as soon as he got home.

…

A week passed, then ten days. Every morning, Anna knew this would be the day that James would come home. Every night, she went to bed disappointed. Disappointed and lonely. She'd enjoyed the comforts of the Mendez mansion just about as much she could stand. It had been totally wonderful at first. Especially having a shower with hot running water. Even if it was just barely a trickle of hot water. Second only to the shower, was the luxury of sleeping in a bed in air-conditioned comfort, something Anna hadn't had the pleasure of experiencing since she left Blue Rapids.

Over the past ten days, Anna had thoroughly explored and examined the entire Mendez estate. She'd been amazed at the totally self-contained power systems on the estate and disappointed to find that the water truck had no more than a hundred gallons of water left. *Maybe he's out looking for water,* she'd thought, when she discovered that the water tank was nearly empty. That had been ten days ago. Now, Anna had a decision to make. There was no longer enough water in the tank for it to even come out of the kitchen faucet.

What if he doesn't come back? She wondered, as she finished the last of the ice cream that she'd decided to have for breakfast. *I can't just wait here forever. Soon I'll be out of water. What then?*

It was time to go home. Time to give up on the dream she'd nurtured for so long. The dream of finding James Mendez alive in Castle Pines. Anna knew she'd actually made up her mind yesterday. Last night, she'd plugged in one of the old Volkswagens out in the car barn. She had her doubts about being able to drive all the way to the Blue River Ranch, even with a full charge. She'd developed a planned route to avoid the mountain passes as much as possible by first working her way north along the eastern edge of the Denver metro area. She thought she'd be able to make her way around the north edge of Fort Collins to Highway 287 north to Laramie. From there, she'd just take the old secondary highways down through Walden and on down to Kremmling.

Just one more thing to do before setting out for home. For a moment or two, she just stared at the blank piece of paper and the pen poised in her hand, ready to write. What did she want to say? What if someone besides James finds the note? Finally, the pen started moving, the words appearing on the blank page:

Dearest James,

I've waited for you to return for ten days. I'm just about out of water, and I can't wait here any longer. When you find this note, I'll still be waiting for you, but I'll be waiting at our secret place. Please come to me soon.

I love you, Anna

Chapter Fifteen

ANNA DIDN'T EVEN look back as she drove out of the gate and started down the hill. She wondered again at the meaning of the army vehicle that would no doubt be sitting in the middle of the road for eternity. She made her way around a curve to a point where the view opened up to reveal the entire city of Denver laid out to the north. That view did bring her to a stop. It had been dark when she'd come up this road, so this was her first view of downtown Denver. Now, in the distance to the north, where downtown Denver should have been, there was nothing but a scene of destruction. It looked like the city had been bombed. She stared at the ruins, trying to make sense of it all. *What the hell happened here?* It was a question that would probably never have an answer. At least, not for Anna.

It took longer to skirt out around the eastern side of the city than Anna had anticipated. She had to make her way around stalled vehicles of all sorts and dead bodies that by now, all looked pretty much the same. There really wasn't much left of the dead but the smell. Ravens, magpies, and buzzards were still feasting on some, most had already been picked clean.

Anna had previously decided to avoid all of the major highways, but seeing how clear and open E-470 looked, she decided to give it a try. It was not just open, it was eerily so. There was not a single stalled vehicle of any kind. It was like someone had cleared it completely of all vehicles. Then, at Pena Boulevard, E-470 was just gone. The interchange ramps and bridges had been blown into piles of rubble. Not only that, but the wreckage of a bunch of military vehicles was scattered throughout the debris. It looked like some kind of convoy had been bombed while crossing the overpass. *Did we have a war?* The question brought to mind the bombed-out bridge across the Snake River back in Idaho. Then she had an even scarier thought. *Was it some kind of germ or biological warfare?* It would make some kind of sense out of the terrible toll the sickness had taken. *How could anything else have killed so many, so quickly? But why not me? Why did any of us survive?*

She was still wondering, still trying to make sense of it all, when she finally got to Highway 287 on the northwest side of Fort Collins. In all that way, she hadn't seen a single living person. Highway 287 wasn't clogged with abandoned vehicles, but it wasn't completely empty either. She had to cross the median several times and use both the northbound and southbound travel lanes. She had just worked her way around a stalled semi when she saw the sign that said Walden, with an arrow pointing to a left turn. Anna had forgotten about Cameron Pass, now she stopped and pondered it. It would be a lot shorter than going all the way up to Laramie and then back down to Walden. If the road was open, that is.

She searched her memory for the only time she'd ever been over Cameron Pass. It had been many years ago when she was just a girl. Her dad and Chuck Pierson had let her ride along on a trip to a ranch on the east side of the pass. She seemed to remember the purpose of the trip was to look at a bull. She couldn't remember now if Chuck had bought the bull or not. What she was really trying to remember was the pass itself. If her memory was accurate, it seemed like Cameron Pass wasn't carved into the mountainside like Berthoud or Vail. From what she could remember, even if the travel lanes of Highway 14 were blocked, she could probably get by on the shoulder or in the borrow ditch. It had already taken longer to get here than Anna thought it would, so she decided to take the shorter route to Walden.

Anna had traveled just over a mile when she saw the green trees that lined the Cache la Poudre River and the old sign that let her know she was on Poudre Canyon Road. Knowing the highway might easily be blocked in a river canyon, Anna decided to keep going anyway. If her way was blocked, it wouldn't be that far back to Highway 287.

She couldn't have been more than five miles up the canyon when she saw them. At first, she couldn't believe it. It had been so long since she'd seen another living human being that she doubted her own eyes. As she got closer, it became clear that there really were four people working in a garden about halfway between the highway and the river.

It was two men and two women harvesting the fruits of a long summer's labor. It reminded Anna of the Farm and those she'd left behind in Blue Rapids. There was absolutely nothing threatening about the four people. They must have felt the same about Anna. They all stopped what they were doing and waved frantically, like they were afraid she wouldn't see them.

The four were already walking toward the road before Anna could even get the car parked. She walked down the shoulder of the road and met the group at the fence that protected their garden. It was a six-foot fence, meant to keep deer from harvesting their precious crop of vegetables.

"I can't believe it!" the first man to reach the fence said. "I was beginning to think we'd never see another soul coming up that road again. I'm Steve."

Steve was short, not even as tall as Anna. He had long sandy blonde hair and a full beard to match. He looked to be around thirty years old. Steve introduced the other three, Mary, Claire, and Mike, before Anna had a chance to say anything.

"I'm Anna." She introduced herself, noticing how strange it was that surnames didn't seem to matter anymore. "It's been a long time since I've seen anyone. Anyone alive," she added. "Are there more?"

"Not here." It was the redhead, Claire, that answered Anna's question. "Just us four, but there's another group a few miles up the canyon. Don't know beyond that, been months since we've seen anybody else besides Josie's bunch."

Claire was probably the oldest of the four, maybe thirty-five or forty. She looked stout and not very feminine. She was the apparent de facto leader of this little family.

"There's seven in Josie's clan," Mary, the youngest looking of the group, added. Mary was a pretty girl. She had long black hair and dark skin. She was built and looked a lot like Anna. If a person didn't know better, they might have mistaken Anna and Mary for sisters. It seemed to

Anna that Mary spoke with more of an affinity for Josie's clan than the rest of the group.

Mike, who looked to be in his mid-twenties, didn't say anything. He just kept staring at Anna, looking her up and down in a way that made her feel uncomfortable.

"Well, come on in," Claire said. "Driveway's just up the road. We'll meet you at the house." Without waiting for a reply, she turned, grabbed Mike's hand, forcing him to follow, and walked away.

"It's lunchtime anyway," Mary said. "Please join us." Then she and Steve turned together and followed Josie and Mike.

Anna could hardly refuse. As much as she wanted to get home, she'd been too long without human companionship to pass up the opportunity to visit with others. Besides, they might know whether or not Highway 14 was passable all the way to Walden.

Claire's clan, as Anna thought of these two couples, had quite a little homestead going. The old house that they occupied had belonged to Claire before the sickness. She'd been a widow, living alone for several years before everyone else died. Her husband had died of cancer some years before the sickness. The others had joined her one at a time after the sickness destroyed their world. As Anna listened to their stories, and she shared parts of hers, she found it fascinating that so many of those who survived the sickness were all doing basically the same thing. Banding together in small groups and relearning to live much as their ancestors had decades or even centuries before. Claire's clan seemed to be reasonably happy living with practically no modern conveniences at all. They did have running water, but it was just water piped directly out of the Cache la Poudre River. They boiled the water before drinking it or using it for cooking. There was a well that used to supply the house with water, but without electricity to power the pump, Claire's clan was stuck with water out of the river.

Claire's clan had a wagon and a couple of horses to pull it. Anna couldn't help but wonder why they didn't just go down to Fort Collins to get PV panels and equipment to supply their own electricity. *Guess none of them knows how,* she thought. As they shared the most wonderful lunch of fresh greens that Anna had eaten since leaving Blue Rapids, she had the thought that she could help them set up an electrical system. *Maybe I can come back and help them later,* she told herself, dismissing any ideas about staying with the group any longer than lunch.

Lunch was long enough for Anna to get a lot of information from Claire's clan. All but Claire, herself, had been living in the Denver area in their previous lives. Anna learned how bombs or missiles had destroyed Denver just before, or at the same time as the sickness was killing everyone. No one knew who, where, or why the city was attacked. Strangely, no one seemed to want to talk much about life before the great dying. Perhaps it was too painful to remember. It was something Anna could relate to. She didn't tell them anything about how she ended up in Blue Rapids, Kansas, either. Some memories are best left buried.

Mike had been the first to stumble into Claire's life. Like the others, he had been fleeing the city that was so full of death that it had become unbearable. Like the others, he had no idea where he was going, just away. Claire had invited him in when she'd seen him walking up the road.

He stayed and became Claire's lover before Steve showed up. Steve had been invited to stay with Claire and Mike a couple of weeks later. He had decided instead to just keep heading up the canyon.

That's where he found Josie's clan and Mary. Mary told Anna about Josie's clan, which had the same problem as the group Anna had left behind in Blue Rapids, too many women or not enough men, depending on how you wanted to look at it. There were only two men and five women in Josie's clan. There had been six women before Steve came along and eventually convinced Mary to go back down the valley to Claire's. Apparently, it hadn't taken too much convincing. One of the only two men at Josie's was Mary's older brother.

Is it love, or just instinct or necessity that still drives men and women together, Anna thought. Steve and Mary really did seem to be in love. Mike and Claire, not so much. Anna could definitely feel the lust in Mike's stare when he looked at her, and she felt sorry for both Mary and Claire. It was evident to Anna that Mike wanted Mary more than he wanted Claire. *This group is not going to last,* Anna realized with a sadness that surprised her. As an outsider, she was probably the only one who could see it. As an outsider, she knew there was nothing she could do about it.

No one in Claire's clan knew for sure whether the road to Walden was open or not. Anna was the first person they'd seen on the road for a couple of months. Claire said she'd seen a few other vehicles go by back when the exodus from the cities first began. She figured the road must have been open at that time because she didn't see any of them come back down.

Anna thanked them for the lunch and the information and told them she hoped to come back and visit one day. Mary gave Anna directions to Josie's place and asked her to stop in and say hi to her brother. Anna said she would, even though she knew she wouldn't. As she drove away, her thoughts were on human nature and what the future would hold for the few people left in this old world.

It was getting late in the afternoon when Anna saw the sign that said Rand, with a left turn arrow. Highway 14 was heading almost due north at that point, and she knew the geography of this part of Colorado well enough to know that cutting through to Rand and then on down to Granby would cut a lot of miles off her trip. The Volkswagen was already down to less than half of its battery capacity. She looked at the old Colorado map just to make sure, then decided to take the old county road to Rand. She wished it was earlier in the day, but Highway 14 had been a pretty slow go. Like most secondary roads in the state, it was pretty dilapidated from lack of maintenance. That was another point in favor of cutting through to Rand. The old county road might be in better condition than the state highway.

Anna didn't make it to Rand. Her luck ran out before the car's battery pack did. She came to a point where a windstorm had blown several large dead trees over, blocking the road completely. From the looks of it, the road had been blocked and unused for a long time. The sun was setting, and Anna didn't know what to do next. She was pretty sure she was closer to Rand than to Highway 14, but if she turned around, based on the battery gauge, she might well end up running out of juice farther away from home than she was now. Studying the map, Anna figured it was less than eighty miles from where she sat right now to the Blue River Ranch. Eighty miles would be no more than four days walking, so she decided to just spend the night in the car and start walking at daybreak. Now that she was up in the mountains, it wouldn't be too hot for hiking during the day.

It was too cold to sleep. It had been so long since Anna had been in the mountains at night that she hadn't really considered how much cooler it was than the low lands. She didn't even have a long sleeve shirt, let alone a jacket or a coat. Thinking it might be nice to have a fire, she rummaged around in her pack for the lighter she knew was there. When she got out of the car, though, she decided it was probably only an hour or two until daylight. She must have slept more of the night than she thought. It wasn't a full moon, but it was definitely light enough to see where she was going. So instead of building a fire, Anna hoisted the familiar pack to her shoulders and set off at a brisk walk.

As light filled the eastern sky, Anna realized just how much she'd missed the mountains. Hiking in the Colorado high country made her feel like she was already home, not just on a journey to get there. Coming around a bend in the road, the forest gave way to a large fenced pasture on one side of the road. The five horses grazing in the meadow saw Anna at least as soon as she saw them. The horses had been at the back of the pasture near a small stream that ran through one corner. They came running across the meadow toward Anna as soon as they saw her.

If there was one thing Anna knew well, it was horses. She could tell at a glance that these were fine animals.

Especially the red Quarterhorse gelding that was in the lead. They act like they haven't seen people for a long time, Anna thought as she walked over to the fence to meet the herd. She held her hands out over the fence, fingers curled into a fist with palms down. The big red gelding reminded her of Chuck's horse at the Blue River Ranch. He timidly sniffed her hand and allowed her to reach up and rub his forehead. Then he stuck out his nose toward her face. Anna exhaled through her nose right at his nostril as she scratched behind his ear.

"What's your name big boy?" She asked, as the other four horses jockeyed for position to get some of her attention.

From where she was, Anna couldn't see any ranch buildings or a house, and she hadn't passed any yet. So, she started walking along the fence line with the horses shadowing her, like she was the pied piper or something. She crested a hill and could see the ranch buildings laid out about a quarter of a mile away. The meadow was cross-fenced at the crest of the hill, so the horses could no longer follow. As she hurried toward the ranch, one of the horses neighed loudly behind her. She was pretty sure she knew which horse it was.

Anna was reasonably sure she wasn't going to find anyone alive on the ranch. She knew she was right as soon as she walked around the corner of the old ranch house and saw the remains lying on the ground with a revolver lying next to it. There wasn't much more than a skeleton left of the man, but the revolver on the ground and the missing part of his skull told the story. He was lying next to a grave. Anna guessed he'd probably buried his wife before killing himself. Did he kill himself because he was sick, or just because of grief? Anna wondered.

She would never know why the rancher had killed himself, but she did know taking horses and tack from a dead man wouldn't be stealing at all.

Chapter Sixteen

ANNA WAS CURIOUS as to whether anyone was still living in Granby, but not curious enough to ride the three miles into town to find out. Instead, she headed west as soon as she got to the intersection with Highway 40. She was getting so close to home, she could hardly stand it. One minute she was filled with dread over what she might find, the next minute, she was consumed by hopeful anticipation.

This was her second day of riding Red Two, which was what she decided to call the horse that she'd "borrowed" from the dead rancher. By the time she found a bridle and saddle, caught Red Two, and saddled up, it had been late morning yesterday before she even got to Rand. She'd left the gate to the pasture open, and the rest of the horses had followed Red Two for a few hours before getting sidetracked by some extra good grass to graze on. Anna rode as far as the old Denver Creek Campground before stopping for the night. It was hard to believe how sore she'd been after eight hours in the saddle. A few years ago, it wouldn't have bothered her at all.

Anna had awakened this morning even more stiff and sore than when she'd crawled into the bedroll the night before. The bedroll had also been "borrowed" from the old ranch. She'd even found a nice warm lined denim jacket that fit well enough to keep out the early morning chill. Now, after a couple more hours in the saddle, her rear end had gone from being sore to mostly just being numb.

Anna stopped and dismounted to stretch her sore legs and to take off the jacket. It was probably just eight or nine, but the morning sun was already plenty warm to shed that layer. Anna tied the coat behind the saddle with her backpack and bedroll. *Should have grabbed some saddlebags,* she thought. The backpack wasn't a very good substitute for real saddlebags. It was pretty awkward and hard to get tied on securely behind the saddle. Windy Gap Reservoir was low, but it did still have some water in it. Anna led Red Two to the water's edge and allowed him to have a good long drink before mounting up and heading west along the shoulder of Highway 40.

It was disappointing and foreboding to ride through Hot Sulphur Springs without seeing anyone at all. In Byers Canyon, several autonomous semis had all stalled out at once, completely blocking Highway 40. "Good thing I've got you instead of that stupid Volkswagen," Anna told the horse, as she made her way past the stalled vehicles.

She wasn't surprised at all to not see anyone in Parshall. Parshall had pretty much been a ghost town for as long as Anna could remember. But Anna was getting worried as she made camp on the bank of the Colorado River just outside the old town. Having not seen anyone or any sign of a living soul since Poudre Canyon, she was becoming fearful of what she might find in Kremmling tomorrow.

...

Anna didn't make it all the way into Kremmling. Seeing the town of Kremmling again, as she came through the last little cut and around the curve that brought the old airport into view, filled her with such elation that it brought tears to her eyes. She pulled Red Two to a stop, and just sat there for a moment drinking in the sight of her old hometown. From there, with the nearest buildings still a mile away, Kremmling looked just as she'd remembered it. All except for the lack of any vehicles moving on Highway 40, that is. As she got a little closer, she could even see a tiny wisp of smoke rising from somewhere on the other side of the airport. *Probably someone's morning cookfire that hasn't gone out yet.* The thought that someone in Kremmling had a fire was absolutely thrilling. Somebody was still alive in Kremmling.

She was trying to figure out where exactly the smoke was coming from. Maybe even the Donovan's. Maybe Will's mother had survived. Their house was definitely in that general direction. The Donovan house was below the hill just off Highway 9. Anna was just about to the airport when she absently looked over at the old Bureau Of Land Management office on the north side of the highway. What she saw there made her involuntarily jerk back on the reins so hard that Red Two almost reared and immediately started backing up.

The old BLM office building looked much as it always had. The difference that instantly chilled Anna to her core was in the parking lot. The flagpole that had always stood in front of the entrance was gone. In its place, there were three large black crosses. The one in the center was taller than the two that flanked it. Just then, the front doors swung open, and two men walked out. Anna could tell that they saw her at the same time as she saw them. She didn't wait to see more. Spinning Red Two like he was chasing a bolting calf, Anna kicked him just enough to put him into a full gallop headed back east along the shoulder of the highway.

Anna kept trying to look back, but at full gallop, it was hard to see whether or not anyone was following. In the fleeting instant that Anna saw the men come out of the building, she had also noticed a couple of vehicles in the parking lot. *We need to get away from the road,* she thought, but it was almost a mile to where the airport security fence ended, and she was able to get away from the highway. She turned Red Two down toward the Colorado River and eased him back into a walk. He was a damn good horse, but a mile at full gallop had taken a lot out of him. Anna scanned the terrain back to the west, back toward Kremmling, as they headed south toward the river. There was no sign of pursuit of any kind, but she kept a head swiveling lookout all the way down to the river and all the way to the other side. The river was pretty low, and it was easy to find a place to cross. What she hadn't counted on was the fence on the other side. Damn, what I wouldn't give for some wire cutters, she thought, as she turned the horse to follow the fenceline downstream toward the Highway 9 bridge. It was less than twenty miles up that old highway to the Blue River Ranch. Less than twenty miles to home.

It wasn't too far downstream to where the fenceline

came to a corner, and the fence went due south. Anna knew that if she followed it, she'd hit the county road in no time. The county road she could follow to Highway 9, that she could then follow home. There was a problem with staying on roads, though. If anyone was looking for her, the roads were the most likely place to search. There was a thick growth of trees and brush dead ahead. Anna took another good look around and made up her mind. She got off of Red Two and led him along a game trail that led into the thick brush. She wanted nothing more than to get home, but she decided to just hide out for the rest of the day and head up Highway 9 after dark. She found an opening with plenty of grass for Red Two, tied him up with a rope, and took off the saddle and bridle. Then she stretched out on the grass to rest and think.

Was she crazy to be so paranoid every time she saw a Modern Times Church? They'd never seemed evil before, but then she really didn't know anything about them. They'd just seemed like another crazy religious sect before Little America. Before the three black crosses painted on the side of Sarge and Curt's rolling slave cage. But, unlike Sarge and Curt, the two men she saw in Kremmling weren't wearing uniforms, and they weren't armed. At least they weren't carrying rifles. Then again, Sarge had seemed unarmed and innocent when Anna first saw him.

There had never been a Modern Times Church in Kremmling or anywhere else on the western slope that Anna knew of. She was sure the first she'd ever heard of it was in Eugene. How did there come to be one in Kremmling? Maybe it wasn't the same, but thinking about it, the one in Eugene had just seemed to spring up after she had arrived.

Perhaps they were popping up all over the country during the past couple of years. She was absolutely sure that she had never heard of The Modern Times Church before Eugene. It was tempting, now that the adrenaline rush of fear was gone, to just ride back into town and confront the place, to find out for herself what it was all about. She ultimately decided to just get home to the BR. Maybe her folks could tell her something about the mysterious church. *If they're still alive,* she thought, and immediately regretted even having the thought that her parents might be dead. More than that, deep down, she felt that her parents were both gone. She'd been trying to deny that feeling for months, but it just wouldn't go away.

…

Other than a noticeable lack of use, the lane from Highway 9 to the ranch looked just as Anna remembered it. The sun had just come up in the east behind her, bathing the buildings of the Blue River Ranch in a bright morning glow. Anna was finally home. After riding all night, after unimaginable months of yearning, she was finally home. She felt an entire kaleidoscope of emotions all at once. The incredible feeling of finally being home was tempered by the fear that she might be the only one. There was no sign of life from any of the buildings up ahead. Somebody had survived after the sickness, though. There was no other explanation for the hay crop having been put up in the big meadow. The sickness had killed everyone in the spring, and the hay wouldn't have been put up until summer. *Then where is everyone,* she wondered.

About halfway up the lane, not seeing any sign of activity, worry settled in a little deeper. The piercing sound of an eagle's scream high overhead startled her. Then she saw movement. It was Blackie, Chuck's dog. The Border Collie came running toward her from the big house, letting out a bark at nearly the exact same instant that another sound, much louder, punctuated the quiet morning stillness. It was a gunshot. Red Two, Anna, and Blackie all seemed to freeze at the same time, as the sound of that single gunshot echoed around them, and a flock of birds took flight from the trees behind the old homestead.

PART TWO

Chapter Seventeen

WHAT THE HELL! She thought. Anna grabbed the pistol on her hip without even realizing it. Then, without drawing the gun, she dismounted and scanned the area. It sounded like the shot came from up behind the old homestead, maybe from the area of the old family cemetery. *Who's shooting?*

Blackie ran up to Anna, with tail wagging wildly. It was amazing how a dog instantly recognized someone that it hadn't seen for almost two years. Anna knelt down and didn't so much pet Blackie, as she embraced the old dog. "What's goin' on, boy?" she asked, still looking up toward where the shot had been fired. She still couldn't see anyone, but, oddly enough, she didn't feel threatened at all. The sound of firearms being discharged had always been a normal part of life on the ranch.

Then she heard a shout. A man's voice, sounding almost hysterical. "Hey! Hey! Hello!" The shouting was coming from where she'd heard the gunshots.

"Hello," she yelled back. She didn't recognize the voice. She was pretty sure it wasn't her dad or Chuck, or either one of her brothers. She started walking toward the sound, leading Red Two, with Blackie running on ahead.

She'd taken just a few steps when she saw what looked like a crazy man come running out of the trees behind the big house. He was waving a gun in the air as he ran toward her. Tears filled her eyes. She dropped the reins and started running to meet the mad man as soon as she recognized him.

Anna and James ran into each other's arms and held on for dear life. Tears were streaming down both of their faces, and Anna was sobbing when she finally pushed away.

"You bastard!" she sobbed. "I hate you! How could you? Why?"

James knew exactly what Anna was asking. He'd asked himself the same thing over and over again and hated himself for the same reasons that Anna did. How could he have just dumped her the way he did? How many times had he thought about the things he could have done - should have done? Having just come within inches of killing himself, James' emotions were as wild and mixed up as Anna's.

"I love you Anna. I love you more than anything," he was able to get out past the lump in his throat.

"If you love me so much, why didn't you ever come back? Never even so much as a call."

Anna's sobbing was tapering off, but the sorrow and pain in those deep brown eyes was almost more than James could bear.

"Please Anna, don't hate me. I had to. He made me do it. It was my dad. It…He…I did it for you and Grandpa. Oh Anna, I'm so sorry."

James looked down at the ground, unable to look at the hurt in Anna's eyes. When he looked back up, the pain was still there, but there was also questioning in those eyes. Eyes that James had feared he would never see again.

"What does Chuck have to do with this?" The sobbing had stopped, but Anna's tear-filled eyes still held the pain that she'd carried for the past three years. "And what do you mean, it was your dad?"

"He made me stop seeing you. He would have taken the ranch. He would have ruined Grandpa…and your whole family."

As soon as he mentioned Anna's family, James regretted that he would be the one who had to answer the question in her eyes.

"They're gone Anna. All of them are gone now. It's just us. We're all that's left."

James never told Anna that the shot she heard had missed his head by mere inches when the gun discharged accidentally. He never told her that if she hadn't shown up when she did, the pulling of the trigger wouldn't have been an accident at all, and the bullet would not have missed. He never told her how close she came to being the sole survivor on the Blue River Ranch.

...

Anna placed the wildflower bouquets on each of the graves and remembered her family. The family that was gone forever. These would be the last flowers of the year. It was either late fall or early winter, she wasn't sure which, but the nights had been getting cold, and the days were definitely getting shorter. There had been a heavy frost that morning. Down at the ranch, she could hear James splitting wood. He'd been at it for hours. *Better get down there and help him stack it,* she thought.

The past month or so, since Anna had been home at the BR, was mostly just a blur. She and James had never once left the ranch. There was so much that needed to be done to get ready for winter. James was willing and able to provide a lot of help, but he still had a lot to learn about living on the ranch and caring for the animals. He was learning, though. Grandpa Chuck had taught him a lot, and he was happier than seemed possible. Anna had to admit to a real feeling of contentment, herself. Other than the grieving that she still felt every day, she was happier than she'd ever been. She couldn't say that life with James was exactly as she'd imagined it would be, but then nothing was as she'd imagined it. No one could have ever imagined the world after the sickness, or the great dying, as James called it.

As she walked down the path from the cemetery to help James stack wood, she thought about all they'd accomplished in such a short time. The immediate pressing concern had been making sure they were ready for the winter ahead. Using the old wood-burning cookstove to boil the jars to can tomatoes and beans had been like working in a foundry. The stove heated the house so much that James and Anna were forced to sleep in the old house on canning days. Sleeping with James in the bedroom from her childhood was strange. Some mornings, it almost seemed like another age. It would take a moment or two to fully wake up and realize she wasn't a kid anymore. To reckon with the reality that, other than James, she was alone in her childhood home.

Anna figured she could probably stand to use James's great-great-grandmother's cookstove through the winter, but come spring, she planned on going somewhere to find enough solar components and storage batteries to upgrade the system. By the time summer rolled around next year, Anna planned to have the electric range back in the kitchen and to have air-conditioned comfort to sleep in.

Thwack! The maul stuck in a particularly large block of fir that was probably too green. "You might need to use a wedge for that one," Anna told him, as she came around the corner of the woodshed.

The woodshed was about halfway between the big house that she and James now occupied and the older original ranch house that she'd grown up in. It was really just an oversized loafing shed, big enough to hold all the firewood that two families would need to get through the winter. Both households had always relied on wood heat to keep the winter at bay. Unlike most of the other ranchers in the area, Chuck Pierson had never made the switch to natural gas.

"Do we have enough yet?" James asked as he rubbed the back of a gloved hand across his forehead to wipe away the sweat that was about to drip into his eyes.

Anna looked at the nearly full woodshed and the pile of split wood scattered around the chopping block. "Plenty," she told him. "That would have been enough for both of our houses."

"Good," James said, "then that damn maul can just

stay right there."

Blackie, who'd been resting in the shade a safe distance from the flying pieces of firewood, suddenly jumped up and let out a single bark. The fur on his back was standing up, as he looked out toward the highway. James and Anna both turned to see what had aroused the dog's attention. Two people on horseback were coming up the lane. They were still way out by the highway so Anna couldn't be sure, but it looked like a man and a woman.

"Blackie, stay!" Anna commanded the dog as she reached down to her hip for the gun that wasn't there. She'd stopped wearing the pistol on her hip once she finally felt securely at home.

"Looks like we've got company," James said as he started walking out to meet the riders. Even from a distance, he felt like he should recognize the two people. As they got closer, and James got a better look at the woman's long blonde hair, he knew who they were. Anna and Blackie followed James out to the barn to meet them. "Hello, neighbors," James greeted the couple as they dismounted.

"Anna, this is Jack and Connie," James did the introductions. "They're two of the neighbors from up by Silverthorne that I told you about," he explained to Anna. "At least I guess you're still up by Silverthorne?" he asked, directing the question at Jack. James may have told Anna about the two couples near Silverthorne, but he hadn't told her everything about his encounter with Connie. Now, he didn't want his body language to reveal that particular little secret.

"Still there." Connie smiled as she answered the question for Jack.

"Just the two of you?" Jack asked, and Anna and James both knew the rest of the unspoken question. Did anyone else survive the sickness?

"My grandpa died after I got here," James told them. "Think it was a heart attack, but I'm not sure."

There was no need for Jack or Connie to say they were sorry or offer condolences of any kind. Everyone had lost so many loved ones that words were unnecessary.

James couldn't help but steal a glance into Connie's blue eyes. Her wistful smile brought the memory of their short intimate encounter in a hayloft immediately back to mind. James had told Anna about staying with Jack and his brother, and Connie and her sister, while on his way from Castle Pines to the BR. He hadn't told her about the early morning sexual encounter he'd had with Connie, though. From Jack and Connie's demeanor, James was pretty sure that Connie had also kept that little secret to herself.

"Please, come in and have lunch with us," Anna told the two. "You must be pretty tired from such a long ride." She intuitively knew there was more about Connie than James had told her, but she also knew how much she had never told James. She'd told him some about being taken captive by Sarge and Curt, but, other than the fact that she'd been raped, she spared him most of the details. She hadn't told him about sharing Charlie with Olivia either. As a matter of fact, she hadn't told him much at all about Charlie. Some things are just better kept to oneself.

They put Jack and Connie's horses in the old log barn with some fresh hay to munch on. Then, they all four went into the big house to share lunch with someone other than each other for a change. Talking with someone other than

James made Anna realize how much she missed other people. It was especially nice having another woman to talk to. And it wasn't just Anna. All four of them seemed to really enjoy each other's company. Seeking out someone besides Ray and Rita to talk to was the main reason that Jack and Connie had ridden all this way. *People are like horses,* Anna thought. *We truly are herd animals.*

James was having similar thoughts himself. The awkwardness he'd first felt at seeing Connie again gave way to a pleasant feeling of companionship with both her and Jack. *No wonder ancient humans always seemed to live in clans or tribes,* he thought. As much as he loved Anna and wanted to always be with her, it was clear that he'd missed contact with others. It was something that he'd never admitted to himself. He, too, was a social animal. He remembered telling Grandpa Chuck that what they were doing without Anna wasn't living, it was just existing. It wasn't until now that he admitted to himself that Anna wasn't enough either. He had always thought she was all he needed. Now, he knew the truth. They could survive together with no other human contact, but it wouldn't really be living. To really live, not just survive, people need people. Looking across the great room at Anna and Connie sitting on the sofa chatting like old friends, James knew that everyone in the room had similar feelings.

"So, what are you planning to do with all the cattle?" Jack's question broke through James' introspection. Jack was obviously referencing the herd of forty-seven Black Angus in the big meadow. When James and Anna had gathered the herd and brought them down from summer grazing in the high country, Anna had been disappointed that they'd only found forty-seven head. "Used to be thousands," she'd told him, and James had wondered what they were going to do with forty-seven, let alone thousands.

"Damn good question. Guess we're just raising a bunch of big grass-eating pets." James answered. "You guys still raising sheep?"

Jack laughed. "Yeah, I'm kind of like you. How many sheep do four people need? I think the thirty-some head we've got is a little too much. I mean, how much lamb can a person stand to eat?"

James couldn't help but laugh, too. As far as he was concerned, he'd rather have beef any day. "Kind of strange, isn't it?" he asked. "Do you think there are people who could use some beef or lamb. Or wool, for that matter. If there are, how would we ever know? More important, how would we ever get it to anybody that needed it?"

James and Jack's conversation was interrupted by Connie. "We better get going Jack, it's going to be dark before we get home."

Neither James nor Jack had noticed how the time had flown. It was already mid-afternoon. "Why don't you guys just stay tonight and ride back tomorrow?" James asked, adding, "We've got all kinds of room. Two houses worth."

"As much as we'd like to take you up on that offer," Jack answered, "we better take a rain check. Ray and Rita would be out looking for us for sure."

"Thank you so much for the hospitality," Connie was telling Anna as they walked out onto the veranda. "I'm so glad I got to meet you."

"Likewise," Anna told her, "wish you didn't live so far away."

"Me too," Connie said. Then, as she took a last look around, "wish our place was this nice."

As Jack and Connie saddled up and started to head home, James and Anna promised to pay them a visit soon.

"I think we should ask them to come and live here," Anna said, seemingly out of the blue. She and James were just finishing what had been a quiet evening meal of beefsteak and fried potatoes. Both had been mostly lost in their own thoughts all through dinner.

"You mean Jack and Connie?" James asked as if she could have been talking about anyone else.

"I mean all four of them," Anna answered. "They can live in the old house. Sounds to me like it's a lot nicer than where they live now."

James didn't know what to say. The idea of having other people around was appealing, but what would Anna do if she found out about that morning in the old hayloft with Connie. What would Jack do? Probably just as important, if they all lived on the same ranch, would it ever happen again? James already felt like that one encounter in the hayloft had been a betrayal of Anna, could he keep it from happening again? He remembered Connie's words that morning, "I'm the one that fucked you, remember." What if she wanted to fuck him again? It hadn't felt at all like that today, but still, he had to wonder.

"I liked them, and I'm sure I'll like Ray and Rita too." Anna's voice pulled James back into the conversation. "Besides, Connie's going to need all the help she can get. She's pregnant, you know."

James didn't know and trying to not show total shock, he asked as casually as he could, "how pregnant? I mean, when's she due? She didn't look pregnant."

"She thinks she's two or three months along," Anna answered, looking obliquely at James as she added, "can't be more than three months. That's about how long she said she and Jack have been together."

Chapter Eighteen

A NNA WAS AMAZED at the warm weather. It seemed like it had to be at least October, maybe even November, but you'd never know it except by the bare aspens and bare, brown cottonwood trees. They'd been riding since just after daybreak, Anna on Pintada and James on Midnight. Each of them was leading another saddled horse behind. James was leading Chuck's old horse, Red; and Anna, Red Two. It had only been a few days since Connie and Jack had been to visit the BR, and now Anna and James were riding up Highway 9 to repay that visit. The two other horses were gifts. When James told Anna that their closest neighbors only had two horses between the four of them, she insisted that they share. There was still a whole herd of horses on the Blue River Ranch. Hell, anymore, there were damn near as many horses as there were cows.

"Do you still think it's a good idea?" James asked, even though he knew what Anna's answer would be. They had talked about it incessantly since Connie and Jack's visit. Anna wanted to share much more than just the two horses. She really did want to share the entire Blue River Ranch.

"You know I do," Anna told him. "Don't know if they'll think it's a good idea, though. Guess all we can do is ask."

"What if they do move into the old house, and then we find out that we don't really get along?" James, himself, wasn't even sure why he kept questioning the idea, but he couldn't seem to stop.

Anna just rolled her eyes and kept riding. She was no longer concerned at all with whether or not asking the others to move to the BR was a good idea, she was thinking about the logistics. Not so much the logistics of getting them moved, but the logistics of the living arrangements once they moved in. The old house that Anna had grown up in didn't have a wood-burning cookstove, just an electric range. It was the same problem that she'd been wrestling with since getting home to the BR. The PV system at the Blue River Ranch was just not adequate. It had only been set up to be an emergency backup for the grid, not the primary power system for the entire ranch.

Maybe she needed to move up the timeline for installing adequate PV power. If the weather stayed this mild, there was no need to wait until spring. Anna knew she was more than capable of putting in a system that could supply all the power the ranch would ever need. She'd proved her capabilities to herself back in Blue Rapids. What she didn't have were the components necessary to build such a system. Where could she find PV panels, batteries, and inverters? And how could she get them home? There were plenty of components down on the front range, but that was a long way to haul stuff in a horse-drawn wagon. Anna was still pondering that dilemma when she saw the wisp of smoke rising from near the old white farmhouse that had to be where Ray and Rita, and Connie and Jack lived.

It hadn't been clear to Anna when James and the others had tried to tell her where the four were living, but now she recognized the old Johnson place. It saddened her to realize that Mr. and Mrs. Johnson were the old couple who the four had buried in their own backyard. Jim and Sarah Johnson had been friends of her parents for as long as Anna could remember. Now, they were all gone. The Johnsons, her parents, so many people just gone. *We're still in shock.* The thought came to her that those who had survived the sickness would probably be in at least a mild state of shock for the rest of their lives. *Why me?* She thought. *Why James? Why the four who are now living in Jim and Sarah's house?* And then she had a much more disturbing thought. *Why did people like Sarge and Curt survive the sickness?* If there was any kind of God anywhere, how could kind, gentle people like Jim and Sarah die while scum like Sarge and Curt were allowed to go on living?

"I don't know," Ray was saying. "I mean, we're all set to spend the winter here. We've got enough canned vegetables put up, plenty of firewood, and god knows we've got plenty of mutton to eat."

"I'm not sure we're even going to have winter," James said. He'd let Anna put the proposal to the other four, and now the whole group was discussing it. It seemed like everyone except Ray was all for it as soon as Anna asked if they'd like to live on the BR. "Besides, we can hitch up the wagon and haul everything you've got down to the ranch," he added.

"Ray, they've even got electricity," Rita added to the argument for the move.

"Well, that might be a little bit of a temporary problem," Anna said. "We don't have enough power to cover everything. Especially on cloudy days. Mostly, we don't have enough battery storage capacity."

Anna went on to explain that the old house they were offering had plenty of electricity for lighting and most things, but not enough to always power the electric range. She told them that she'd planned to add power next spring, but maybe they could do it sooner.

"Guess electricity would be nice," Ray argued, "but do we really need it? Rita and Connie made candles out of tallow, we've got the old wood-burning cookstove. Granted, this old house is small, but we've got plenty of room for the four of us."

"We don't!" Connie exclaimed. "We don't have plenty of room. Ray, I'm pregnant." She looked over at Jack, whose expression left no doubt that it was news to him. "I'm sorry, Jack, I should have told you sooner. We're going to have a baby, and I don't want to have it here."

Rita walked over and put her arm around her sister's shoulders. It was pretty clear that she already knew Connie was pregnant. "We're going to live at the BR," she said flatly to Ray and Jack. "If you want to come along, that's fine. If not, that's fine, too."

...

The six of them rode along behind the herd of sheep. The four people weren't really herding the flock. Connie and Rita's dogs did most of the herding, keeping the sheep moving along at a good steady pace. Anna hoped the sheepdogs, Mutt and Jeff, would get along well with Blackie, who James and Anna had forced to stay back at the ranch. After Rita's ultimatum made up Ray's mind, the group had decided to get the four moved as quickly as possible. Just because they hadn't had any snow yet, didn't mean they wouldn't get any at all.

After the decision was made yesterday, Anna and James had spent the night in the same hayloft where James had slept before. Early the next morning, before daylight, he even got lucky again. Only this time, the roll in the hay was with Anna instead of Connie. That was a good six hours and at least as many miles ago.

James had never followed a herd of sheep before. It was a lot different than herding cows. When the sheep were bunched close together, they seemed to move in waves. Looking down at the backs of the herd was like looking into gently rolling waves on the ocean. Once, he was so mesmerized by the waves of moving wool that it made him feel seasick. Now, he knew better than to stare down at the swirling mass. *Guess it makes sense to get the herd moved first,* he thought, wondering if cattle and sheep could share the same pasture, or if they'd have to keep them separate.

"Can they stay in the big meadow with the cows?" he asked Anna, who was riding next to him. "Or will we have to keep them separate?"

Anna laughed. "They'll be fine with the cows," she told him. "It's the dogs I'm wondering about. Blackie's pretty used to having the run of the place all to himself."

Anna couldn't help but notice that Jack had hardly said a word since Connie told all of them that she was pregnant. He was even riding by himself, keeping his distance from everyone else. The other five were bunched up riding along together talking, but Jack was on the other side of the right of way, bringing up the rear a few horse lengths behind the others.

"What's with Jack?" Anna asked no one in particular. "Seems like he should be excited about being a father."

"He's just afraid." It was Connie that answered. "He already lost a son and a wife to the sickness. He'll come around, I'm the one that should be afraid."

"Jack will be alright," Ray joined in. All of them talking quietly enough that the conversation wouldn't carry back to Jack. "And you're right, Connie. You should be afraid. Much as I'd like for Rita to have a child, I'm afraid of what could go wrong. It's not like there's a hospital or even a doctor around. Or even a midwife for that matter."

That pretty much shut everyone up for a spell, and they all rode along lost in their own thoughts. Anna couldn't help but look at James. *I want to have his baby.* It was something she'd known, if only instinctively, since before the first time they made love. The instinct to procreate in this time of so much death was something that nearly everyone must be feeling, but Anna knew it was more profound than that. It wasn't just that she wanted to bring new life into this world, she wanted to have their baby, his baby. *Does he want it, too?* she wondered. *It doesn't matter. At least not as long as I have this implant in my arm.* She tried to guess how much longer the implant would prevent her from becoming pregnant. She'd had the implant for almost three years, which meant it was about due for replacement. *What happens if I just leave it in there? Probably not a good idea,* she thought. But how was she going to get rid of it? Like Ray said, there wasn't a doctor around anywhere. At least none that anyone knew of, and she couldn't hardly cut the damn thing out herself. She felt the small lump under the skin on the inside of her left arm. *I'll get Connie or Rita to cut it out.*

"Does it seem like there are more eagles than there used to be?" Rita asked, opening up a whole new subject for conversation. She was looking up, and the others followed her gaze to where two golden eagles were riding the thermals high above.

"Guess I haven't noticed," James was first to answer. "Do you think there are more than there used to be?"

"Don't know, really." Rita laughed. "It's just something Sam told me once. Sam was my fiancé before." She didn't have to say before what. "He'd been going to that new church in Montrose. I think they called it the Modern Times Church or something like that. Anyway, he said the church was founded by some kind of modern-day prophet who predicted that some kind of plague would end the reign of man on earth, and then the eagles would return." She laughed again, a sad short laugh this time. "Guess he was right about the end of man, wonder if he's right about the eagles. It doesn't seem to me that we've ever had any noticeable shortage."

The question of whether or not there were more eagles now than before, hardly even registered for Anna, but the mention of the Modern Times Church immediately caught her attention. "Did it have three black crosses?" she asked. "The church, I mean. The church in Montrose," she added, seeing the blank look on Rita's face.

"Matter of fact it did," Rita answered. "Don't they all have the three black crosses?"

James knew why Anna was so interested in the Modern Times Church, but Anna hadn't told the rest of them. As she gave Ray and Rita the bare outlines of her ordeal with Sarge and Curt, and the three black crosses on the side of the transport cage, Jack rode up to draw even with the rest of the group. He must have overheard some mention of the church. Anna didn't go into detail about being raped, but she said enough to leave no doubt. She also told them about the seemingly fantastic plot to basically start a new confederacy.

"That can't have anything to do with the Modern Times Church," Jack said. "At least not the church that I knew. I only went to a few of their meetings. But the church in Glenwood, and the people who went there, were nothing at all like that."

"So, what was that church all about?" Anna asked. "It seems like it just sprung up everywhere, all at once."

"I guess that's true," Jack said. "The one in Glenwood couldn't have been there more than a year or two when my wife talked me into checking it out. Looking back on it, I think it was just a product of the times. On the other hand, that Mystic Martin sure did hit the nail on the head."

"Mystic Martin," James laughed. "What's a mystic martin?"

"The prophet. That's what he called himself. I know, pretty weird, right? Weird or not, though, he did prophesy the end of the world, or at least the end of the world we used to know." Jack sounded sold on the guy.

"Hasn't pretty much every religion predicted the end of the world?" James asked. "What makes this Mystic Martin so special?"

"Well, like I said, I only went to a few meetings myself, so mostly I only know what my wife told me. I can tell you it did seem different than any other church I've ever known anything about. For one thing, they didn't seem to have any belief in a god or gods at all."

Anna was spellbound as Jack told them what he knew about the Modern Times church. The three black crosses had nothing to do with the cross or crosses that had always been a symbol of Christian religions. Rather, he said, the black crosses represented three ages of man. The first cross on the left, less than half as big as the middle cross, was for humankind's early development when we were more in balance with the rest of the world. The big center cross represented the modern age, from about the time of the industrial revolution to recent times. A period of time when humans, or humankind, outgrew the entire planet. Dominating and destroying the natural world that had nourished life in the earlier ages of man. And the third cross, "have you noticed it's even smaller than the first?" he asked. "The third cross is now, I guess. Mystic Martin apparently didn't just prophesy the end of the world, he predicted when it would end."

"Wait a minute," James interjected. "Are you telling me this Mystic Martin not only predicted the great dying, but when it would happen?"

Jack laughed. It was good to see him laugh. He'd been so morose since Connie told him she was pregnant. "Well, when the tsunami hit the east coast before anyone was even sick, my wife told me this is it. Martin's right, she told me. The end time is here." Jack's demeanor grew sullen again. "Before she died, she wanted me to take her to that church.

She was too sick by then. Maybe I should have taken her anyway."

The entire group became introspective and rode on in silence for a while before Anna had to ask Jack another question. "Did Mystic Martin have anything to say about what happens to us now? I mean, the ones of us that are left."

"He said we would return to the old ways of community, that people weren't meant to live separate lives, but should always be part of a community."

"I guess we're doing the right thing then," James said, "forming our own little community."

"I need to go to Kremmling," Anna said.

Chapter Nineteen

IT WAS EERILY STILL and silent, like a soundproof blanket had covered the world. Anna got out of bed quietly, hoping to let James sleep. She didn't open the curtains on the bedroom window but instead slipped quietly downstairs for a look outside at the foot of new snow covering the ranch. *Guess we won't be going back to the old Johnson place today,* she thought. *Won't be going to Kremmling, either.* She looked out at the giant, softly falling flakes of snow. It was just starting to get light, but it was snowing so hard that she couldn't even see the old house just a couple of hundred yards away. What an unexpected wonder. She tried to remember the last time she'd seen this much snow. It had to have been years and years ago.

"Looks like a fairy tale, doesn't it?" James startled her. She hadn't even heard him slip up behind.

"It does," she said. "It's been a long time."

James put his arm around Anna's shoulders, and they stood side by side, gazing in wonder as the flakes started to get smaller and taper off. The old house slowly materialized as the snowfall ended. James could see a light shining from one of the windows. That seemed as odd as the snow. The old house had been dark and empty for as long as he'd been living in the big house. *It must be half a year now.* The thought took him back to a much earlier time. A time when he and the world were both so much younger. A time when the woman standing beside him was just a girl who lived in the old house that was now occupied by new residents.

It was chilly. "Guess we better build a fire," James said. He pulled Anna into a tight warm hug and held her briefly before letting her go and crossing over to the kitchen side of the great room to get a fire going in the cookstove. "Hard to believe it's cold enough for a fire to actually feel good," he told Anna. "Especially as warm as it was yesterday."

The clouds had been building, and the temperature dropping yesterday evening while they put the sheep in with the cattle in the big meadow. It was dark by the time they got the four newcomers somewhat settled into the old house. Now, Anna could see a wisp of smoke rising from the chimney of the old house. *Good thing we made sure they had firewood,* she thought.

The snow completely stopped falling by the time it was fully light. All six of the newly created Blue River clan traipsed out through the snow to throw some hay to the sheep and cattle. Fortunately, they didn't even need to hitch up the wagon to haul the hay. They just had to use pitchforks to throw it over the fence from one of the loose stacks that James and Chuck had put up a few months ago.

"Should we haul some hay to the horses in the north pasture?" asked James. Caring for livestock in winter was one more thing that James had yet to learn. Anna, Rita, and Connie all told him no at about the same time.

"The north meadow wasn't mowed," Anna told him.

"The horses can paw through the snow to plenty of grass," Rita said.

Feeling the warm sun on her face, Connie added, "Snow'll be all gone by this evening, anyway."

The exchange brought out an irony that was mostly lost on the men, but not the women. This little band of people was made up of three men who were less knowledgeable than any of the three women when it came to surviving in this new reality.

By the time they were finished feeding, the sky had begun to clear, and the sun started melting the snow at a phenomenal rate. True to Connie's word, by nightfall, the BR had changed from a winter wonderland to a muddy mess.

The windows were all wide open in the big house. Cooking the group's first dinner together on a woodburning stove in what was now, temporarily at least, a communal kitchen had completely overheated the entire house.

"We have got to get enough power to stop using this damn thing," Anna said, referring to the stove that was still putting off way too much heat. "I think I know where to get enough batteries for storage. There are two semis stuck in Byers Canyon that have more than enough battery capacity. Getting the batteries out and getting them home might be tough, but the real problem is going to be finding PV panels and controllers, and inverters, for that matter."

"Why go all the way to Byers Canyon?" Ray asked. "Plenty of trucks on I-70, and it's a lot closer."

Anna had already guessed there would be trucks on I-70. She had another reason to go in the other direction, though. What she really wanted was to find out who and how many had survived in Kremmling. Now that it seemed like the Modern Times Church was not a threat, she really wanted to find out if any of her friends from town had lived through the sickness. There was even a chance that Dr. Ming was still alive. Or, maybe one of the nurses from the clinic.

"What about the solar farm up by Frisco?" Jack asked. "Could we get any components from there?"

Anna didn't know anything about a solar farm near Frisco. "What solar farm?" she asked.

Jack said the power company had installed a large array of PV panels just outside Frisco three or four years ago. He didn't really know anything about it, other than that it was visible from the interstate, and some of the few rich people that still maintained mountain homes up by Breckenridge had complained mightily when it went in. The "not in my back yard" crowd didn't want a solar farm detracting from the mountain views.

Anna was considering the possibility of being able to get parts from a commercial solar installation when a downdraft forced a puff of smoke from the cookstove. *Definitely worth checking out,* she thought. Then she had another thought. *If there were still summer homes for the wealthy near Breckenridge, wouldn't some of them also have PV systems?* Thinking about wealthy people's homes led to another thought. *There might even be a usable vehicle and charger we could borrow.*

...

It was quite a procession that made its way up Colorado 9 from the BR to the Johnson place the next day. James, who was extremely grateful that Chuck had taught him to drive the team of draft horses, and Jack, who'd never been on a horse-drawn wagon before, were in the seat of the old wagon. They were led by three border collies, who seemed to know exactly where they were going. Four horseback riders, three women and one man, followed along behind at a leisurely pace.

There was not even a trace of yesterday's snow left, but the tops of the peaks were still white in the distance. The plan the group had put together was to spend the night at the Johnson place and then, tomorrow, while the other four loaded up the wagon, Anna and Connie would ride up to Frisco to see what they could find in the way of PV power supplies. James hadn't liked the idea of two women going off alone, but Anna had patted the pistol on her hip and pointed out that Connie had her trusty old 30-30 rifle in her saddle scabbard.

It was a long round-trip ride from the old Johnson place to Breckenridge and back, so Anna and Connie set out before sunrise. Jack was right about the abandoned semis on I-70. The two women ran into the first of them as soon as they got past the burnt-out remains of Silverthorne. They stopped, and Anna studied the first one to see what she thought it would take to get the batteries out of the truck. One thing she didn't want was to come all the way back from the BR to steal batteries and find that she hadn't brought all the tools needed to do the job.

Satisfied that she knew what tools to bring when they came back for the batteries, she and Connie rode up the interstate to where they could see the PV array off toward where Dillon Reservoir used to be. What was left of Dillon

Reservoir was a lot more ruinous to the picturesque beauty of the scenery than the solar farm had ever been. What had once been a large lake was now mostly bare ground with little pools of water remaining in the very lowest areas. Anna could remember seeing the reservoir full of water once when she was very young. In her mind's eye, she could still see the sailboats in the distance. Boats that hadn't been on that lake for at least ten years now. *Guess Denver doesn't need any water now,* she thought, remembering her dad telling her that all of that water wasn't even enough to satisfy the needs of the capital city. The concept of there being enough people to drink Dillon Reservoir dry had been unimaginable to her three or four-year-old self.

They had to cut through the fence that surrounded the PV farm, but Anna had planned on that. She had brought both wire and bolt cutters. Jack was definitely right. It wasn't the largest solar farm by any means, but there were enough PV panels to power a small town. And better yet, they were less than five years old. In use, they should last another twenty-five years or so. Anna had the thought that if she could get them all and store them away somewhere out of the sun, she'd have a lifetime supply of panels and then some. Of course, storage would still require batteries, but there was a lifetime supply of those in the trucks on I-70.

"Will they work?" Connie asked.

"We can make these panels work just fine," Anna answered. "If we can find the rest of what we need, that is. Do you know if there is, I mean was, any kind of electrical supply places anywhere around here?"

"Sorry," Connie laughed. "I'm not from around here.

Not only that, I don't know much at all about electricity. After the power went out, I figured we'd just have to live like my great-great-great-grandparents did. You know, before electricity."

"Kind of tough, isn't it? Living like our ancestors did."

Connie really laughed at that. "Why do you think I was so anxious to move to the BR?" she asked. "After a couple months at that old Johnson place without any power or running water, I was ready to go anywhere." She looked thoughtful for a moment before continuing. "At first, I thought going back to the old ways might be a good thing. I mean, look at how badly we screwed up the planet with all of our modern conveniences."

Anna smiled. "Guess we did really blow it, didn't we? It's ironic that just about the time we finally stop killing nature with fossil fuels, nature finally gets around to killing most of us."

"Yeah, as much as I hate to admit it," Connie said, "the world's probably a better place without so many people in it." She rubbed her hand on her tummy, where new life was now growing. "What will life be like for our children? I mean, won't they have to learn to live without all of this?" She pointed at the rows and rows of solar panels.

Anna thought about it before replying, "Not if I can help it. We may not be able to manufacture any more of these, but we can certainly use what's already here."

"I'm glad you can," Connie said, as she started to get back on her horse. "Thanks Anna. I don't know where we'd be without you."

Anna, holding the reins of Pintada in one hand, didn't mount up, but looked up at Connie, who was already in the saddle. "Does Jack know?" she asked. Connie didn't answer, though she knew what Anna was asking. She blushed a little as Anna held her gaze. The answer was plainly written in Connie's blue eyes. "It's okay," Anna finally said. "I don't think James knows either. I mean, he may wonder, but he doesn't know the baby is his."

"I'm so sorry, Anna." Tears welled up in Connie's eyes. "I didn't know you. I didn't know anything. It just happened. It…" she looked down and mumbled, "I'm sorry."

"I'm not," Anna said the words with such truth of conviction that it surprised her as much as it surprised Connie. "The men don't need to know," she added, as she stepped into the stirrup and mounted Pintada. "Sometimes the men don't seem to know much, anyway."

Connie couldn't help but laugh through her tears. Anna crowded Pintada close enough to Connie's horse to reach over and give Connie a hug. "We can help each other raise James' children," Anna said. "I plan on having his children myself someday, you know."

Connie hugged Anna back. "My baby could be Jack's, you know. It was only that one time with James. Oh Anna, it'll never happen again. I promise."

Anna let go of Connie and looked into her eyes. "You probably shouldn't be making promises like that. Never's a long time. We can't know the future any more than we can know for sure who's baby you're carrying. Let's just promise each other to make our shared future as good as it can possibly be."

"That I can promise," Connie answered. "I'll help any way I can, but you'll have to tell me how."

"First thing, let's see what we can find in Frisco and Breckenridge," Anna said over her shoulder, as she rode back toward the highway.

They didn't find much in Frisco. Anna found it especially odd that there didn't seem to be anyone alive, or even any indication that anyone had survived in Frisco. It seemed like since there'd been some survivors almost everywhere else, why not here? The grocery stores didn't even look like they'd been ransacked at all. There were a few human remains scattered around, but they'd been dead so long that scavengers had pretty much picked the bones clean.

"Shouldn't we get back?" Connie asked when Anna turned toward Breckenridge instead of heading back to the interstate. It was already late morning, and a good half day's ride back to the Johnson place.

"Guess we should," Anna answered. "But something isn't right here. Let's just take a quick ride up to Breckenridge first."

About a mile up the road toward Breckenridge, Anna struck gold. There was a huge building supply store that not only had lumber but all kinds of electrical and plumbing supplies. The store had all of the breakers, switches, wire, and everything else Anna would need to put together a good power system. *Sure wish I had that old propane-powered truck that me and Charlie found in Blue Rapids,* she thought. She'd found everything they could possibly need. Everything except something to haul it all back to the BR. *Maybe we can find something in Breckenridge.*

Something was still bothering Anna as she talked Connie into continuing on up toward Breckenridge. It was the way people's remains seemed scattered in the wrong places. Like most of them had died outside instead of sick in bed. A few dying outside seemed reasonable, but there were definitely more than just a few. She was pondering the question of why so many were outside when the three black crosses came into view. Anna stopped Pintada, and Connie, who'd been riding side by side, continued on a little before stopping and looking back at Anna.

"What's wrong?" Connie asked.

Anna forced herself to relax the reins and gently nudge Pintada with her heels to start walking again. "Sorry, those three crosses still freak me out," she answered as she caught up, and the horses started walking side by side again. "Guess I just need to get over it." She forced a laugh. "What's one more old abandoned church?"

"That church kind of creeps me out, too," Connie said. They were just passing by the driveway that led up to the church's parking lot. "Something about the way it just sprang up everywhere all at once. It always seemed like a cult or something to me. Guess most religions are basically just cults, though."

Before Anna could respond, the peace and quiet of the valley were shattered by a girl's scream from inside the Modern Times Church. Then a girl's voice yelling, "You can't. She's too little! I won't let you." The girl sounded hysterical.

Anna was off of Pintada in an instant and had her pistol in her hand practically before she realized it. Connie was almost as quick to dismount and pull the 30-30 out of the saddle scabbard. Then, a man's voice yelled, "give me back my gun. I'll kill you, you little bitch."

The sound of two gunshots followed in quick succession and then another scream. Anna was running toward the front door of the church when the door opened, and a man stumbled out, clutching his abdomen. He looked more deranged than anyone Anna had ever seen. Sarge and Curt both had crazy eyes, but this man made them look sane. His hair was sticking up in every direction, the blood spilling out between his fingers was only adding to the filth of the chambray shirt. But the eyes were what Anna would never forget. They were the craziest eyes she had ever seen. Having obviously been shot, fear in his eyes would have been normal, but not the wide-eyed total insanity that was so obvious. The man almost made it to the first step of the porch before falling face-first down the steps. If he wasn't dead before he fell, the way his head hit the concrete walk at the bottom of the stairs surely would have killed him.

As the man fell away, Anna was face to face with a young girl pointing an assault rifle at her. The girl was almost as filthy as the dead man had been. Her stringy long blonde hair looked like it hadn't been washed in ages. She was wearing some kind of dirty denim dress that might as well have been a sack. She appeared to be a pre-teen, or maybe in her early teens. The girl's pale blue eyes weren't crazy. They were just terrified. The tears streaming out of those eyes were leaving trails through the layer of dirt on the poor girl's face.

Anna lowered her pistol. She couldn't have shot the girl if she wanted to. "She's too little," the girl mumbled, as she too lowered the weapon in her hand and let it drop to the floor. "I couldn't let him fuck her too. She's too little," she said between sobs, as she sank to her knees and then just kind of folded over frontwards.

Anna holstered her pistol and rushed up the stairs, thinking maybe the girl was wounded. "Are you hurt?" she asked as she knelt beside the girl. The girl, head down, just continued to sob. Anna put her hand on the girl's shoulder, as a younger girl came out of the door and knelt down to hug and hold the first girl. The younger girl was at least two years younger than the first girl, who was obviously her older sister. Both girls were sobbing.

"You saved me, Misty," the younger girl sobbed. "You really did it. You saved us. He won't ever kill anybody else. Not ever again."

Anna looked up from the two sobbing girls to see Connie standing over the dead man. Connie's normally pale complexion had turned pure white. She backed away from the body on the sidewalk and bent over and wretched. "Jesus, the smell!" she got out between heaves.

The stench was definitely overpowering. Anna wasn't sure how much was plain old body odor and how much was the blood and guts spilling from the dead man's body. She gently lifted the two girls to a standing position and led them back inside the church. If there was anyone else there, they would surely have made themselves known by now.

Inside the church, the first thing Anna noticed was the lights. The church had electricity. "Is there anyone else here?" Anna asked the two girls. The girl's sobbing had subsided, but they were probably both in shock. Anna didn't really expect an answer, the building just seemed empty.

"Just us now," the younger girl surprised Anna by answering. "He killed the rest."

They were in what must have been the main meeting room of the Modern Times Church, but it seemed more like a business conference room than a chapel. There was a small stage with a podium at one end of the room, with two rows of long tables and cushioned chairs filling the rest of the space. The tables and chairs had once been arranged so that seated people could face each other across the tables or turn sideways to face the podium. Now, the room was a total mess. Some chairs were still in place at the tables. Some were laying scattered about like they'd been knocked over and left. Some were even broken. The tables, chairs, and walls were riddled with bullet holes, and the brown stains of old dried blood were everywhere. Anna looked around at the scene of what must have been a massacre. A massacre that had happened quite a while ago. *Where are the bodies?* She wondered. Then she noticed the dried streaks of blood on the floor, all leading to a closed door at one side of the room. Anna decided she had no desire to see what was on the other side of that door.

"Can we go home now?" It was the older girl, the one named Misty. Her voice was totally flat, with no emotion.

Anna looked at the girl's blank stare and could not imagine the trauma and horror these two young girls must have been through.

Connie, who'd followed the others into the church, took Misty's hand and started back toward the entrance. "Sure," she told the girl, "let's go home."

Anna took the younger girl by the hand and followed Connie and Misty. "I'm Anna," she told the younger girl. "What's your name?"

"Mandy," the girl answered. "Mandy Carlisle."

"Well, Mandy Carlisle, where is home?" Anna asked, as they walked toward the two horses that were patiently trying to graze on some old grass at the side of the road. Not an easy feat with a bit in their mouth and reins dragging along the ground.

"Up there," Mandy said, pointing in the general direction of Breckenridge.

"Have you ever ridden a horse?" Anna asked.

"Oh sure, that's how we got here, but our horses ran off. Can we really go home?"

It was heartbreaking for Anna to tell Mandy she'd take her home, knowing that for Mandy, there would never really be any going home. At least not any kind of home the young girl had ever known before.

Mandy didn't do much talking except to give directions, and Misty might as well have been mute. Anna mostly thought about the trauma these two girls must have endured. Being a rape survivor herself, she could not imagine what it must have been like for Misty, who must have been raped repeatedly by the crazy man. And poor Mandy, the insane bastard was apparently going to rape a girl that hadn't even reached the age of puberty. How Misty had been able to get the gun and kill that man, they might never know, but if any man ever needed killing, it was the one they left lying face down in front of the Modern Times Church.

It was a mostly silent ride for a couple of miles up Highway 9 before Mandy directed them to take a paved driveway that disappeared into the trees on the west side of the highway.

"Are your parents alive, Mandy?" Anna knew the

answer before she asked, but she needed to get it out in the open. She knew they'd have to take the two girls back to the BR. There was no way she could stand to leave them here alone.

"Mom died," Mandy answered, and then got quiet again.

"He killed him." It was Misty, not Mandy, that continued to answer. "That's what you want to know, isn't it? He killed our dad just like he killed the others."

"Who was he?" Connie wanted to know, or maybe she just wanted Misty to keep talking; to get her out of the dark place she was in.

Neither Misty nor Mandy answered right away. They seemed to be lost in thought for a few moments before Misty said, "I don't think he was from here. He just showed up at the church. He just walked in with that gun and, and…" She burst into tears again.

Everyone fell silent again, except for the sobs coming from Misty. They rode around a bend in the driveway and came upon three horses grazing at the side of the drive. All three were saddled with rope halters on their heads but no bridles.

Mandy saw the horses at about the same time as Anna did. "Peanut!" she squealed. "Look, Misty, it's Peanut."

One of the horses was a buckskin with a dark mane. *That one has to be Peanut,* Anna thought. The other two horses were white. All three were pretty animals, but the saddles they wore were twisted and dirty. H*ow long have they been trying to rub off those saddles?* Anna couldn't help but wonder.

Misty raised her head and stopped sobbing as soon

as she saw the horses. The nearly instantaneous change that came over her was so profound it was amazing. Anna couldn't help but smile at the sight. Here was a girl who loved her horse as much as Anna loved Pintada.

"Which one's yours?" Anna asked.

"Cloudy," Misty answered. And then she even smiled. She didn't even wait for Connie to stop before swinging her leg up over the horse's rump and sliding to the ground.

Anna stopped Pintada to let Mandy off, and watched as the two girls walked right up to the horses. The horses seemed to be as happy to see the girls as the girls were to see them.

"We should have brought the bridles," Misty said. She took hold of a halter in each hand and started leading the two white horses up the drive. "We should have known the horses would come home," she told her little sister, who had a grip on Peanut's halter, and was following alongside.

Anna almost laughed out loud. It was hard to tell if Mandy was leading Peanut, or if Peanut was pushing her along. The phenomenal change that came over the two girls made her think about the power of love. Not just between people, but between people and animals. She reached down and patted the side of Pintada's neck and remembered how much she'd missed her horse when she was away at college.

The driveway, which had been climbing steeply, worked it's way around a switchback and then, after a short straight stretch and another curve, came out on the cleared top of a hill. There was an impressive looking house at the end of the drive, an even more impressive barn and corrals off to one side, and a large metal shop on the other. Misty and Mandy led the horses straight to the barn as Connie and Anna followed.

With their own horses tied up loosely at the hitching rail in front of the barn, Anna and Connie helped the Carlisle girls get the other three horses unsaddled and into stalls. Mandy seemed to want to get to the house, but Misty, just as Anna herself would have been, was intent on caring first for the animals. Like any good old-fashioned horse barn, this one had a hayloft. Anna helped Misty break a couple of hay bales and throw the hay down through the openings into the horse's troughs. Then, back down on the ground floor, to Anna's amazement, Misty opened the spigot on a yard hydrant and, using the attached hose, filled a water bucket in each stall. Must be a well, Anna realized. But, also power for a pump.

"I'll put them out in the paddock later," Misty said. "After I have a chance to clean them up."

Following Mandy and Misty toward the house, Anna glanced back over her shoulder at the barn and saw the source of electric power. The entire south-facing gambrel style top of the barn was covered with a solar roof. *Must be storage batteries somewhere,* she thought, and made a guess that the large metal shop contained some kind of battery room.

Connie and Anna were both surprised when the two girls didn't go straight into the house but walked around the side to the back yard. There, for a moment, they stood silently, with heads bowed at an obvious grave in the back yard.

"It's our mother," Misty explained. "This is where Dad buried her."

"Do you have any other family?" Connie asked.

Misty put her arm around her little sister, as she answered. "No, I guess just me and Mandy live here now." Then she looked up at Connie. Almost pleading, she asked, "Do you want to live here with us? We have lots of room," she added.

Connie and Anna both smiled at the invitation. "We'd love to," Connie answered, "but we already have a home."

"And we have other people waiting for us," Anna added. "It's a long ride, and we have to get back before they get worried about us. But you can come, too."

"I don't want to go," Mandy practically screamed. She ran to the back door of the house and disappeared inside.

"We can't stay here alone, can we?" Misty said. The forced maturity of one so young was heart-wrenching.

Fighting to hold back her own tears, Anna knelt down in front of Misty and took hold of her hands. She looked up into the face of the girl who was so much older than her years. "No," she told her, "you can't stay here alone. But I promise you can come back. When you're a little older, you can come back here to live if you want to."

Misty bent down and gave Anna a hug. There were tears in both their eyes, but Misty was no longer sobbing. The young woman and the even younger girl, who had both been through so much, just held each other in a silent embrace for a long time.

Finally, Anna stood up. "It really is a long ride," she said. "We better get started."

"We should take my Dad's truck," Misty said. "We can load the horses in the trailer." Anna and Connie both stared at the girl in shocked surprise. "If you can drive it," Misty added.

Chapter Twenty

ANNA WOULD LIKE to have seen the look on James'
face when he came out of the Johnson place and saw
a truck with a horse trailer coming down the road. It was
probably about like the look on hers when they opened
the shop doors at the Carlisle place, and the truck and
trailer were sitting there side by side. Both the truck and
the trailer were plugged in, and both were fully charged
and ready to go. Anna had never seen a truck-trailer combo
like this one, but it didn't take long to figure out that
they were truly designed to work together as a unit. The
combination vehicle was like a small electric semi-truck
with massive battery capacity. There was not only a huge
battery compartment under the fifth wheel and cab of the
power unit, the entire floor of the four-horse trailer housed
a separate battery pack. When Anna first pulled the truck
out and connected it to the trailer, the combined indicator
gauge said it had over a thousand miles of range.

It was just a thirty-minute drive instead of a three-hour
ride on horseback, but it was still late afternoon when Anna
parked the truck at the Johnson place. Anna and Connie

had allowed Mandy and Misty to have baths and change clothes while they put four horses in the trailer and got ready to go.

"Well I'll be damned," James said by way of greeting, as Anna climbed out of the driver's seat. He wasn't sure what to say when the back doors of the truck opened, and two young girls got out, one on either side of the truck.

Anna gave James a quick hug and then stood back and introduced him to Mandy. Meanwhile, Connie was introducing Misty to Jack, Ray, and Rita over on the other side of the truck.

"Misty and Mandy are going to come live with us," Connie announced to the group.

"Just for a while, though," Misty was quick to add. Anna had promised the girls that someday they would be able to go back home. She hadn't said how many years away someday might be.

Anna put her hand on Mandy's shoulder and said, "someday, these young women want to go back home to Breckenridge. They have an absolutely beautiful home, and I promised them they could go back. Who knows, they have such a nice setup there, I might want to go live with them myself." She winked at James and gave Mandy's shoulder a slight squeeze.

Mandy looked up at Anna and smiled. "Really," she said hopefully. "You might come live with us."

Anna smiled down at her. "Maybe," she said. "Someday."

The thought had actually crossed Anna's mind that the Carlisle place was, in some ways, set up better than the BR. It was already comfortably self-contained, with plenty of power and well water. As Anna had checked it out, she'd realized that the Carlisle place had never been on the grid to begin with. So, when the lights went out most everywhere else, nothing changed at all at the Carlisle residence. The problem, though, was it was just that, a residence. There was no pasture or even a garden. Mandy and Misty's parents must have been quite wealthy to own and maintain a place like that, but it was only self-contained as far as water and power were concerned. Food, for both the people and their animals, had to be imported instead of grown on-site.

Anna had thought about the Carlisle home a lot while driving from Breckenridge. The vehicle she was driving was nearly perfect for the BR's needs. The only thing that could have made it better would have been all-wheel drive. But then again, as rare as winter snow was anymore, maybe that wasn't even a factor. Anna's first thought regarding the truck was that she should move some of the electrical systems, including the chargers for the truck and trailer, from the Carlisle home to the BR. She'd already changed her mind by the time they got to the Johnson place. No, much like she'd left the bomb shelter intact back in Blue Rapids, leaving the Carlisle place intact was a better option. It was less than forty miles from the BR to the Carlisle place. Anna would just have to charge the truck and trailer there when needed. With a fully charged range of well over a thousand miles, it wouldn't need to be charged very often. When it did, she and James and the two Carlisle girls could just spend a night or two there instead of at the BR.

Right now, what was needed was getting people, horses, and a wagon load of possessions back down to the Blue River Ranch. The group had previously planned to spend another night at the Johnson place before riding home tomorrow. Having the truck changed all that. The old horse-drawn wagon was already loaded up for the trip back, but there was no good way to pull it, other than with the team of draft horses. So, they decided to put the two Belgians in the Johnson barn, and make two trips with the truck to get the people and the other horses on down to the BR before nightfall. Tomorrow, Anna would drive James back up to get the horses and wagon.

…

With the Carlisle truck to transport components, and the entire Blue River clan pitching in to help, it took about a month to complete the power system on the ranch. Anna even had extra PV panels, batteries, and other components safely stored in the shop before ending the solar salvage runs to Frisco.

During that time, Connie's pregnancy was starting to show, and Anna was becoming more and more envious. It was strange how she could shrug off not being jealous of Connie for having sex with James, but couldn't help being envious of her pregnancy. The desire to have her own baby was growing faster than Connie's belly.

"I have to go to Kremmling," Anna told James. They were still lying in bed, basking in the afterglow of morning lovemaking. She leaned up on one elbow and looked at James. "Maybe the doctor's still there. I need to get this stupid implant out so we can have a baby."

James smiled up into Anna's bright brown eyes. "Thought you said we could cut it out right here," he said. "How hard can it be?" He reached over and felt the tiny lump on the inside of Anna's arm.

"I suppose we probably could, but we need to find out about Kremmling. I need to know who's still there."

The sounds coming from downstairs told the two lovers that Misty and Mandy were already up. Caring for the two young girls had turned out to be no trouble at all. Misty, aged by trauma, was so much more mature than her twelve years of age. She not only did most of the caring for herself, but she also took care of her little sister, too. The only indication of the PTSD that the young girl was undoubtedly suffering was the occasional breakdown into uncontrollable sobbing. Anna would hold her and try to comfort her through those times and, once the anguish passed, Misty would seem rejuvenated and energized once again.

Anna, who had sat up on the edge of the bed, thinking she should get downstairs to help the two girls fix breakfast and then deciding that Misty was fully capable, twisted back around to look at James. "It's not just me, you know," she told him. "Connie's going to need someone, too."

James had wondered about the possibility that he might be the father of Connie's baby, but he thought that possibility was known only to himself and Connie. Like most men, he had no idea what a powerful force women's intuition could be. Besides, the odds of that one encounter making Connie pregnant seemed pretty slim. "What if the doctor in Kremmling didn't survive?" he asked.

"I don't know," Anna answered. "What I do know is that no one on this ranch has any experience delivering a baby. Even if Dr. Ming is dead, there might be somebody in Kremmling to help. We know some people are still living there."

"Two people. You only saw two men, and they were coming out of one of those churches that seem to be home to some really crazy people. What if they're like those two you ran into in Wyoming? Besides, Connie isn't going to have her baby for a few months yet. Maybe we should wait a while before we risk going to Kremmling."

Anna stood up and started toward the door. "I'm going to Kremmling," she said over her shoulder. "I hope you'll come with me."

It was a cold day. *It has to be about Thanksgiving,* thought Anna, as they got closer to Kremmling. She wished she had kept track of time so she'd know what day it was, but then again, what difference would it make to anything. She could see wisps of smoke rising above the hills before they even got to the point where Kremmling came into view.

"Looks like somebody's there," James said.

"More than I would have guessed," Rita added from the back seat. "That's at least four separate fires."

There were four of them in the truck, Jack and Connie had stayed home with Misty and Mandy. All four were armed, even though Jack tried to convince them there was nothing sinister about the Modern Times Church. Even Misty agreed with him. Apparently, the Carlisles had been members of the Modern Times Church. When she'd finally opened up to Anna about her ordeal in Frisco, she said the crazy man she'd killed was a total stranger to the members of the Frisco Chapter of Modern Times. Misty had no idea where the man had come from, or why he killed everyone but her and Mandy. That was just one more mystery that would never be solved.

As they topped the rise in the highway where Kremmling and the Colorado River Valley came into view, all four of them were wondering the same thing. How many people were living in Kremmling, and what kind of people were they? By the time they got to the Colorado River Bridge, Anna could see that like before, at least one column of smoke was rising from the southwestern part of Kremmling where Will's mother, Sharon, lived. *First stop, Sharon Donovan's house,* Anna thought.

Seeing that smoke really was rising from the chimney of the ancient white clapboard four-square where Will grew up, brought Anna wildly mixed emotions. She had always loved her potential mother-in-law at least as much as she'd loved her potential husband. Sharon Donovan was a strong-willed, independent woman that Anna looked up to from the day they first met. The great joy Anna felt at the thought that Sharon had survived was tempered by the sorrow of having to be the one to tell her that her only son was dead.

When Anna stopped the truck and stepped out in front of the Donovan house, and Sharon Donovan came out of the front door, Anna didn't have to say a word for Sharon to know that her worst fear had been realized. Anna rushed through the gate in the old white picket fence that surrounded the Donovan home. Sharon met her in the middle of the yard, and the two embraced and held each other while Anna's companions got out of the truck. When Anna gently held Sharon Donovan at arm's length and really looked at her, the effects of the great dying, as James called it, were obvious. Sharon Donovan was not a large woman. Anna stood nearly a full head taller than Sharon, but now, it seemed like she had shrunk even more. Her short sandy blonde hair had turned totally white, and she looked much older than Anna knew her to be. It was like Sharon had aged twenty years in the two years since Anna last saw her.

Sharon wiped at the tears in her eyes with the back of her hand and said, "Come on in, it's too cold to be standing around out here. Why are you all carrying guns?" she added, seeing that Ray and Rita both had rifles, and James had a pistol.

"Long story," Anna said. "Let's talk inside." Ray, Rita, and James put their guns back in the truck following Anna's lead as she unstrapped the gun belt around her waist and placed it in the console. Then, they all followed Sharon Donovan into her home.

"I wanted to come and tell you sooner," Anna told Sharon, referring to Will's death, "but when I came into town and saw two guys come out of that church with the three black crosses, I just kind of freaked out. I'm so sorry, Sharon."

Sharon looked at Anna, perplexed by what she'd just said. Then she looked at Anna's three companions, who were seated across the room on the sofa, to see if there might be a clue there as to why two men coming out of a church would cause Anna to freak out. The small living room was arranged with the sofa and the two easy chairs that were occupied by Anna and Sharon in a sort of semi-circle, all facing the woodburning stove that was throwing out way too much heat. The only information Sharon could take in from looking at the three people sitting on the sofa was that all three were too hot.

"Maybe you should open that window behind you,"

Sharon told them before turning her attention back to Anna. "Why would a couple of guys coming out of the church freak you out?" she asked.

Though Anna dreaded reliving the traumatic experience again, she told Sharon, without going into too much detail, about being kidnapped and held in a cage with three black crosses painted on the side. She was careful not to say anything about being raped, and she skipped entirely the time spent in Blue Rapids. Having never told James about her romantic entanglement with Charlie, she wanted to just avoid the subject of Blue Rapids altogether.

"You poor girl," Sharon said, rightly guessing that Anna had left much out of the story of her long journey home. "I wish he could have been buried here," she said, completely changing the subject. "We buried everyone, you know, the whole town. Put 'em all in one huge grave. It was quite an undertaking," she rambled on, looking at the three on the sofa. "Will should have been buried with the others," she finally trailed off into silence, looking off into a distance that no one else could see.

Anna allowed Sharon a few moments of silence before bringing her back to the present. "Sharon, how many people survived here in Kremmling?"

"Well, let's see." Sharon seemed to be counting them off in her head. "I guess fourteen right here in town, if you count the kids. There's the Schumachers, Richard, Jean, and their daughter Sam. Then there's Donna Farris."

"Mrs. Farris?" Anna interrupted the recital of names. "Mrs. Farris is still alive?" Mrs. Farris had been Anna's high school biology teacher. *She has to be at least seventy-five,* Anna thought.

"Yes, she is," Sharon answered. "She taught you and Will both, didn't she?" Sharon didn't even wait for an answer before starting, once again, to list the names of Kremmling's survivors. "Then there's Johnny Garcia. God bless Johnny. If it wasn't for Johnny, well Johnny and Richard, if it wasn't for them, we'd be packing water out of the river instead of having it come right out of the tap. Sure is a good thing the town switched over to solar power and that wind turbine for the water and sewer plants. You know, it was really controversial when we did that." Sharon was getting sidetracked again. "Wish we would have taken the whole town off-grid, so I could have electricity. The natural gas quit working, you know."

Anna couldn't stand it anymore. "What about Dr. Ming?" she asked. "Is Dr. Ming still here?"

"Oh yes, Dr. Ming's still here." Sharon looked askance at Anna, and then at the three on the couch. "Are you sick, dear?" she asked Anna.

"It's my sister," Rita answered before Anna could respond. "My sister, Connie. She's not sick. She's pregnant."

"Is Dr. Ming at his clinic?" Anna asked.

"He's probably at the church," Sharon answered, like everyone should know that not only was Dr. Ming usually at the church but which church that might be.

Sharon agreed to ride to the church with them since it was almost lunchtime, anyway. "I've never seen a truck like this," she said, while Anna was trying to figure out what lunchtime had to do with the church.

"Which church?" Anna asked, as she started to pull away from Sharon's house.

"You know, The Modern Times Church," Sharon

answered. "Where the Bureau Of Land Management office used to be."

To everyone but Sharon's surprise, there were two vehicles parked in front of the Modern Times church. Anna recognized one of the vehicles as being Sherriff Larson's old Jeep, but she didn't recognize the pickup truck that was parked next to it.

"Is Sherriff Larson still alive?" Anna asked. Sharon hadn't said so earlier.

"Oh no," Sharon answered, "he's buried with the rest of them. Richard usually drives the old jeep now. It's kind of like our public transit system. Guess he won't have to pick me up today, though," she added, as Anna parked next to the Jeep.

"What about the pickup?" James asked, stepping out of the truck with his revolver in hand.

"That's Johnny's truck," Sharon answered. "Well, it is now. You won't be needing that here," she said, seeing the gun in James' hand.

James hesitated before putting the revolver in the console with Anna's gun. "Why don't you two wait here for just a minute," James said to Ray and Rita, who were both holding their rifles between their knees. They both nodded their heads, letting James know they understood what he was saying.

As soon as James and Anna followed Sharon into the church, it was apparent what being almost lunchtime had to do with anything. The smell of cooking food greeted them in the foyer, and in the main room, the room that would have been a chapel in most old churches, tables and chairs were set up for dining. There was no one in the dining hall, but voices could be heard coming from an open double doorway that obviously led to a kitchen.

"Need some help?" Sharon asked through the open doors as she led James and Anna into the kitchen. "We have guests for lunch."

There were four people in the commercial style kitchen, which, like the dining hall, was brightly lit by overhead electric lights. The two men were leaning against a counter, talking, while two women were apparently doing all of the work. As Anna and James walked in behind Sharon, the only person Anna recognized turned away from the large pot that she'd been stirring.

"Oh my god!" the little old gray-haired woman exclaimed. "Anna Duran!" She didn't even bother to put down the spoon in her hand before rushing across the kitchen to hug Anna.

Anna hugged her back, careful to avoid the dripping spoon. "Hi, Mrs. Farris," Anna said to her favorite high school teacher. "It's so good to see you...to see you..." Anna's voice trailed off, and Mrs. Farris continued the thought.

"To see me alive?" she smiled. "It is amazing, isn't it? And stop calling me Mrs. Farris. Mr. Farris has been dead for twenty years now. This is a new life. I'm just Donna from now on, okay?"

"Okay, Donna," Anna answered, though it felt really strange to call her old teacher by her given name.

"Anna, do you know Samantha?" Donna asked before Anna could say anything else. Then she proceeded to make introductions all around.

"And this is James Mendez," Anna gestured toward

James standing uncomfortably in the doorway. "He's my..." once again, Anna was at a brief loss for words as she glanced at her once future mother-in-law.

"It's alright, Anna," Sharon told her. "I know Will's dead."

"I'll get the others," James said, backing out of a somewhat uncomfortable situation.

"Where is Dr. Ming?" Anna asked, after James left the room.

"Probably in his office," Johnny Garcia was first to answer. Then, after seeing the puzzlement on Anna's face, "down the hall, last door on the left."

"Guess I better go round up the others for lunch," Anna heard Richard Schumacher say as she headed down the hallway to find Dr. Ming.

...

Anna felt the bandage on the inside of her arm, where Dr. Ming had removed the implant. She thought about all they'd learned in Kremmling. James was driving home. Ray and Rita were mostly silent in the back seat; everyone lost in their own thoughts. Besides the gift of having the implant removed, Anna clutched another treasure in her lap. A gift from Dr. Ming. It was a calendar. A real multi-year calendar, with the days all marked off right up to today, which Dr. Ming had assured her was the third of December. Her guess that it was about Thanksgiving had been pretty close after all.

Anna pondered the fact that there was nothing sinister at all about the Modern Times Church. Quite the opposite, in fact. The truth about the Modern Times Church, as told by the Schumachers, was that it was indeed founded by a man who called himself Mystic Martin. Mystic Martin founded the church to respond to the end of mankind's reign on earth. He had apparently foreseen the sickness that would wipe out most of mankind, and his followers built churches that, using modern technology and renewable energy, had only one purpose; sustaining those who lived through the great dying. The Modern Times Church had pretty much nothing at all to do with religion. Calling it a church was the easiest way to ensure tax-free status and to use America's freedom of religion laws to accomplish things that would have otherwise been impossible. Each chapter, as they called their individual groups, built their own building. Or, as in Kremmling, repurposed an existing building, with some guidance from the church, which was headquartered in California. The standard features of all of the chapter houses, besides the three black crosses, were renewable energy production and storage, a water well and septic system, a good supply of non-perishable food, and a community meeting place.

The Kremmling Chapter of the Modern Times Church had, since the sickness, truly become the center of the community for the survivors. Being the only place in town, besides the water plants, that was totally self-contained, it had become the community kitchen, gathering place, and doctor's office. Dr. Ming had moved what he could of his practice because the old health clinic didn't have any electrical power.

Over a wonderful lunch of homemade stew, Anna had been discussing with Dr. Ming the possibility of getting power to the old clinic. Johnny Garcia, overhearing their conversation, had asked, "Why not the whole town?"

Johnny, it turned out, had been Kremmling's water utilities supervisor before the sickness. He had some ideas about using a large PV array that was up by Wolford Reservoir to supply power to the whole town. Since most places in Kremmling had relied on natural gas for heat and cooking, and natural gas was no longer flowing, converting to electricity seemed like a perfect idea. If it could be accomplished, that is.

Anna had been impressed by Johnny Garcia's intelligence and resourcefulness. The only problem was, he had very little expertise when it came to electricity. Water and sewer systems were his domain, and he was the first to admit that he didn't know enough about electrical power systems to put his ideas into practice. Anna had promised to check out the feasibility of making his dream a reality when she next came down to Kremmling.

Anna absently fingered the bandage on her arm again, thinking about the fact that it was likely she would soon be pregnant. The thought was thrilling, but the thrill was tempered by what Dr. Ming had told her. When Anna told Dr. Ming she wanted to have a baby, he responded with a question. "Did you notice Lisa Smith?" he'd asked. Anna had noticed the quiet young woman sitting at the other end of the table at lunch. Lisa looked to be no more than a few years older than Anna, and Anna couldn't help but notice that she hardly ate a thing and didn't join in the conversation at all. "She lost a baby boy a little over a month ago." Dr. Ming said. When Anna mentioned that was well after the sickness had killed everyone else, Dr. Ming went on to explain that Lisa had given birth to a healthy baby boy right there in his office. The child seemed perfectly fine for three days before coming down sick. Really sick. Within a single day, the child went from being totally healthy to dying of the exact same symptoms that killed everyone in the great dying. "That baby died of V-1 just like everyone else," Dr. Ming had said. He didn't know how that was possible, and he didn't have a lab to prove it, but he was absolutely sure that was the case.

What if we're it? Anna thought, still fingering the bandage on her arm. *What if we're the last? What if babies can't survive?*

Chapter Twenty One

JAMES CAUGHT A MOVEMENT out of the corner of his eye. It was mid-morning, February fifteenth, according to Anna's calendar. He and Jack and Ray were feeding the mixed herd of cattle and sheep. He had just stabbed his pitchfork into the loose stacked hay for another load to throw over the fence when the movement out on Highway 9 caught his attention.

At first, when he looked up, he wasn't sure what he was seeing. He stared, not quite believing his eyes. "Hey Ray, do you see that, or am I hallucinating?" he asked. Ray was working closest to him on the same side of the stack. Jack, working on the other side of the stack, couldn't see the strange object coming up the highway.

"Jack, come here," Ray said, sticking his pitchfork in the ground and rubbing his eyes as if to clear away an illusion.

"What the fuck is that?" Jack muttered, coming

around the haystack to get a view.

It looked like a crane coming up Highway 9 from Kremmling. A crane that was being followed by some kind of car pulling a small RV. It seemed strange that only the top half of the crane was visible behind a slight rise, while most of the SUV style vehicle and towed trailer behind it were visible clear down to the top of the wheels. It created the illusion of some kind of large off-road crane being followed by a car and trailer that were floating in the air.

As the men watched, the crane came up out of a dip, and the illusion was shattered. It was indeed a relatively large off-road crane, but it was pulling two separate trailers behind it. One looked like some kind of flatbed without much on it. The second trailer carried the SUV and RV camper. *Looks like a Rivian,* James thought. *Looks like Dad's Rivian. No, can't be.* He was headed back toward the house with the other two right behind him before the crane even turned off the highway and started up the lane to the BR.

"Thought maybe I should return your car," the man said as soon as he climbed down out of the crane.

Jack and Ray watched as James ran up to the stranger and grabbed him in a bear hug. "Dave Ortiz," James said, stepping back away. "How the hell did you ever find me? And what the hell is that thing you're driving?"

"This, my friend, is how you travel anywhere you want to go in this day and age." Dave gestured toward the crane. "It's a Link-Belt 9045 E. You find something blocking your road, you just move it out of the way. You wouldn't believe how many roads I've opened up between here and Montana. And finding the Blue River Ranch, that was easy, once I got to Kremmling. Some guy in a Jeep with a sheriff's star on it gave me directions."

"Must have been Richard Schumacher," James said. "He isn't really a sheriff, you know."

"Yeah, I figured that. He told me that him and some guy named Johnny could sure use some crane work, but I told him it would just have to wait. I told him I had a long-overdue appointment at the Blue River Ranch."

James looked from the crane to the two trailers behind it, and then he saw a door swing open on the RV trailer. Two women stepped out of the RV onto the deck of the second trailer. Jack and Ray also saw the women get out of the RV, but neither one of them had any idea why James burst into laughter. He slapped Dave on the shoulder and stopped laughing long enough to say, "Mission accomplished, I see. Looks like that replenishing the earth thing might be working out for ya." One of the women who got out of the RV was obviously very pregnant.

"Not mine," Dave said over his shoulder as he hurried back to help the pregnant woman down off the trailer.

By that time, everyone on the BR had gathered around Dave and the two women. Introductions were made all around. "Feel like I already know you," Dave told Anna, shaking her hand. "James used to talk about you a lot."

The two women with Dave were Charlene Dixon and Rachel Cosgrove, both from Billings, Montana. Connie and Charlene immediately started discussing and comparing their pregnancies. Charlene said she figured she was due in about a month, so Connie was a month or so behind.

Anna listened to the conversations around her, but the engineer in her couldn't help but study the way the electric crane and trailers were set up. The first trailer was a flat-bed, at least forty feet long. The crane just had a pintle hook, so the trailer was attached by using a fifth-wheel dolly. But the solar PV system that was built on the deck of the flatbed is what was really fascinating. The entire trailer was covered with PV panels mounted flat on top of a steel box that was about a foot high. The box undoubtedly housed an enormous bank of storage batteries.

"How much storage capacity?" Anna asked Dave. "That looks like a huge battery pack."

"Ten actually, it's ten separate battery banks. Makes it easier to charge." Dave was obviously proud of the crane and trailer set-up. "Five thousand kilowatt-hours altogether. Plenty of storage, but she could sure use a lot more PV. Guess I should have added another trailer full of panels."

"You add much more to that train, you'll have to put it on rails," James said, hearing Dave and Anna's conversation. "Don't see how you can turn it around as it is."

"Good point," Dave laughed. "Takes about forty acres. How big did you say this ranch is?"

"Way more than forty acres, but don't be getting in a hurry to turn it around. Let's get inside out of this damn wind." The wind wasn't really that cold for February in the Colorado mountains, at least not by historical standards. The temperature was probably right at freezing, but Mandy and Misty were neither one wearing coats.

There was a lot of space in the great room of the big house, but it felt pretty cozy with eleven people gathered together. As the warmth from the woodstove chased away the chill from being outside, the people inside sort of separated into two groups. The women, all but Anna, gathered around the woodstove on the large L-shaped sofa, while the men and Anna were seated at the dining table. Mandy and Misty gravitated toward the two pregnant women on the couch.

Anna caught herself trying to listen to two separate conversations at the same time. Charlene and Rachel were both from Montana, and Connie and Rita were comparing how recent history had unfolded in Montana compared with Colorado. With Misty and Mandy listening attentively, the four women were trying hard not to re-traumatize the two young girls.

"What I can't figure out," Anna heard Rachel say, "is why V-1, that's what Dave says it's called, why did V-1 kill so many more men than women. From what I've seen, I bet there are over twice as many women now as there are men."

She's right, Anna thought. *It was the same in Blue Rapids. More women than men.* She looked around the room at the four men and seven women, counting Misty and Mandy. At Blue Rapids, there had been six men and nine women before she herself left, and in Kremmling, there were seven women, four men, and three children. Two girls and a boy.

"Our mom got sick, but not Dad," Mandy volunteered, catching the gist of the conversation. "He didn't get sick, the devil killed him."

That brought the conversations on both sides of the room to a momentary standstill until Misty, giving her little sister a disdainful look, said, "I told you, Mandy, that man was not the devil. He was just a really bad man."

"Well, Misty killed the devil." Mandy was mostly undeterred until she saw the look her sister gave her. "Okay, Misty killed the really bad man. He wanted to fuck me like he did Misty, but she stopped him."

"Shut up Mandy, you promised not to tell." Misty burst into tears and ran down the hall to her room. Anna got up and followed her without saying a word.

"That sounds like some pretty bad shit," Dave said quietly to the table.

"Ain't that the truth," Jack told him. He lowered his voice even more, to try to keep Mandy from hearing. "That crazy son of a bitch that Misty shot, not only killed their dad, near as I can tell, he killed everyone that survived in Frisco and Breckenridge."

James, shaking his head and bringing his voice back up to the level of normal conversation, said, "Anna ran into some evil guys, too. Guess V-1 or whatever you want to call it, spared the bad right along with the good."

"Yeah, there were some in Montana, too," Dave told the group. "Called themselves The New Army Of God. Near as I can tell, the main tenant of their religion, if you can call it a religion, is white supremacy. Guess they're the main reason we didn't stay in Montana."

"Well, I don't think the crazy SOB in Frisco was anything but that," Connie said. "Just a totally insane loner. I don't think he had anything to do with any new army of god, or any other army. Or God, for that matter."

The men didn't realize that Connie and the other women over by the stove were even listening to their conversation. James, knowing much more about Anna's ordeal than the others, wanted to know more about the white supremacists. "How many were there?" he asked. "White supremacists, I mean."

"Not that many," Charlene said. There was only one

conversation going on in the great room now. "I'd guess no more than fifteen or twenty at that church outside Billings. Wouldn't you say, Dave?"

"Yeah, sounds about right," Dave answered.

Based on the size of the surviving population in this part of the world, fifteen or twenty people at one church seemed like a lot to James. "Jesus, is everybody in Montana a white supremacist?" he asked.

"Oh, hell no," Dave said. "They're just a small minority holed up at that church. But I'm afraid they're the leftovers from the ones that started the revolution. I guess my biggest fear is that more like-minded followers of General Korliss will get together and really start some trouble."

The main thing that James heard was the part about fifteen or twenty people being just a small minority. "How many people survived in Montana?" he asked, hoping maybe there were places less ravaged by V-1 than Colorado.

"They're not from Montana," Rachel spoke up. "The New Army Of God, I mean. I never heard of it until after everyone died, and strangers started moving in."

Rachel, Dave, and Charlene went on to explain that Montana, at least the Billings area that Charlene and Rachel were from, hadn't fared any better than anywhere else during the great dying. Most everyone that Charlene and Rachel knew before had died. Rachel and Charlene, even though they were both from Billings, had never even met until they ran into each other on the road as they were leaving the city. Billings may have been small compared to Denver, but there were way too many dead people for the survivors to deal with. So, most everyone that survived just left.

Rachel and Charlene hadn't walked that far from Billings when they came across a couple of other women and a man digging graves in a field near the Yellowstone River, just outside of Park City. Glad to see others still alive, Rachel and Charlene stopped to visit and ended up staying. They helped the other three, none of whom were from around there, bury the farm family that had all died in the big old farmhouse. Then the five of them took up residence. That was just a few weeks after the great dying. Apparently, more and more people found the Park City area appealing over the months that followed.

"I wasn't the only one headed north," Dave said. "By the time I got there, must have been at least a hundred people living in and around Park City. Gotta admit it was a pretty nice spot. Far enough from Billings to escape the smell, but close enough to acquire almost anything a person might need. That's where I got my crane."

"I'm not sure any of them were from Montana," Charlene added, in reference to the people who settled in Park City. "I think the men, and it was just a few men to start with, that moved into that old church up toward Billings, were from California or Arizona."

"They got there before me," Dave said. "Probably no more than four of five people there until they put those three black crosses out front. Those crosses were like a magnet to attract scum."

"Wait." Anna came back into the room just in time to hear about the three black crosses. "You mean they were part of the Modern Times Church?"

"No, you missed the first part," Dave answered. "They call themselves The New Army Of God, and their crosses are different."

"What do you mean different, you said three black crosses?"

"You know, the crosses are just different. The Modern Times Church has the one large cross in the center that's really more like a T. The New Army Of God's crosses are all the same size and all definitely cross-like."

Anna's mind flashed back to the crosses on the mobile cage she'd been enslaved in. They were definitely the same size. *So Sarge and Curt didn't have anything to do with The Modern Times Church,* she thought. It was a huge relief. All this time she had thought there had to be a connection, but there wasn't. "So, there's nothing wrong with The Modern Times Church," she mumbled, as much to herself as anyone.

The others looked questioningly at Anna before Dave continued his narrative. "More and more people kept coming up to Montana from all over, like it was the promised land or something. Most just seemed like normal people, but a few fell in with that New Army Of God bunch. They basically turned it into a compound. Put up a wall around the whole place with armed guards at the gate."

"Do you know if they had any women?" Anna asked.

"I did see a couple of women coming and going from the place," Rachel said. "I guess some women must have joined them."

"No," Anna clarified, "did they have any kidnapped women? Any slaves?"

"Not that any of us would know about," Charlene answered. "They would never have let any of us through the gate. Like we'd ever want anything to do with any of them anyway."

"They had a big sign out front," Dave explained. "It said, white is might, white is right. Don't know if they had any slaves, but I know they didn't think us people of color were good for anything else."

"What about the rest of the community? I mean, you said this Army of God was just a minority. Was the whole community racist?" James asked.

Dave laughed. "Most of the rest of the community looked just like us. And the ones that looked like Connie and Rita there, they didn't want to have any more to do with the New Army of God than we did."

James looked over at the contrast between the four women seated by the stove. Connie and Rita with blonde hair and blue eyes were the only purely white looking women in the room. Charlene had dark ebony skin and kinky black hair, and Rachel was one of those women whose ethnicity is hard to distinguish. She may have been Native American or Hispanic, or Asian for that matter. She was definitely not white, though. "But you said you left because of the New Army of God. Sounds to me like that group of Nazis was way outnumbered, why leave?" James asked Dave.

Dave seemed to look for the answer somewhere off in space before he said, "They're like cancer. That little compound is just the early stage. Just a small tumor now, but they're insidious. Eventually, the cancer will grow enough to destroy that community. Remember me telling you about General Korliss' rebellion in the Army? It started the same way. Just a small group to start with. But once that cancer metastasized, the whole country was screwed."

"I thought they were all back in Kentucky," Anna said.

"The New Army Of God, or whatever they call themselves. I didn't think we'd ever have to worry about people like that out here."

"Don't think we do," James told Anna. "I think we're all pretty safe right here." Then to Dave, "I'm glad you're here. I hope you and Rachel and Charlene will stay. If not with us, at least close."

Charlene gave a little gasp and put her hand on her belly. "Hope it's just a kick," she said.

"Maybe we should take you into Kremmling to see Doctor Ming," Anna told her. She didn't tell anyone that she wanted to see Dr. Ming herself. She didn't want to tell James she was pregnant until she was absolutely sure, herself.

Chapter Twenty Two

WHAT WE REALLY NEED *is a computer wizard,* Anna thought. She was studying the computer-controlled switching systems at the large solar array near Wolford Reservoir. Dave and Johnny were there with her. As was James, who seemed unwilling to let her out of his sight once he found out she was pregnant.

Dave, Charlene, and Rachel had been living with James and Anna for two weeks now. The big house at the BR, with five full bedrooms, had initially been built for a much larger family than had ever lived in it. It was not, however, designed for multiple families under one roof. With five adults, one pre-teen and one teenage girl, all living there now, the big house didn't seem so big anymore. Not that it felt uncomfortable. That was one of the strange aftereffects of the great dying. Having multiple family units all living together seemed more normal now than each family living in separate homes.

This was the second trip to Kremmling since Dave's arrival at the Blue River Ranch. It had been two weeks since Dr. Ming told Anna that she was definitely pregnant, and he told Charlene that she was due any time now.

Wonder why Sharon and Mrs. Farris still live alone. It seems like they'd be better off together. Anna's mind was wandering. She focused back on the problem at hand. "If we can figure out how to bypass all of these remote computer controls," she told the guys, "we don't have to move any of this."

"Guess I'm not much help when it comes to computers," Dave said. "Wish I was."

"Another one of my weaknesses, too," Johnny added. "Give me pipes and valves and filters, and I'm your man. Computers, forget it."

"Don't look at me," James added, "my experience with computers is minimal at best."

The Wolford Reservoir solar farm was much more than Anna had expected. Not only was it an extensive array of PV panels, it also had a utility-scale battery bank. The system was big enough to power a lot more than just Kremmling, and there was enough storage to make it through many days without sunshine. Best of all, it was already tied to the grid that had fed Kremmling power before everything shut down. And not just Kremmling. If Anna could figure out how to do it, she could isolate it from the overall grid and convert it to a smaller area-wide network that could feed electrical power to Kremmling, and even the BR. *We could probably power up Granby and the whole Fraser Valley,* she thought. *Wonder if there's anybody over there.*

"Have you had any contact with anyone from Granby?" Anna asked Johnny. Maybe, just maybe, someone from Mountain Parks Electric had survived. And, just as important, the computers that controlled this whole system would be located at Mountain Parks Electric in Granby.

"Can't say as we have," Johnny answered. "I tried to drive over there once, right after everything went down, but Highway 40 was blocked by a couple of dead semis in Byers Canyon, and the old county road from Parshall over to Hot Sulphur Springs hasn't been passable for years."

"What's in Granby?" James asked.

"Mountain Parks Electric," Anna told them what she'd been thinking. "The computers that control all of this. And maybe, someone that knows something about the Mountain Parks Electric system."

"Only one way to find out," Dave said. "Let's go get my crane and open up that canyon."

Back in Kremmling, any plan to go pick up Dave's crane was put on indefinite hold. They had left Charlene with Dr. Ming for a thorough check-up. When they got back to his office, Charlene was in labor.

"Don't know how you did it," Dr. Ming told them, "but you got her here at exactly the right time. Of course, this being her first baby, and since she just started early labor, it's probably going to be a while."

Since Dave was the only one who knew anything about his crane, and he wasn't about to leave Charlene alone with Dr. Ming, the power project was put on the back burner. Anna and James agreed to make the run back up to the BR to pick up the things Charlene would have brought with her, had she known this was going to be anything more than just a checkup.

The old Rivian SUV was really proving its worth. It was a lot more nimble at missing the potholes in Highway 9 than the Carlisle's truck. What would have been at least an hour's drive in the truck took only about forty-five minutes in the Rivian.

Rachel insisted on going back to Kremmling with them, so she could be with her "sister," Charlene. This caused a little bit of a row because Mandy wanted to go, too. For reasons unknown, Mandy had become almost instantly attached to Rachel. It was like the ten-year-old girl had picked Rachel to be a surrogate for her dead mother. And Rachel had been more than willing to fill the role. Separating the inseparable wasn't easy, but Rachel finally convinced Mandy to stay with Misty. She gave the young girl a hug and told her, "If you need anything, Connie will be right next door."

"I had a little girl once." The statement from Rachel, who was riding in the backseat, came out of the blue. "Think that's why I'm getting so attached to Mandy."

Anna turned half around in her seat, shocked to hear that Rachel had once had a child. "You didn't tell us you had a daughter," Anna said.

"I haven't told anyone," Rachel answered. "Not even Dave or Charlene. I don't know why I'm telling you." She had her face turned away from Anna, looking out the side window of the car as she spoke. "Guess I just wanted to forget about Amy. Seemed easier. It doesn't work, though. You don't ever lose a child, you know. Once you give birth, that child will be with you forever. Even if your baby only lives for a year. It probably wouldn't have mattered if she'd only lived for a few minutes. I think it must be the nine months before the child is born that does it. You just can't forget someone that you carried around inside your own body for that long. I sure hope Charlene's baby will be okay." She trailed off into silence without ever turning to look at Anna.

"I'm sorry," Anna said. It seemed there wasn't much else to say. "Sorry you lost your daughter."

Rachel turned away from the window to look at Anna. There were tears in her eyes as she said, "I need to tell Dave myself. Please don't tell him and Charlene."

James and Anna both promised to keep Rachel's secret. By the time they got back to Kremmling, Rachel's tears had all dried up, and she was back to being her usual self. *How do we just go on living with so much loss?* Anna thought, and then she looked at James. She put her hand on her lower belly, where she knew his child was growing inside her. *It's hope. As long as we live, there's hope. Right up to the end, we just go on hoping for a better future.* She watched Rachel hurry through the door of the Modern Times Church. *If we ever lose that…if we lose hope, that will definitely be the end.*

...

"Anna, wake up." It was James, gently shaking her. What a strange dream, she thought. She'd been flying. Vast reaches of the earth, opening up below her. She was somewhere over the plains, soaring toward mountains in the distance. Flying was effortless. It was as though she didn't have a body to propel through the sky. Just an ephemeral self that had only one goal. She had to reach those mountains in the distance. The mountains were home. It was time to return home to the mountains.

Where am I? she thought, seeing the strange surroundings come into focus. Then she remembered. "Guess I fell asleep, huh?" she said to James.

He was smiling. "It's a boy," he said. "Charlene has a new baby boy."

Anna sensed that it was very early in the morning. The windows of the Modern Times Church looked out on a dark world. Inside the building, the LED lights in the lounge area where Anna had fallen asleep had been dimmed to a soft glow. She stood up and stretched. Anna and James were the only ones in the lounge. She headed down the hall toward Dr. Ming's office, with James right behind her.

Dr. Ming's office in The Modern Times Church building actually consisted of several rooms that had once been offices for the BLM. One of the offices had been set up to be a small maternity ward. Dave and Rachel were already there, of course. Dave and Dr. Ming on one side of the bed, and Rachel on the other. Everyone in the room looked happy. Everyone except Charlene, who simply looked exhausted. She held the swaddled newborn close to her breast. The baby was asleep. "We should let them rest," Dr. Ming said to everyone and to no one in particular.

"Is the baby healthy?" Anna asked Dr. Ming once they were back out in the hall. Dave had stayed in the room with Charlene and the baby. Instead of leaving with the others, he just sat down in the easy chair that was next to the bed.

"Mother and child both seem perfectly healthy." Dr. Ming answered. Then looking directly at Anna, "Lisa's baby was born healthy, too."

"Who's Lisa?" Rachel asked.

"Lisa Smith." Dr. Ming answered. "She had the first baby born here, after, after, you know. Anyway, that was a couple of months ago. Lisa's baby seemed perfect for three days."

"And?" Rachel asked.

"On the fourth day, Lisa's baby developed a terrible fever and the other symptoms of V-1. There was nothing I could do."

Chapter Twenty Three

FOR ANNA, the road through Byers Canyon was filled with both hope and fear. She hoped they would find the means to switch on the power. But there was a fear now that Anna took with her everywhere. Like tinnitus, never drowning out other sounds, but always present just beneath the surface, Anna constantly carried the fear that the baby growing inside her would end up like Charlene's, and Lisa Smith's before that. Charlene's baby only survived two days before the sickness took it. Anna couldn't imagine carrying a child for nine months, only to have it die two days after birth.

Today was the twenty-fifth of March. Charlene's baby boy had died exactly two weeks ago, on the eleventh. Anna looked over at James, who was riding in the passenger seat. *Is he afraid, too,* she thought? He hardly ever let her out of his sight even though she was barely two months pregnant. Protecting her from any harm that might befall her during pregnancy was one thing, but no one could protect their baby from an invisible disease that wouldn't even make itself known until after the baby was born.

Anna's mind wandered back to the private talk she'd had with Dr. Ming after Charlene's baby died. That talk was as much at the root of her fear as the death of poor Charlene's infant son. Anna had pressed Dr. Ming to tell her what he knew or even what he guessed could be causing newborn infants to suddenly die, apparently of V-1.

"I'm no virologist or epidemiologist," Dr. Ming had said. "But then, even the epidemiologists couldn't understand V-1." He'd rummaged around in a file cabinet by his desk and brought out a single sheet of paper. "This is the last report I got from the CDC. I barely got it printed before the coms went down. Guess it's a good thing I'm old-fashioned, or I probably wouldn't have printed it at all."

Anna read the report and then re-read it. Some of the medical and scientific terminologies didn't mean much to her, but the gist of the document was that the CDC basically didn't know much more than anybody else. The best scientific data on V-1 at the time of the report suggested that it was some kind of totally new, previously undetected virus. The previously undetected part was the key to its lethality. Apparently, nearly everyone in the world carried the virus in their system and had for some time. No one knew if it was months or years. The scientists didn't know how long ago humans were first infected with V-1, nor did they understand why it suddenly turned lethal at the same time all over the world. What they did know was that it killed more men than women. The data suggested that V-1 could possibly kill ninety-nine percent of humans on earth, and up to seventy percent of the one percent remaining would be women.

"But what about the babies?" Anna had asked after reading the report for the third time. "Why does it kill the babies?"

Dr. Ming's answer was basically no answer at all. "The scientists who wrote that report were probably gone by the time any babies were born. And, even if any of them are still alive and able to continue their research, how would they ever disseminate the data?"

Anna looked at the report again before asking Dr. Ming, "What do you think? What could have made a virus so lethal? And why babies?"

Dr. Ming had stared off into space, searching his own mind before answering, "I wish I knew, Anna. I really wish I knew."

Coming out of Byers Canyon into Hot Sulphur Springs, Anna's thoughts turned to Charlene. She wondered how long it would take the poor woman to recover, if ever. It wasn't just Charlene, either. Dave just wasn't the same as before. He took it as hard as if he really was the father. Dr. Ming tried to tell them they should try again. That those who were still in their reproductive years needed to keep having children. Without babies, if no children could survive, our species was doomed to extinction. He was right, of course. Anna knew that what he said was true, but the intellectual knowledge of the truth didn't override the purely emotional fear of the possibility of losing a child.

It wasn't just Anna that feared for an unborn child. Connie, who was due in a month, hadn't been herself since Charlene's baby only survived two days. She was going crazy, trying to figure out a way to keep the same thing from happening to her baby. When she asked Dr. Ming if he had any ideas, he told her to pray if she was a religious person. "How could anyone still believe in God?" she'd asked Dr. Ming. "Any God. What kind of god would allow so much death?"

There had been no sign of anyone at all in Hot Sulphur Springs where they left Dave's crane. They left the crane after Anna assured them Highway 40 was open from there to at least Windy Gap Reservoir. The road was as empty as Anna remembered. Driving past Windy Gap, a mostly dried up lake that had once been a wetland bird's paradise, Anna thought about all that had happened in the past five or six months. It seemed impossible that less than six months had passed since she rode Red Two down this stretch of highway. Her thoughts turned to all of those who were gone. The family she'd hoped to find at the BR. The grief in finding they were all gone. *At least I found James,* she thought. *His baby has to live.* She unconsciously put her free hand on her belly again. *He just has to.* And then she was struck by the way she assumed the baby was a boy.

"What the hell is that?" Anna's thoughts were interrupted by Dave's exclamation from the back seat. He was reaching up between the seats, pointing toward Granby.

Anna and James both looked where he was pointing. It was something shimmering in the mid-morning sun, something in the sky. As they watched it rising higher above the hills, all three realized it was some kind of airplane.

"Now there's a sight I never expected to see," James said.

"Guess there's at least one person alive in Granby," Anna added.

Dave was studying the plane as it made a wide circle and headed back toward where it came from. "Looks like an old Eviation, or maybe a Sonex," he said. "Pretty small, whatever it is. Probably just a two-seater."

"So, you think it's an E-plane?" Anna asked.

"That'd be my guess," Dave answered. "There might still be some good av-gas around, but I'd have a hard time trusting it. And it definitely wasn't big enough to be one of those commercial hybrids, if any of those are even still flyable."

Just after crossing the Colorado River bridge near the Fraser River confluence, Anna saw the people before she saw the garden. There were most definitely survivors in Granby. It looked like there were at least twenty or thirty people working in what had to be the biggest garden Anna had ever seen. What was once a hay meadow or pasture had been converted to food crops for people, not animals. *A community garden,* Anna thought. *Like the one in Kremmling, but at least five times as big.*

The garden, more like a truck farm than a garden, had an eight-foot fence built all around the perimeter to keep out deer and elk. There was a parking and hitching area adjacent to the garden. Surprisingly, there were two electric vehicles parked near the open gate to the garden, along with about fifteen horses tied up to hitching rails. The people, most of whom had been bent over planting or pulling weeds when Anna first saw them, were all standing and staring at the Rivian as Anna pulled into the parking area. The scene reminded her of a prairie dog colony with the animals all standing at attention, studying an intruder, ready to sound the alarm, and dive into their holes if the intruder proved to be dangerous.

"I believe this is the most people I've seen in one place since the great dying," James said.

"Most since Montana, anyway," Dave said, leaning up from the back seat to get a better view.

"Nice garden, too," Anna mumbled as she glanced at the clock on the dashboard. Almost 10:30 if the old clock was still accurate, and already eighty-two degrees according to the thermometer. *Not even April, and it'll probably hit ninety today.* The thought was anything but comfortable. Anna remembered her mother telling her they used to not plant most things until the end of May or even early June to avoid a killing frost. *Now, they'll start harvesting in early June. If they don't run out of irrigation water first.*

Everyone in the garden headed toward the gate as Anna, James, and Dave got out of the Riv. Having a strange vehicle pull into their little parking lot had to be a novel experience.

A dark-haired woman wearing an old beat-up straw hat was in the lead and seemed to be the de-facto leader of the group. She wasn't a young woman, the wrinkles in her dark brown skin attested to that. She had the look of one that has never been a stranger to hard work outdoors under a scorching sun. The bent and wrinkled straw hat on her head matched the woman perfectly. Both had a lot of wear written all over them.

"Hello strangers," the woman said, as they all met at the gate. "Been a while since we've seen anybody but us around here. I'm Ruth Aguilar, and this," she gestured with one arm at the rest of the people gathered behind her, "is the Granby gardeners." She laughed. "Least they're learning to be gardeners."

The group of people crowded around Ruth were, for the most part, younger than her. The group seemed to be about two-thirds women and one-third men. A few of the women were really just teenagers, and two boys were even younger than that.

"Hi Ruth," Anna, as usual, took the lead, "I'm Anna Duran." She took the woman's calloused old hand in hers and introduced James and Dave. "We're from the Blue River Ranch south of Kremmling. Well, I'm the only one originally from the BR," she clarified. "But James and Dave live there now."

"So you must be Clyde Duran's daughter. Well, I'll be. I can see a little resemblance, but you must take more after your mother. Is Clyde," the old woman hesitated. It was still difficult to ask who had died.

Anna shook her head. "No, I'm the only one of my family that survived."

"What about Chuck, is he still with us." Ruth Aguilar seemed to know a lot about the people of the Blue River Ranch.

James answered that one. "No, Chuck was my granddad. He survived the…the great dying, but then he died. I think it was a heart attack."

"Well I'll be," Ruth said, again. "You must be Noni's son then. Noni?"

"She's gone, too," James answered the one-word question. "Died of cancer, just like my grandmother." The woman hadn't asked about James' dad, so he didn't volunteer any other information.

"How do you know the BR?" Anna asked.

"Oh, I imagine everybody that grew up in these parts knows something about the Blue River Ranch. Guess I did know Clyde Duran and Noni Pierson better than most, though. We all went to school together over in Kremmling." For just a moment, Ruth seemed to stare back in time. "Doesn't even seem like the same world now." Then, coming back to the present, "What brings you young folks over to Granby after all this time?"

After Ruth heard about the possibility of getting electric power back up and running in the valley, she was more than happy to help. And it wasn't just Ruth. The Granby gardeners, as Ruth had called them, were about as excited as any group of people Anna had ever seen. One of the women said that her husband had worked in IT for Mountain Parks Electric before, but he got sick and died along with everyone else. "Liz might help, though," the woman said.

"Who's Liz?" Anna asked.

Ruth answered before the other woman had a chance. "Liz is the one person in this valley that'll be going hungry if she doesn't stop tinkering with that stupid airplane long enough to help with this garden."

"Liz was a lineman for MPE," the other woman added.

"Line person," a man standing near the front of the group said. "Liz wouldn't like being called a lineman."

"Like I give a rat's ass what Liz would or wouldn't like," Ruth told the man. "Come on," she said to Anna, "I'll take you to her."

On the drive to the Granby airport, Ruth gave Anna, James, and Dave a quick overview of the status of Granby and the nearby surrounding area. Other than a few people who were too old to help with growing food and Liz McClure, the Granby gardeners were all that remained of the living in Granby itself. Apparently, there were a few people up in Fraser and a few more in the Grand Lake area, and no more than a dozen scattered out on the ranches in between. As seemed to be the case everywhere, more women in Granby survived the sickness than men.

"How'd you get lucky enough to have two men?" Ruth asked Anna with a wink.

They told Ruth about the other people now living on the Blue River Ranch, and the people who were still living in Kremmling. Ruth was especially interested in Dr. Ming. Apparently, no one with any kind of medical background had survived in Granby. When Dave told Ruth about Charlene's baby dying, she became visibly upset. "I'm sorry," she told Dave. "Same thing happened to Yvette a couple of months ago. She had a fine baby boy. All on her own. No doctor, no midwife, no nothing. The baby seemed as healthy as a horse for a couple of days. Then he just got sick and died. It's like that sickness that took everybody is still here. Still here, just waiting to kill off anybody born to replace those who are gone." Everyone was silent for a moment before Ruth brightened and said. "They'll be glad to know there's a doctor in Kremmling, though. Three of the other women back there are pregnant, and the rest of them are trying their damndest to get that way." She laughed out loud. "I'd be tryin' too if I was just a few years younger."

Anna hadn't told Ruth that she herself was pregnant, and decided not to. Instead, she switched to the subject at hand. "Do any of you have electrical power?"

Ruth laughed at that. "Mostly just horsepower," she said. "Oh, there are some places around with solar power. That's what keeps those EVs you saw charged up. Just pull through the gate there." The gate through the security fence at the Granby airport was standing wide open. "And then there's Liz, here," Ruth continued. "She's got more solar working here at the airport than anywhere else I know of. Even more than at the Modern Times Church. At least, I think she has more."

The drive through the gate led between a couple of hangars. "Liz'll be in this hangar on the left," Ruth said. Anna turned left as she came out onto the apron in front of the hangars. Sure enough, the big doors on the front of the hangar were wide open. The cavernous space inside would have been adequate for a much larger plane or several small ones, but there was just one little airplane sitting near the back of the vast space.

Anna stopped just outside the hangar door, and a woman stepped around from behind the lone airplane as everyone got out of the Rivian.

"Well, well," the woman said, seeing Ruth get out of the passenger side. "You come to drag me back to the farm?"

Ruth refused to take the bait. "No, I think we may have found a better project for you. This is Anna, James, and Dave from Kremmling, and they have an idea you might be interested in."

Liz McClure introduced herself since Ruth had failed to do that part. "What kind of an idea would I be interested in?" she asked, the skeptical look on her face suggesting she probably wasn't really interested in much of anything. Other than her airplane, that is. She was obviously interested in that.

Anna wasn't the only one to pick up on Liz McClure's attitude. "Is that a Sonex?" Dave asked, walking toward the little plane.

"Sure is," Liz told him, as she fell in step beside him. "Restored it myself."

"Really?" Dave sounded impressed. "Don't think I've seen one of these since I was a kid."

Liz looked at Dave with a little more interest than she'd shown before. "You a pilot?" she asked.

"No, my dad was. Took me up in one of these babies once. I must have been seven or eight years old at the time. Thought I wanted to be a pilot after that." Dave took his eyes off the little plane and smiled at Liz. "Never worked out, though."

"How do you get enough power to charge the batteries?" Anna asked, taking advantage of the opening Dave had created.

"Panels on the roof." Liz pointed up at the ceiling without ever taking her eyes off Dave.

Uh-Oh, Anna thought. *Dave has definitely got her attention.* Liz McClure seemed a little older than Dave, but not much. Probably in her late twenties or early thirties. She may not have been the most attractive woman in the world, nor even in the hangar, for that matter. But the coveralls she was wearing and the disheveled hair that she ran a hand over masked some hidden charms. Charms that were now directed at Dave.

Interestingly to Anna, Dave seemed interested in Liz as well. *Jesus, that's all he needs. Like two women aren't enough already.*

"What about the grid? Couldn't we get at least part of the grid online?" Anna asked.

Liz finally broke eye contact with Dave to look at Anna. "Grid's dead," she said. "Dead as all those people that used to keep it going."

"Well, Anna here thinks we can resurrect it," Ruth told the younger woman. "Seems like that'd be a lot more valuable than tinkering with an old airplane all the time."

Ruth didn't really like Liz, and the feeling was reciprocated. That was evident to all. Dave broke the tension once again. "Seems to me we should be keeping technology alive as much as we can. Airplanes included. Otherwise, we'll all be living in caves before you know it."

Is it even possible, though? The question triggered by Dave's statement hit Anna hard. *Can we really keep technology alive?* And then, another even more profound question, *should we?* After all, it was modern technologies that got the world into this mess in the first place. It was nearly ninety degrees in March, and the mega-drought in Colorado showed no signs of easing anytime soon. *But it's not like we want to burn any fossil fuel. And there are hardly enough people left to make much of an impact on the climate, anyway.* She put her hand on her lower belly, conscious of the other life growing there. Aware of the desire, of the need, to bring new life into this dying world. *But what if new life can't survive in this world?* She forced the question and the fear out of her mind. *First things first, let's get some electricity flowing in this valley again.*

. . .

Working together without any computer experts among

them, they decided the best solution was to eliminate Mountain Park Electric's centralized computer control system. After their somewhat inauspicious first meeting, Liz McClure proved to be invaluable. Not only Liz but her little airplane, too. They couldn't eliminate the system's computer controls without some new switching gear. Switching gear that was nowhere to be found locally. Liz, however, knew of a warehouse in Casper, Wyoming, of all places, where she figured they could acquire the necessary gear.

After discussing the range of the airplane, the size and weight of the switches, and whether flying to Casper was better than driving, Dave agreed to fly up to Casper with Liz to get the switches. Instead of a two-day trip by Rivian, it was no more than a three-hour roundtrip flight.

Anna and James were waiting at the Granby airport when the little plane came into view. Seeing that silver speck in the sky was a huge relief. Seeing Dave and Liz together after they exited the plane, Anna found herself wondering how well Rachel and Charlene were going to take to sharing Dave with a new sister wife.

"You two seem pretty happy," Anna said. "I presume you found the switches."

James just looked at Dave and shook his head. What else the two had found was just as evident to James as it was to Anna. "So, do we need to make room for another woman at the BR?" James teased his friend when they were far enough away for Liz not to hear.

"No," Dave chuckled, "but I might need to spend some time over this way once in a while."

"Maybe you can take flying lessons," James told him.

Liz, who had just walked around the plane with Anna,

heard that last part. "I think that's a great idea," she said. "I'd love to teach you to fly, Dave."

. . .

Anna watched as Liz tightened the last connection. It was the first of April. *Sure do hope we're not all April Fools,* she thought. The two women were alone at the Wolford solar farm. James had reluctantly agreed to go back down to Kremmling with Dave. The two men, along with Johnny Garcia and Richard Schumacher, were tasked with watching for problems when the power was switched back on. They'd taken every precaution they could think of to prevent any potential issues. But the power had been off for nearly a year, no one could know what might happen when it was suddenly switched back on. It took several days, but the residents of both Kremmling and Granby had gone from building to building shutting down all of the master switches or pulling the main fuses on every house or business from Kremmling to Fraser.

The four major substations that connected the local grid to the high voltage transmission lines had all been disconnected from the overall electrical grid. All that remained now was throwing the right switches in the proper sequence.

"Have they had enough time?" Liz asked, wondering if everyone was in place in Kremmling. Ruth was supposed to have a detachment in Granby doing the same thing as the men in Kremmling. Watching for any little problems with the power to keep any minor issues from becoming a catastrophe. With no fire departments or fire trucks, an electrical fire would definitely be catastrophic.

"I think so," Anna answered. "Go ahead."

"Oh no. This is your idea; you get to do the honors."

"May have been my idea," Anna said, "but we couldn't have done it without you. Let's do it together." Anna grabbed Liz's hand, and they threw the first switch together. As Anna started to guide Liz's hand to the second switch, Liz stopped her. She pulled Anna's hand back away from the switch.

"Boy, would I have been fired for that. Back in the day, I mean. First safety rule, don't touch anyone else while you're working with live power, and always assume the power is live." Liz pulled Anna back away from the switchgear. "Let me do it. No point in all three of us getting fried," she said, looking pointedly at Anna's belly. Liz threw the rest of the switches herself, while Anna watched from a few yards away.

With no indication of any problems on their end, both women jumped in the car. Anna and Liz were giddy with excitement, anxious to get down to Kremmling to see the results of their handiwork.

"I really envy you, Anna," the statement was totally out of the blue. They were about half-way back to Kremmling. "I'd give just about anything to have Dave's baby."

"You and a couple other women I know," Anna answered. "You do know about the others, right?"

"Honestly, I don't care. Actually, I'd like to meet Rachel and Charlene. From what Dave says, I think I'd like them. What about you? I mean you and James. What if he decided to up the odds of fathering children? There are plenty of women that would jump at the chance, you know."

Anna did know. The more she saw of this new world,

the more obvious it became that the imbalance between the number of men and women would require major structural change to the old status quo. Monogamous pairs of people just didn't make sense when women outnumbered men by at least two to one.

"I don't know," she told Liz. "I honestly don't. I do know that Dave living with two women at the same time is probably more normal now than the way the rest of us on the BR are living. I mean three apparently monogamous couples in a world where there seems to be at least twice as many women as men isn't very sustainable, is it?"

Liz laughed. "I know it's not working that way in Granby," she said. "Hell, I think Ruth even gets laid once in a while."

"What about you Liz, were you married before?"

"Way before. I got married when I was twenty-two, divorced two years later. I've been a free agent ever since. Up until the sickness, anyway. Dave's the first since my last boyfriend died. Just never could see much in any of the men that survived in Granby. That's why I was working so hard getting my plane ready. I haven't told anyone else this, but I was just about ready to leave Granby when you guys showed up. If you'd waited another day or two, you wouldn't have found anything but an empty hangar at that airport."

"Why? I mean where would you go?"

"I don't know for sure." Liz turned her head to look out the side of the Riv, thinking about the question before answering. "Probably just somewhere north. I just knew I had to find somewhere that I wanted to live." A slight smile played across her face as she turned back to Anna. "That's not exactly right. I had to find someone to make living worthwhile. Someone to make me want to bring new life into this nearly dead world."

"Maybe there is such a thing as fate," Anna told her, though she was having trouble believing it herself. "Maybe things do happen for a reason."

"Maybe," Liz said. "Tell you one thing, though. When it comes to having Dave's baby, I am definitely not leaving that up to fate. Working hard to bring that about myself," she laughed.

Anna laughed with her and then drove in silence for a spell before saying, "None of them have made it, you know. None of the babies born since the sickness have lived."

Liz's only reply was to stare silently out the window, and Anna drove in silence. Both women lost in their own thoughts. One hoping to beat the odds with a baby on the way. One who wanted nothing more than a chance at those odds herself.

Chapter Twenty Four

IF ANNA HAD a religious bone left in her body, she would have been praying. It would have been a simple prayer, please God, let Connie's baby live. She was sitting in a comfortable chair in the waiting room of Dr. Ming's old clinic. With electric power for the equipment all restored, the clinic was a much better healthcare facility than the Modern Times Church in the former Bureau of Land Management building. The clinic even had an ultrasound machine. A couple of weeks ago, Connie had been the first person since the power went out to know the sex of her baby before it was born. Connie was giving birth to a baby girl.

James was sitting next to Anna. Ray and Rita were sitting on the other side of the waiting room, and Jack was back in the delivery room with Connie, Dr. Ming, and Lisa Smith. Dr. Ming had convinced Lisa, who had once worked in a dental office, to be his assistant. Being sixty-four years old, Dr. Ming knew the little community would need someone to provide care after he was gone. There wasn't much chance of a trained healthcare professional showing up in Kremmling ever again. He would just have to teach someone else everything he could in whatever time he had left. Lisa was the someone he'd chosen.

Anna sat with her hands resting on the slight bulge of her belly. It was both comforting and frightening to feel the changes happening to her body. Random thoughts swirled around inside her head as she waited. *Would the baby growing inside her survive? Would Connie's? If the babies did survive, what would their world be like?* It was a question that had always plagued expectant parents, is it right to bring new life into this world? For Anna, before the great dying, or V-1, or whatever one wanted to call it, the answer had been a resounding no. The pre-plague world was not a world fit for a child, not for any child.

Now, bringing new life into this new world was what she wanted more than anything. *Is it just instinct?* She thought. *Is it just our species' drive for survival?* She looked at James, sitting next to her asleep in his chair. *Is that what love is, too? Just another way for ancient instincts to drive procreation.* Somehow, it didn't seem right that reasonable, rational humans could be manipulated by instincts that predated us as a species. *Right or wrong, that's the way it is.* The realization was a little bit unsettling. Were human beings no different than any other species of animal, driven by instincts that could even overpower our supposedly much larger brains? There was no stronger drive than the drive for survival. Not for the survival of the individual, any individual, but the survival of homo sapiens. The continuation of the species was what really counted.

Anna looked across the room at Ray and Rita, who were also both asleep in their chairs. They'd been waiting for a good twelve hours now. The window above Ray and

Rita showed the glow of first light beginning in the east. *Wonder why Rita hasn't conceived yet?* The question in Anna's mind sparked another thought. *One of them must be infertile.* That, in turn, brought another realization. *They'll both have to try with other partners.* The instinctual drive to procreate would allow nothing less. *Emotions such as love and jealousy don't stand a chance. Not against the unrelenting instinctual need to bring new life into this world.*

Anna's thoughts were interrupted by the sound of a door opening. Dr. Ming stepped into the room with a big smile on his face. The others all awoke at the sound of the opening door, and Dr. Ming told them mother and baby were both doing well. He said they could go back for a brief visit, but it would be best if just two at a time went back to the small maternity ward.

"Do you think it will be different this time?" Anna asked, after Ray and Rita left the waiting room.

Dr. Ming and James both knew exactly what she was asking. A slight frown momentarily furrowed Dr. Ming's brow before the smile returned. "Where there's life, there's hope." He answered.

...

It was the third of May. A day like no other in anyone's memory. Today, one week after giving birth, Connie and baby Michelle were coming home to the BR. Anna was so excited she could hardly contain herself. Michelle, born into some kind of plague-infested world, was alive and healthy. Dr. Ming, who had resisted letting the baby out of his sight, finally relented. If she didn't get sick in that first week, she was probably immune. None of the other babies had survived more than four days. Besides, if the baby did get sick, there was likely nothing he could do about it, anyway.

James and Anna were sitting on the veranda, watching the sun climb above the hills in the east. James had a cup of the chicory root brew that he still called coffee. Anna was sipping a glass of water. The hot chicory beverage that James enjoyed every morning didn't seem to go too well with morning sickness. Rita had left before dawn. She'd taken the Rivian into Kremmling to pick up Connie, Jack, and baby Michelle. Ray was somewhere out above the north pasture guarding the flock of sheep. The herd was a lot smaller now than it had been a week ago. Last week, while everyone was in Kremmling with Connie, a bear had torn through the flock of sheep.

Anna had heard stories of bear attacks on sheep before, but the carnage was worse than she could have imagined. When a bear gets into a herd of sheep, it doesn't just kill one or two of the sheep to eat. It kills as many as it can and just leaves them lay. Fresh mutton isn't what the bear is primarily after. The dead sheep and lambs are just the raw ingredient of what the bear really wants. A meal of mutton isn't fit for a bear until the dead sheep's carcasses are fly-blown and crawling with maggots. The maggots are the delicacy that bears crave, not the mutton.

Everyone's first instinct had, of course, been to kill the bear when it came back to feast on rotting mutton. Oddly enough, Rita, who grew up raising sheep, was the one that talked them out of it. "Probably a sow with cubs," she'd said. "What are we going to do with all these sheep, anyway?"

What are we going to do with the sheep and the cattle? Anna wondered. *Leftovers from a world that no longer exists.*

She thought about the vast number of animals the world had once required to feed and clothe billions of people. *How many animals, from chickens in chicken houses to pigs packed together like sardines, had perished along with the billions of people?* That was another sobering thought. The world, once home to many billions of humans, was probably now inhabited by no more than a few million survivors. There were possibly fewer people scattered around the globe now than had inhabited any one of the world's largest cities before. *How many eons have passed since this old world contained so few people?*

How many of the cows and calves will come back down from the high country this fall? They had just let the cattle wander off toward the mountains on their own this year. The older cows and bulls had made the trek year after year until it was just part of their nature. The new calves just followed their mothers. The calves were most susceptible, of course. Most of the cows, and probably all three bulls would be back down by winter. But some of this year's calf crop would end up feeding non-human predators. *Kind of a strange relationship,* Anna thought. *People and cattle. Without people needing meat and dairy, cattle don't really have much of a place in this world.* The BR herd that had wandered up to the high country was about ten times as many cattle as everyone on the BR and in Kremmling combined could ever possibly use. Granby had their own old outlying ranches supplying them. Anna was sure that was the case all over the west. There were no doubt some people somewhere that could use some beef or dairy, or wool, but there was no way to find them, let alone get the products to them. *No, in this new world, just as well allow the non-human predators to have most of the livestock.*

"Looks like Dave's back," James said, interrupting Anna's thoughts.

She looked out at Highway 9. It was indeed the Carlisle's truck and trailer coming up the road from Kremmling.

"Dave's back," Anna hollered at the screen door.

Charlene and Misty came out to watch the truck coming up the lane. Rachel and Mandy were with Dave and Liz in the truck. Charlene hadn't taken to having a third "wife" in Dave's little family quite as well as Rachel had. Mandy, who hardly let Rachel out of her sight, had insisted on going along to get Liz's things from Granby. They had been gone for a couple of days. It was quite a project to dismantle the PV system and charging apparatus for the Sonex plane, but Liz wasn't about to leave the airplane in Granby.

"Can I stay here?" Misty asked as the truck came up the lane. Dave was in the process of moving his family up to the old Carlisle place above Frisco. He'd already cleared a long straight section of old Highway 9 between Frisco and Breckenridge to use as an airport for Liz's plane. There was a big barn just off the highway that they planned to convert to a hangar and charging station.

"I thought you wanted to go home," Anna said.

Misty sat down next to Anna. "I like it here with you," she said. "I did want to go home, but not anymore. I don't think I want to live with Dave's family."

"I know what you mean," Charlene said from behind them. "Don't get me wrong. Dave's been good to me, but I kind of like it here myself."

"What about Mandy?" Anna asked Misty, trying to ignore Charlene's input. Anna had a feeling that Charlene wasn't so much leaning away from Dave as she was leaning toward James. "You know Mandy's going wherever Rachel goes."

"I know," Misty answered. "But I'm almost a grown woman now. Mandy needs someone to take care of her. I don't. Besides, it's not that far. I can go visit whenever I want. Please. Please let me stay here with you."

James got up and started back into the house. "Looks like I better get some more chicory brewing," he said, totally ignoring the women's conversation he had just overheard.

Dave looked out toward Kremmling again. "Thought they'd be right behind us," he said. Dave, Liz, Rachel, and Mandy had stopped in Kremmling, and Jack had told them that Connie and the baby were just about ready to leave. Now Dave was anxious to get on up to Frisco. "Dr. Ming said he just wanted to give the baby one more quick checkup."

The whole group had just finished a breakfast of lamb chops, fried potatoes, and awkward conversation. James and Dave, each with a cup of chicory in hand, walked out toward the fully-loaded truck and trailer.

"You know I haven't, with Charlene, I mean," James told Dave. The two men were by themselves out by the truck.

Dave laughed at the change of subject, or maybe just to relieve some tension. "You're not the only one. Far as I know, Charlene hasn't had sex since long before she lost her baby. Now, I think she's afraid to get pregnant again."

"Well, I just want you to know that I had nothing to

do with her deciding to stay here, that's all."

"Yeah, I know," Dave said. "Guess there's no more understanding women now than there ever was." He laughed again. "Difference now is, each of us has a lot more of 'em to not understand."

James couldn't help but laugh at the absurdity of the truth in that statement. How could anyone reasonably expect relationships to be the same now as they were before? With the entirety of the only society they'd ever known now gone, how would the survivors, and more importantly the children of the survivors, reorder this new world. *What will life be like for our children?* It dawned on James that that question was one that every parent who ever lived had probably asked themselves. That and, *how do we make this a better world for our children?*

"Here they are now." Dave motioned with his chin at the Rivian that was turning up the lane to the BR.

"The power went out in Kremmling," was the first thing Jack said as he and Rita got out of the car and scrambled to help Connie out with the new baby. "Dr. Ming's office went dark right in the middle of the exam. Couldn't have been more than five minutes after you left," he told Dave.

The entire house emptied out as soon as the Rivian came up the lane. There may never have been another group of people so excited to see a newborn baby come home. Everyone was crowded around Connie and baby Michelle when Rita asked, "Where's Ray?"

With everything else going on, no one had noticed that Ray hadn't returned from his overnight sheep guarding duty. Usually, he would have been back home shortly after daybreak. The sheep were reasonably safe from predators during the day.

As Rita asked the question, she looked off toward the north pasture, to where they had moved the herd. Anna, with her back to the north, seeing a look of horror come over Rita's face, quickly turned around. A horse was walking slowly up the path toward the barn. Anna instantly recognized Red Two. His head was down, dragging the reins from the bridle along the ground. He wore a saddle, an empty saddle where Ray should have been sitting.

Chapter Twenty Five

NO ONE WOULD ever know what caused Ray to fall or be thrown from the saddle. As Rita said, "he never was a very good rider." It didn't take them long, following Red Two's tracks, to find him. He was lying flat on his back, his head next to the bloody rock that had smashed the back of his skull on impact.

It was so hard to believe that he'd been killed by a freak accident. After surviving the great dying to come to such an end seemed so unfair. *Fate,* thought Anna. *Was it just his fate? Are we all just fated to who knows what?* She thought of the life growing inside her. A life that seemed so much more precious now after the loss of another man. Anna was sure the child she carried was a boy. She would bear a son. The world needed men. How could fate deny her the chance to bring one into the world? *There is no rhyme or reason to fate,* she thought. And the thought frightened her. What if humankind was fated to simply fade away? To simply become extinct like all the other species driven to extinction by a human race that would, in the end, destroy itself.

Anna and Liz were almost to Kremmling. Just the two of them, alone in the Rivian. It was just after noon. They'd left everyone else at the BR, grieving, after burying Ray early that morning. Ray was the first person buried in the ranch cemetery that wasn't related to the Piersons or the Durans. It was just over twenty-four hours ago that the joy of a new baby on the ranch had turned to sudden sorrow. Both Anna and Liz would have preferred to be back at the ranch, but they had another responsibility. The two of them had brought electricity back to Kremmling, and the two of them knew it was up to them to keep the power flowing.

"What if we weren't here?" Liz asked. The question seemingly coming from nowhere. "I mean, what happens when we can't keep the power on anymore?"

It was part of a question Anna had asked herself many times. *What happens to him,* she thought of her baby, *when all of the old technologies are finally gone?*

"Guess people will just have to go back to the old ways," she told Liz, wondering *what old ways?* even as she said it.

They stopped and picked up Johnny Garcia at the water plant before going on out to the Wolford Reservoir solar farm. Liz and Anna agreed that, of all the people in Kremmling, Johnny would be the best bet to learn the power system.

As it turned out, other than learning what breakers and switches to check if it happened again, Johnny didn't get much of a lesson on this trip. It took about fifteen minutes to get the power back on, but Anna knew it wouldn't always be so simple. For the first time, she really thought about how hard it was going to be to teach the children of this world everything they needed to know to keep the power flowing.

Back in Kremmling, after dropping off Johnny at the water plant, they stopped at Dr. Ming's office for Anna to have a quick check-up and to give him the bad news about Ray.

"Do you think the power is going to be reliable now?" Dr. Ming asked Anna. "I mean if I was trying to do some kind of emergency surgery or something…" He just let the "or something" trail off into the ether.

"We need to get you some emergency backup," Anna told him. "If any place needs it, this clinic does. We need to salvage some batteries and find an inverter and controller, so you have at least a couple days' worth of battery backup."

"Sure hope you can get it set up quickly, this place is about to become a full-time maternity ward. Jackie Adams from Granby is due in about two weeks, and there's two more over there that aren't far behind. I just hope V-1 is finally behind us now. Before Connie's baby, I was starting to think the human race would just go extinct."

On the way back to the BR, Anna and Liz decided they would have to get Dave to clear old Highway 40 all the way from Granby down to I-70 and then I-70 on into Denver. It wasn't just electricity that the clinic needed. Dr. Ming would also run out of medical supplies someday, just as the people of the valley would eventually run out of other things. Baby clothes and diapers being high on the list of things that people would need if procreation continued at its current pace. The old Walmart stores in Granby and Frisco wouldn't supply what everyone needed for much longer. No, they would have to start making salvage runs down to Denver. The metro area could provide most everything they needed for a long, long time to come. *But not forever* was the thought that lodged in Anna's mind. *Someday, it will all be gone.*

...

Just barely over a year ago. In retrospect, it didn't seem possible to James how much had transpired since the last time he was at the Mendez estate in Castle Pines. "I should have buried her at the ranch," he told Anna. They were standing in the old flower garden turned cemetery, paying respects to Noni. Like most spaces in the Denver area, dryland weeds were taking over the old garden. There was one giant tumbleweed growing right on top of Julie's grave that James found particularly troubling. "That's Julie's grave," he said, pointing out where he and Dave had buried his last girlfriend.

In the month just past, James had told Anna all about Julie and the other women he'd known. He even told her about the sexual encounter that he'd had with Connie. He was surprised when Anna told him she already knew about that. In turn, Anna told James all about Charlie Day and about being a semi-willing participant in a polygamist relationship in Blue Rapids.

"Did you love her?" Anna asked.

"I guess I did. But not like I love you."

"Strange, isn't it?" Anna thought out loud. "Love, I mean. Love, lust, sex. What was it that brought about monogamy as an ideal? It certainly isn't the norm in most of the animal world."

James thought about it before replying, "I don't think it's natural for humans either." He laughed. "People may have preached monogamy, but I don't think very many ever truly practiced it. At best, the old norm was serial monogamy. One sex partner at a time, but any number of sex partners over time."

"Guess that's true," Anna laughed. "Doesn't seem like it makes much difference, does it? I mean, what's the difference between having multiple partners over time or having them all at the same time."

James put one arm around Anna and placed his other hand on her swelling tummy. "Well, at least with one at a time," he said, "you always know who the father is."

"Come on," Anna said, "let's go see what we can find."

Dave and Liz were waiting for James and Anna inside the Mendez house, where it was a little cooler. In the year that had passed, the uninterruptible power supply of the Mendez estate had finally stopped working, but it was still cooler inside than out. This was the first supply trip since Dave finished opening the road. The four of them had driven the Carlisle truck and trailer down early that morning.

"We could probably fix the power," Anna said when she and James were back inside.

James took one last look around the home he'd known for most of his life. "Why bother?" he said, "I don't think I'll ever be back." With that, he turned and left home for the very last time.

With a trailer full of supplies, some medical, but mostly baby clothes, shoes, boots, and an inordinate amount of disposable diapers, they turned onto Highway 40 from I-70 just as the sun was going down.

"Wonder if there's still anyone in Georgetown?" James

asked. He told the others about seeing a couple of people there from a distance, way back when he'd first made the trek from Castle Pines.

"Guess next time we should run up there and see," Dave said. In the past month that they'd spent clearing the highways enough to make this trip, they hadn't seen anyone between Fraser and Denver. That trend had continued today. Searching and salvaging through a metro area the size of Denver without seeing another living soul really brought home just how isolated their little community was.

As they made their way around the switchbacks on Berthoud Pass, Anna wondered if isolated communities like Kremmling-Granby and Blue Rapids would survive. *Can our species even survive?* It was a question she'd been thinking a lot about. The recent births at Dr. Ming's clinic provided hope. The two women from Granby had both given birth to healthy baby girls, neither of which showed any sign of V-1, or whatever the sickness was that had taken all the earlier babies. There were now three new baby girls in their little community. *But no boys* was the thought that made Anna wonder about the survival of the species. *We need more men,* she thought. *We need you to grow up healthy,* she silently told the baby boy growing inside her womb.

Chapter Twenty-Six

THE THERMOMETER on the dashboard read 112 degrees. It was the twenty-eighth day of August. Anna was due in about six weeks, and she was totally miserable. The unrelenting heat wave gripping the valley would have been bad anytime, but the heat made being eight months pregnant almost unbearable. James was driving, and the two of them rode mostly in silence. The weekly trip down to see Dr. Ming was routine now. After the ultrasound confirmed what Anna's intuition already knew, that she did indeed carry a baby boy, Dr. Ming was as concerned about the health of Anna's baby as anyone. There had been two more births in Dr. Ming's clinic during the past two months. Another totally healthy baby girl and one baby boy that lived for only three days. Four baby girls born in the valley and no baby boys.

The valley had also recently lost another one of the older men. One of the men from Granby had died of an apparent heart attack. The longterm viability of the entire Middle Park community seemed more and more in peril, and Anna was becoming ever more fearful for her unborn son. As her due date approached, she found herself wishing she could just keep her baby secure in her womb, safe from a world of dying men and boys. *Maybe we really are doomed,* Anna thought. Looking down at not much more than a trickle of water as they crossed the Colorado River bridge didn't help her state of mind at all.

"That's different," James said as he parked next to a strange old SUV parked in front of Dr. Ming's clinic. It was definitely a different vehicle than any they'd seen in the valley before.

The strange car put both James and Anna on edge. Who was it? *Probably just one of the Granby bunch,* Anna thought. *The Granby Gardeners,* she corrected herself, remembering Ruth's name for that community. *Who knows how many old cars might be hidden away somewhere?* She found herself taking her pistol out of the console anyway. Having the old S&W.40 in her bag gave her a feeling of security, warranted or not.

There was, as it turned out, nothing threatening at all about the two women sitting in the waiting room. Women that neither James nor Anna had ever seen before. One was Black, and the other either Latino or Native.

"Where are you from?" Anna asked after the two women introduced themselves. *Strange question,* she thought as soon as the words left her lips. *Where are you from before? Or, where are you from now?*

"We came here from Montana." Constance, the large Black woman, said. Constance and the other woman, Mary, were both in their mid-twenties. Other than age, the only common physical trait shared by the two women was the fact that they were both females. Constance was a big woman in every way. Not obese by any means, just exceedingly large. Mary, on the other hand, was a petite, extremely attractive young woman. Where Constance was over six feet tall, Mary was probably no more than five-four. Constance was probably north of two-hundred pounds, while Mary would be lucky to go much over a hundred.

"Dr. Ming said we would be welcome to stay here in Kremmling," Mary said. "Even after Lenore and our baby can leave." She looked at Constance before adding, "if we want to stay, that is."

"We have some friends that came down from Montana," James had to think for a second to remember where in Montana. "Somewhere close to Billings, Park City, I think."

"Wow, that's where we were," Mary brightened. "Guess it's still a small world after all."

"Too small," Constance said. "Too small for the likes of those trying to take over Park City. Dr. Ming says none of those New Army Of God people are around here. Is that true?"

James and Anna told the two that no one in the area had anything to do with the New Army Of God. They also assured them that Dr. Ming was not the only one that would welcome them into the community. Everyone in Middle Park would be glad to see them stay.

After James and Anna's reassurances, the two women really opened up and shared their story. The three women had fled increasing persecution in Park City. Apparently, The New Army Of God was growing and starting to take over the entire Park City area. And they weren't just taking over land and property. They were trying to make what

Mary said they called "a whites-only paradise" in Park City.

"That New Army of God bunch is trying to drive people of color out of the area. And it isn't just Black people like Constance," Mary told them. "It doesn't matter what color you are if you aren't lily-white."

"If you ask me," Constance said, "they don't want us out. They want us to be slaves. Just like before the Civil War. Think they're some kind of superior beings just because they're white."

"They want you to be slaves," Mary told Constance. "They just want to kill those of us that are sexually diverse." After looking at James and Anna to gauge their reaction, she continued. " I guess that was the final straw, the lynching," Mary looked down, remembering the horror. "When we found Scott hanging from that overpass, we knew we had to leave."

"Poor Scott," Constance said. "He had the misfortune of not only being Black but also being gay. Guess there isn't much worse than a gay Black man, as far as the New Army of God's concerned."

Anna's own memories of her encounter with The New Army Of God were too painful. She had to change the subject. "Is Lenore pregnant then?" she asked.

"She was," Mary said, glad to talk about something else. "Now we have a baby boy. Daniel. Born right here two days ago."

Anna couldn't help but notice the ring that Mary fidgeted with as she spoke. "Is Lenore your partner?" she asked.

"We're married," Mary held up her hand to show off the ring. "Been married for three years now. Kind of a strange concept anymore, isn't it? Marriage, I mean. Almost as strange as a couple of lesbians having a baby." She looked for any signs of disapproval on James and Anna's faces before laughing and adding, "Me and Lenore wanted to have a child before - you know before," she paused before continuing, "anyway, we always planned for one of us to have a child using a sperm bank. The problem was, we could never agree on which one of us would actually get pregnant, but then," she paused again. "After - I mean now, it just seems like we need all the babies we can get. I tried to get pregnant too, but Lenore got pregnant first. Guess I still want to get pregnant myself someday," she confided. "Not that I relish sex with a man." She looked directly at James. "No offense," she said.

James laughed. "None taken," he answered.

Anna knew exactly what Mary was feeling as far as her desire to have a child, it was that same maternal instinct that seemed to afflict almost every woman that survived the great dying. The drive to reproduce so the species would survive was something common to all women, regardless of sexual orientation. She had the thought, *for men, it's probably not much different now than it's ever been. Wonder how much they understand about what it is that drives them to do or say damn near anything to get laid.* Anna looked at James, then she turned back to Mary, and asked the question that was foremost in her mind, "Is the baby healthy?"

"He is," Mary answered, but she had a concerned look on her face. "At least he was. What's going on around here?" she asked. "Why did Dr. Ming make me come out here just because Daniel had a little touch of fever?"

Anna's heart dropped. *Not another one, please not another one,* she thought. Anna didn't want to be the one to have to tell Mary about the other baby boys that had all died shortly after birth. Even more than that, she didn't want to know herself. But how could she not know? How could she just unknow what she already knew? How could she maintain the belief that the baby she carried would be okay when another baby boy was probably dying right now back in the maternity ward. Anna couldn't help it, she burst into tears.

Mary's expression changed from concern to bewilderment, and finally to fear as James started trying to explain, "It's just that baby boys haven't made it yet. They just..." he was saved from having to continue by Dr. Ming opening the door and stepping into the waiting room.

Anna didn't need to hear the sounds of a woman sobbing back in the maternity ward to tell her what the look on Dr. Ming's face made all too clear. Dr. Ming walked over to Mary, who stood up and was looking at the door. The closed door that had now shut out the sobs of her lover.

"There was nothing I could do," he said softly, but not too softly for Anna and James to hear.

Chapter Twenty Seven

THE GOLDS AND REDS of autumn were almost gone. The aspen trees were nearly bare, the whole world fading into the drab grays and browns of winter. Anna walked the lane from the house out toward Highway 9, James by her side. This daily walk out to the highway and back was the only exercise she had allowed herself lately. The baby was due any time now. The baby was the only thing that mattered. The depth of Anna's worry about the upcoming birth, and the health of the baby, was as deep as any ocean. She couldn't stop thinking about it.

The horses, cattle, and sheep were all in the big meadow now. The hay crop had been put up months ago. *Wonder why we bother,* Anna thought about the hay. She tried to remember the last winter with enough snow to keep the animals from being able to just graze their way through until spring. *October seventh, I've been back here for just about a year now.* Anna spent a lot of time thinking lately. She thought about the events of the year just past. The first year of a new world on the Blue River Ranch, and the year before that, when the old world came to an abrupt end.

The pain in her lower back seemed worse than usual today and walking more difficult. They were less than halfway out to the highway when she felt something different, a pain that seemed to radiate from her lower back and spread through her swollen belly. She gasped and stopped walking, her hands holding her stomach, which seemed harder and tighter than usual.

"Anna, are you alright?" the concern in James's voice matched her own anxiety.

Having never experienced childbirth before, Anna couldn't be positive, but she was pretty sure. "I think it's time," she said. "We better turn around."

James carefully pulled her left arm up over his shoulders and reached around her back with his right hand to give her support and help her walk. He led her not to the house, but straight to the metal shop building where the Rivian was all charged up and ready to go. With Anna securely buckled up in the passenger seat, he pulled away from the shop and only stopped at the house long enough to run inside and grab the bag that was packed and waiting.

"It's time," he told Charlene and Misty, who were sitting at the bar having a snack. No one was in sight over at the old house, and James didn't want to take time to figure out where they were. "Charlene, why don't you come with us now. You can drop us off at the clinic and bring the Riv back for the others. Misty, tell the others where we went." The calm, collected demeanor James displayed was utterly at odds with the chaos swirling through his mind.

The emotional storm hidden behind James' façade wasn't lost on Charlene. She jumped up immediately. "Better let me drive," she said.

As Anna was helped into Dr. Ming's clinic by James on one side and Charlene on the other, she wasn't sure which was more terrifying, the fact that she was about to give birth, or the harrowing race from the Blue River Ranch to Kremmling that she'd just experienced. *Should have just driven myself,* she thought.

Lisa was seated at what had once been the receptionist's desk at the clinic, studying what was undoubtedly some kind of medical textbook. Dr. Ming's school of medicine was in full swing. Seeing Anna being helped through the door, Lisa leaped to her feet and grabbed the wheelchair that was always sitting near the front desk.

"Dr. Ming's at the church," Lisa told Charlene, as they eased Anna into the chair. There was no reason to specify which church. "Please go get him." She wheeled Anna back to the delivery room with James firmly in tow.

…

"I want to call him Alpha," Anna said, as she rearranged the cover over the new baby boy that was nursing at her breast. "He's the first. The first baby boy to survive. The first male child to inherit this new world."

Dr. Ming was filling out some kind of birth certificate form that he'd dug up from some archive somewhere. He looked up at James for affirmation. There was no way for Dr. Ming to know James and Anna had already been over this too many times to count. From that first ultrasound showing Anna's baby was a boy, James had wanted to name him Charles, after his grandfather. Anna's early choice was Clyde, after her father. They'd considered Charles Clyde, but Anna always seemed to balk at naming her son Charles. James didn't know why. For him, Charles was his grandfather and his great grandfather before that. That the name might remind Anna of Charlie Day didn't even occur to him. Yesterday, he had been as surprised by the name, Alpha, as Dr. Ming seemed to be now.

"I wanted to name him Charles," James told Dr. Ming. The way he said it, Dr. Ming could see that James had already given up on that.

"Maybe we should just leave the name blank for now," Dr. Ming said. "He is just barely two days old."

Anna knew what Dr. Ming was saying. Maybe it would be better to not give the child a name for a week or so. If the child didn't survive, it might be easier to bury a nameless child than one who had a name. Like a child was meaningless until it was given a name.

"His name is Alpha," Anna said, firmly but without malice. "Whether you write it down or not." Then she looked from Dr. Ming to James. "I'm sorry James, I just can't name our baby Charles." She looked up at the ceiling, remembering another Charles. Not Chuck Pierson, but Charlie Day back in Blue Rapids. Olivia would have had Charlie's baby by now. Anna hoped it was a boy. She hoped her Alpha wasn't truly the first. She hoped that another baby boy had already survived back in Kansas.

"Alright, Anna," Dr. Ming asked, "what about the surname, Mendez, or Duran."

"Pierson or Duran," James stated firmly. "I won't have my child named Mendez."

Anna and Dr. Ming both looked at James. Anna knowing why James didn't want Alpha named Mendez, Dr. Ming, not understanding at all.

"None," Anna said. "Alpha is just Alpha. I don't think

surnames from the past have any meaning anymore. The old world is dead. Just Alpha is good enough for this world." She looked down at her baby boy, who had stopped feeding.

Dr. Ming stopped writing. "I guess you're right," he said. "There's probably no reason for a birth certificate, either. Look at how many have died without a death certificate. I guess I'm just too old for a totally new world. Alpha, I hope you can make a better world than the one we did." He put down the pen and reached over to gently place his hand on the back of the newborn's head. Dr. Ming's hand nearly recoiled of its own volition before he could steady it. The hand that had touched hundreds of babies during a lifetime of medical practice was much too sensitive to miss the telltale signs of the beginning of a fever.

If you enjoyed *The Flight To Blue River*, please take just a moment to review the book on Amazon. Reader's reviews and comments mean the world to me. I read them all and cherish each and every one.

Thank you so much for reading!

About the Author

Marcus Lynn Dean is an avid reader who has enjoyed writing since childhood. He has published three books and has more on the way. Book Three of the Thermals Of Time trilogy will be released in 2021. Marcus has lived and worked in every region of America except the far northeast. He currently resides in his once and always home state of Colorado. Correspondence with readers is always so much more than welcome - marcus.dean@lastditchpress.com

CPSIA information can be obtained
at www.ICGtesting.com
Printed in the USA
FSHW020702210421
80660FS